War 1812

Battle
at
Horseshoe Bend

I0562251

DAVID WRIGHT

Published by Boson Books

An imprint of Bitingduck Press
Formerly an imprint of C&M Online Media, Inc.

ISBN 978-1-938463-19-8
eISBN 978-1-938463-20-4

For information contact
Bitingduck Press, LLC
Montreal • Altadena
notifications@bitingduckpress.com
http://www.bitingduckpress.com
Cover art: "Treed," by David Wright
www.davidwrightart.com
The Treaty at Fort Jackson was copied in whole from that at the Battle of Horseshoe Bend National Military Park.

Author's note

This book is a work of fiction with a historical backdrop. I have taken liberties with historical figures, ships, and time frames to blend in with my story. Therefore, this book is not a reflection of actual historical events.

Books by Michael Aye

Fiction

<u>The Fighting Anthony Series</u>

The Reaper, Book One

HMS SeaWolf, Book Two

Barracuda, Book Three

SeaHorse, Book Four

Peregrine, Book Five

<u>War 1812 Trilogy</u>

Remember the Raisin, Book One

Non-Fiction

What's the Reason for All That Wheezing and Sneezing

Michael A. Fowler and Nancy McKemie

This book is dedicated

to a dear and longtime friend, Stephen Lieupo and his family. Steve is a hunter, fisherman and has not let life's obstacles slow him down. He is a "man's man." Keep your powder dry, Steve!

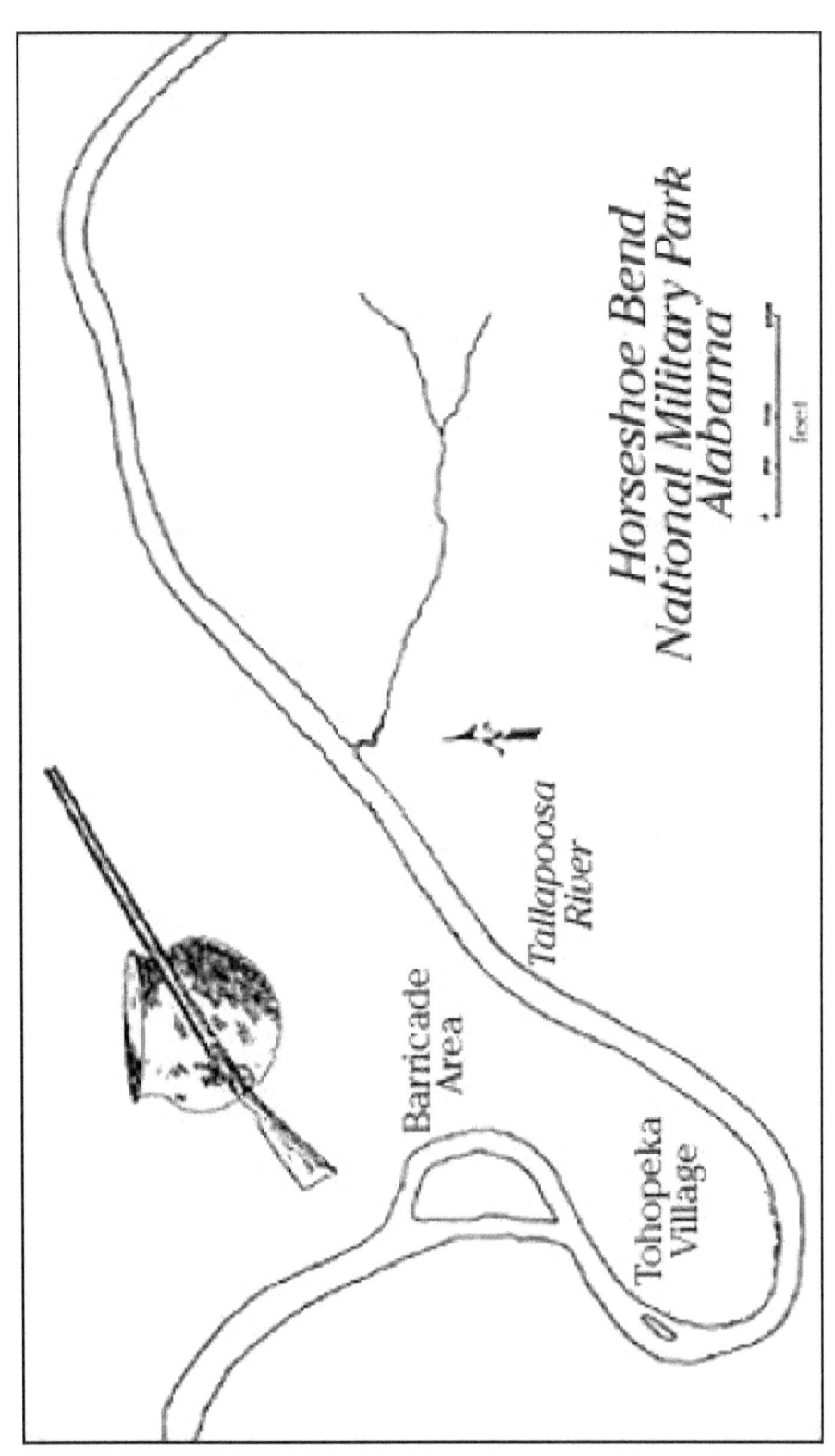

Horseshoe Bend
National Military Park
Alabama

Tallapoosa River

Barricade Area

Tohopeka Village

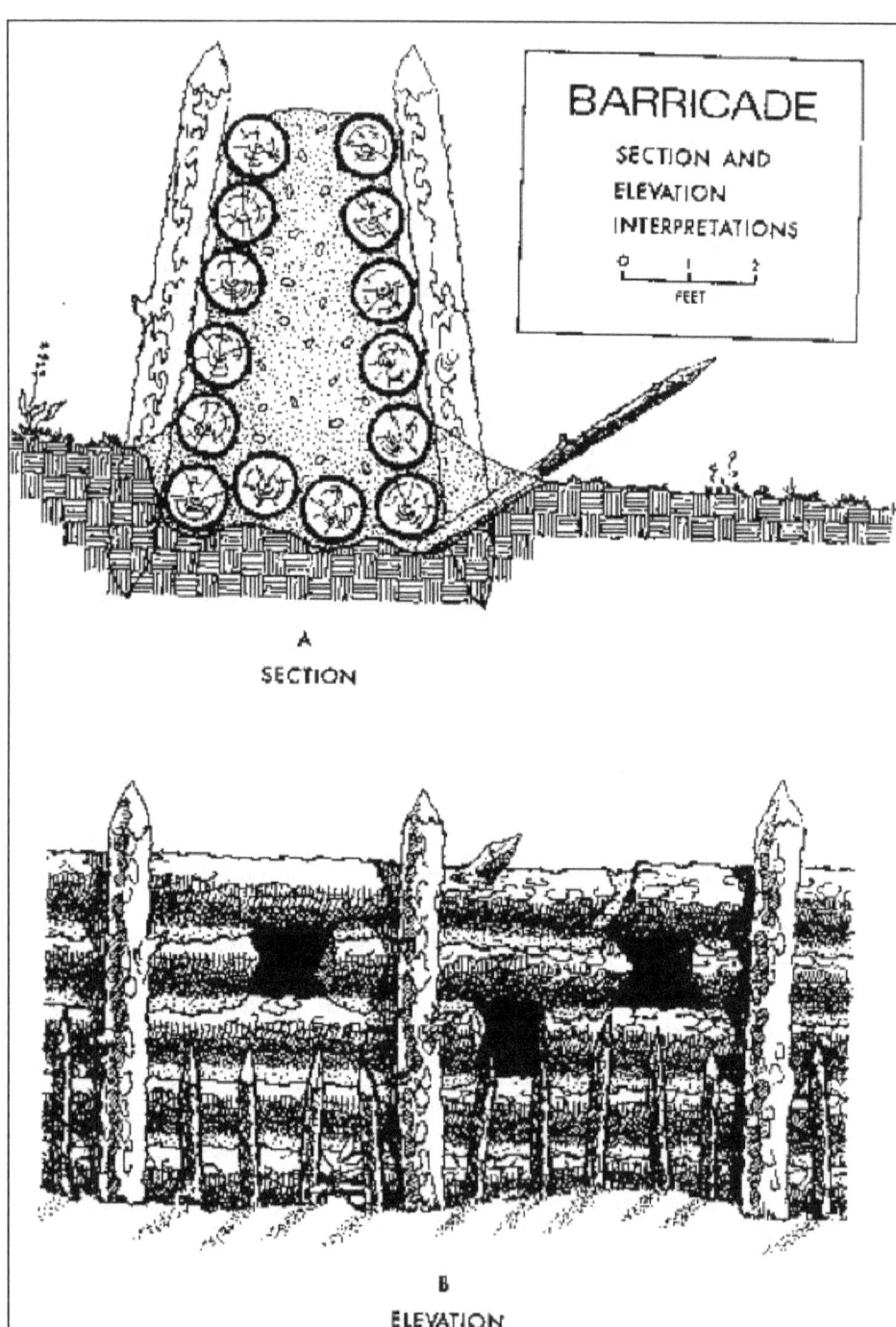

BARRICADE

SECTION AND
ELEVATION
INTERPRETATIONS

0   1   2
FEET

A
SECTION

B
ELEVATION

Tecumseh's Speech to the Creek Council

(as told by Samuel Dale)

IN DEFIANCE OF THE white warriors of Ohio and Kentucky, I have traveled through their settlements, once our favorite hunting grounds. No war-whoop was sounded, but there is blood on our knives. The Pale-faces felt the blow, but knew not whence it came.

Accursed be the race that has seized on our country and made women of our warriors. Our fathers, from their tombs, reproach us as slaves and cowards. I hear them now in the wailing winds.

The Muscogee was once a mighty people. The Georgians trembled at your war-whoop, and the maidens of my tribe, on the distant lakes, sung the prowess of your warriors and sighed for their embraces.

Now your very blood is white; your tomahawks have no edge; your bows and arrows were buried with your fathers. Oh!

Muscogees, brethren of my mother, brush from your eyelids the sleep of slavery; once more strike for vengeance; once more for your country. The spirits of the mighty dead complain. Their tears drop from the weeping skies. Let the white race perish.

They seize your land; they corrupt your women; they trample on the ashes of your dead! Back, whence they came, upon a trail of blood, they must be driven.

Back! back, ay, into the great water whose accursed waves brought them to our shores!

Burn their dwellings! Destroy their stock! Slay their wives and children! The Red Man owns the country, and the Pale-faces must never enjoy it.

War now! War forever! War upon the living! War upon the dead! Dig their very corpses from the grave. Our country must give no rest to a white man's bones.

This is the will of the Great Spirit, revealed to my brother, his familiar, the Prophet of the Lakes. He sends me to you.

All the tribes of the north are dancing the war-dance. Two mighty warriors across the seas will send us arms.

Tecumseh will soon return to his country. My prophets shall tarry with you. They will stand between you and the bullets of your enemies. When the white men approach you the yawning earth shall swallow them up.

Soon shall you see my arm of fire stretched athwart the sky. I will stamp my foot at Tippecanoe, and the very earth shall shake.

Prologue

When I am old and gray I will be
One of those people that say
I remember when I did and not someone
Who say I wish I would have

—William D. Weatherford
(Chief Red Eagle)

Fort Mims August 30, 1813

"H*ENRY... HENRY PARRISH. WHAT are you doing riding in here in such a rush for? You're kicking up a cloud of dust." The old scout looked at the man addressing him. The soldier seemed to stagger and appeared half drunk as he shaded his eyes to look up at the man on horseback. It was not quite noon yet.*

Trying to control the horse he'd raced into the fort on, and at the same time not get tangled in the lead rope of his pack mule, Henry spoke, "Zach, by gawd, you have to get them gates closed. The woods are full with more Red Devils than fleas on a cat's ass."

"Shh!" Zach replied, placing his fingers to his lips in an exaggerated manner. "The major done had two slaves tied up and the lash put to their hides for telling lies."

"Lies... lies, damn it man, this ain't no tall tale. The woods is busting wid Injuns."

"What's going on, Sergeant? What's all this shouting about?"

"It's one of General Claiborne's old scouts, Major. Claims he spied a passel of Injuns."

"Claim... Damn your soul, man. I don't claim nothing. It's a fact. A pure, honest-to-God fact. Major," Parrish turned his attention to the major, "You don't get those gates closed, you're gonna have a bunch of dead folks here about before the sun goes down."

Major Beasley snorted and spoke to the sergeant, "More fabrication, sheer fabrication."

Parrish shook his head in disgust as he looked over the fort's grounds. Children were playing, men were working, and a woman was calling her family to eat while another toted a bucket of water. One man walked past him leading a pair of oxen, and a group of soldiers were playing cards on a barrel. How many would survive the day? Seeing two men he recognized, Parrish made to call out, but neither Dr. Osborne nor Captain Middleton heard his call as the cook began clanging the dinner bell. Above the clang of the bell, war whoops filled the air, sending a chill down Parrish's back. Arrogant ass, the scout thought, now the major and a lot of others were gonna get their briskets full of Injuns for a noon meal.

Turning in the saddle, a shiver ran through Parrish. Even he was not prepared for what stormed toward the unsuspecting fort. Through the gate not thirty yards away, a thousand warriors charged. Major Beasley gave a startled cry and raced forward to close the gates. It was useless, the gates had been held open by a large pile of dirt on each side. Major Beasley, with sword in hand, made it almost to the gate when he was shot in the stomach by one warrior, then tomahawked by Red Eagle.

Arrows flew into the open gate and Parrish's mule brayed loudly. Turning, the wild-eyed mule jerked the lead rope from its owner's hand, spilling him to the ground. The mule fell dead as multiple arrows impaled its body. Taking a chance to glance back at the gate, Parrish could still see Indians pouring out of the nearby ravine and across the open ground into the fort.

Soldiers alerted from the war whoops and sounds of gunfire were now trying to make a stand against naked hordes of painted savages. It was useless as they were quickly overpowered, the Indians pausing only long enough to scalp their victims.

Seeing a warrior chase a little girl, Parrish quickly took aim with his long rifle and fired., He hit the warrior in the back, shattering his spine and causing him to fall on the little girl. As she was trying to crawl out from under the Indian, Parrish rushed over and grabbed an arm, pulling the girl from under the dead weight. He'd just gotten the little girl loose when she screamed. Sensing a presence, Parrish ducked and heard a 'whoosh' as a tomahawk swept past his head. Having not had time to reload, Parrish used his rifle as a club. He drove the butt plate into the Indian's throat. The brave sank to his knees, gasping, and Parrish finished him off, crushing his foe's skull with a powerful swing that hit the man above the ear. Sweeping the little girl up, Parrish ran toward the south wing of the fort where Captain Jack and a company of riflemen were putting up a brave fight. Racing for cover, Parrish was overwhelmed at the carnage already inflicted. He tried to shield the little girl's eyes as a young boy was seized by the legs and his brain was bashed out, his head slammed against the log wall of a hut. A pregnant woman was dragged out of one of the small houses and held by two braves as another opened up her belly with his knife. Another woman was tomahawked as she tried to pull away braves that were raping her teenage daughter. Men were being scalped at every turn, some before they were dead.

Fires were set as shrieks and cries of pain and anguish mingled with the war cries of Indians and curses from soldiers. The Indians' thirst for blood seemed insatiable, as warriors who had grown up with whites and were their friends only a week ago now butchered them with reckless abandon. On the north side, Captain Dixon Bailey put up a heavy defense as his men repulsed the Indians time and time again. However, the number of savages was so great they had fallen back until they could no longer do so. The pickets and houses that had for a time offered some protection now swarmed with bloody savages, their weapons dripping blood from their butchery. Still the soldiers fought on, in spite of seeing the death and mutilation of their families and hearing the piercing screams continuously fill the air.

Parrish had fired his long rifle until the barrel was so hot he couldn't touch it. A soldier next to him fell as an arrow found its mark. He fired the dead man's musket until he was out of powder and shot. His face blackened and eyes burning from spent powder, Parrish glanced over to where Captain Middleton and his men had been fighting. He felt a lump in his throat as he realized all were dead. Suddenly, there seemed to be a lull in the fighting. Captain Jack looked at his watch; it was a quarter to three.

Gathering the few soldiers that remained, they entered a small house at the rear of the fort.

"Henry."

"Yes, Captain."

"You think this is over?" Parrish shook his head no. "Me neither." Then in a louder voice, the captain continued, "I don't see none of us surviving. The only chance that little girl clinging to you has got is to get you out of this fort. We ain't got any axes but we have bayonets and tomahawks. If we can open up a hole big enough for you to get out of here with that child, you hightail it and don't stop."

Parrish was too choked up to answer and just nodded, knowing the soldier was right. They both knew the only chance the little girl had was for them to quickly open an escape route. In ten minutes time, a hole barely big enough for Parrish to squeeze through was completed. Taking a quick last look out of the front window burned a memory in Parrish's brain he would never forget. Strewn bodies, ground turned dark with blood, buildings burning, and the smell of burnt flesh drifted on the wind. He would never forget the sight. He didn't want to forget. 'Vengeance is mine,' sayeth the Lord, but Henry Parrish planned to lend a hand if the Almighty spared his life this day.

Captain Jack was back at the scout's side, "You'd better go, Henry."

Parrish nodded and shook the man's hand, "I won't forget, Captain."

"You'd better not. Now get that girl and get gone." Looking at his watch, the captain said, "Its 3 o'clock. Were it five I would stand a tankard."

About that time a soldier shouted, "Here the Red Devils come again, Captain." The man turned to his captain as blood gushed from his neck where he'd been hit by ball. "Oh God! I'm a dead man, Captain."

As the braves rushed the remaining resistance, Henry carried the girl out the back wall of the fort. Smoke from the burning buildings helped cover their escape. Tired and out of breath, Parrish paused by a cypress stump and set the girl down. Rising, he found himself face to face with a warrior. Fresh scalps dangled from the Indian's belt, and his body was blackened from dried blood. Parrish immediately recognized the brave. They had drunk, hunted, chased squaws, and smoked together in the past.

"Gray Eagle," Parrish said without thinking.

"Go," the Indian said and pointed toward Tensaw Lake. "Go to the lake, after dark go down river. Gray Eagle does not make war on women and children. Parrish, you remember this. We were friends in the past. No more. Weatherford say this. He now Red Eagle, he war chief. You take girl and go. You have no girl, we fight." Parrish stood silent and only nodded. "We meet again, we fight," Gray Eagle said and then drifted away through the smoke. As he moved away, Parrish saw the pucker wound in the warrior's belly; he'd been shot. They might meet again, but Parrish doubted it. Picking up the little girl, he headed through the swamp toward the lake.

Chapter One

THE SQUAWK OF SNOW geese overhead caused the two riders to glance skyward. "Late heading south," Moses mumbled. Jonah's nod of agreement was barely perceptible. The eastern skies were heavy with snow, and bitter cold penetrated their heavy blanket coats, causing a constant shiver. The battle of the Thames was not a week past. General Harrison's army had won a wonderful victory over the British. Jonah and Moses had been part of Colonel Richard Mentor Johnson's brigade that had gone into the swamp after Tecumseh and the Shawnees. It had been touch and go for a while, with the Americans suffering heavy losses. Colonel Johnson had been shot many times, but the surgeon said he'd live. Now, most of the militia had broken up and were headed home; their part was done. Jonah and Moses had made a lot of good friends with the Kentucky volunteers. They would be missed. Like the Kentucky volunteers, Jonah and Moses had completed their mission for President Madison. As the president's agent, Jonah had pushed and prodded General Harrison into action, finally putting an end to the British and Shawnee threat in the Northwest Territory.

A few flurries of snow drifted with the wind. As the men rode down a gentle slope, Jonah spoke loudly to be heard over the wind, "That's the creek where the Indians tried to ambush us, isn't it?"

"Yeah," Moses replied. "We were lucky that farmer's wife alerted us."

"Wasn't we though," Jonah replied. "If this is the creek, the farm is not far away. Maybe they'll put us up for the night."

"They should," Moses agreed. "They gave shelter to Tecumseh and his bunch."

"Man will do a lot when he is scared," Jonah threw out.

"Yeah, there's that."

The horses paused to paw at the slushy ice at the creek's edge. After a quick drink and encouragement from their riders, the animals, under a sky filling with dark clouds, moved on. After a couple of miles, the men topped a rise and there lay the farm they had remembered, not a half a mile away. As the two drew closer, the braying of a mule and lowing of cows could be heard from the barn.

"Feeding time," Moses volunteered and then added, "probably milking time too."

The men rode up to the house as the snow started to fall in earnest. Before they could dismount, a man opened the door holding a musket in his hand. He looked the pair over, not sure what to make of Moses. Half black, half Creek Indian, with scars on his face from the smallpox, Moses' features were enough to cause any man to take a second look. It had the opposite effect on the squaws they happened upon however. He seemed to have a certain charm that caused them to flock to the man.

"We're part of General Harrison's army," Jonah volunteered. "We are headed home."

"You beat the Redcoats?" the farmer asked.

Nodding, Jonah added, "And the Shawnee. Tecumseh is dead."

A change came over the man, like a look of relief. The farmer continued to stand in the doorway almost in a trance when his wife opened the door wider and looked at the men. Recognition was instant as was a sudden look of fear. She didn't want her husband to know she'd warned the soldiers of the Indian ambush.

Seeing the woman's fright and thinking quickly, Jonah spoke, "I know it's not every day strangers ride up, Madame. But we are half-frozen and the weather is getting worse. If it's not too much of an imposition we'd like to stay over the night."

"Even if we have to stay in the barn," Moses added.

The man seemed about to say no, so Jonah tried another direction. "We'd be glad to pay for room and board."

"In coin?" The farmer asked.

"In coin," Jonah stated.

"Hush," the woman said. "There will be no talk of money. It's the only decent thing a person could do on such a night. It's only Christian."

"Thank you," Jonah and Moses replied. "We'll just put our horses in the barn if that's all right."

"Of course," the woman said. "Supper will be ready in half an hour."

"It may be the Christian thing to do," Moses whispered once they were in the barn, "but I bet we don't get out of here without the husband expecting a generous offering in his plate."

THEIR STAY TURNED INTO three days and nights. Snow filled the air and covered the ground. Water froze and had to be heated to water the animals. At times it was almost like blizzard conditions and the barn could barely be seen from the house. Jonah and Moses lent a hand caring for the livestock, and after the first day, the farmer and his wife seem grateful to have someone to talk to and help out. Food was limited: carrots, dried beans, potatoes, bacon or ham from the smokehouse, cornbread, and fresh milk. The chickens seemed to be off what they usually laid.

"It's the weather," the farmer advised. "Happens every time."

Because of this, Moses and Jonah declined the offer of eggs at breakfast. They did have plenty of maple syrup, which Moses poured liberally over his cornbread. Coffee was offered only in the morning.

On the second night, the farmer broke out a jug and passed it around. Their guests were somewhat surprised when the wife took a long pull from the jug before replacing the corncob. Jonah had seen women consume before but it was usually wine or sherry and in a glass. Times were tough, however, and niceties tended to go by the way. On the morning of the third day, the farmer asked why the men were taking the route back home that they were, when a much more southerly route would see them home faster.

Smiling, Moses answered, "Jonah has a woman waiting for him in Sandwich, gonna make her his wife." A look of horror came over the farmer and his wife.

"What is it?" Jonah asked. "What's the matter?"

Pausing to collect his thoughts, the farmer replied. "After Harrison's army pulled out, an Indian raiding party attacked Sandwich. They killed several people, men and women. They burned and pillaged the village, making off with food, guns, blankets and such. Before General Cass and his men could respond, they were gone."

"We have to go," Jonah said as he stood up.

"We can't," Moses replied placing his arm over his friend's shoulder. "We wouldn't last an hour out there. Besides, we don't know that Anastasia has come to any harm."

"We don't know she ain't either," a gloomy, worried Jonah mumbled.

"I do know if she needs help we won't be in any shape to offer it if we don't wait till the weather clears."

"You are right as always, old friend." Rising from the table, Jonah made his way to the room he was sharing with Moses.

"I'm sorry," the farmer said. "Maybe I should have kept the news to myself."

"He would have found out soon anyway," Moses said trying to reassure the man he had not done wrong. "This way he'll have a clear mind when we get to Sandwich and find out if any action needs to be taken or not. I do want to thank you both for the hospitality you've shown a pair of strangers."

"Only the Christian thing to do," the woman said for the second time.

The weather was cold but clear the next morning when Jonah and Moses rode out. Jonah had been very quiet and it surprised Moses when he leaned over and asked, "Did you leave an offering?"

Smiling, Moses responded, "Yes, a most generous one."

Chapter Two

I'M SORRY, JONAH, WE did the best we could. Guards were posted. I lost three good men to that raiding party. I can't tell you how many times I had asked Anastasia to move closer to my headquarters, but she refused. She could have even stayed in the little cottage out back where you and Moses stayed. Again, she refused, preferring her own home."

Jonah, with Moses at his side, stood before General Cass, who was doing his best to explain the disappearance of Jonah's lady. He was doing a poor job of it. He and Jonah had become friends, and now he felt he'd let his friend down. He'd been rehearsing his comments since the raid, since Anastasia went missing, knowing he'd have to face up to his friend. All the rehearsing had been wasted when you looked into the man's cold stare knowing he held you accountable regardless of the excuses.

"Well, you didn't find a body, so that means she's alive," Moses volunteered, coming to the general's aid and trying to soften the blow to Jonah.

"That's right," Cass said, "we searched the trail the savages took for several miles, Jonah. We didn't find any signs of d... of anything distressing."

Not trusting his emotions, Jonah turned and walked out of the general's office. Moses paused, letting his friend get out of hearing and then spoke, "He's taking it hard now, General, but when the shock has worn off and he's had time to think on it, he'll realize there was nothing you could have done. Anastasia should have accepted the cottage where she would have been protected. She didn't and that's that. Now, we'll see if we can find her."

General Cass put down the cigar that he'd been smoking and held out his hand, "Thanks for understanding, Moses. The cottage is open if you'd like to stay there tonight."

"I'll talk with Jonah about it, General, but I'm afraid the place will have too many bad memories. We'll look around maybe, talk to some people and then be on the trail."

"We already…" Cass paused, and then started over. "Of course, you know we did that, but Jonah will feel the need to go over it again."

Moses nodded. "We could use a few supplies, sir, if any are to be had."

"By all means, I'll speak to the sergeant. Safe travels, Moses, and I hope your search will be successful."

Outside the headquarters, Jonah stood by his horse, and leaned on his saddle. Rising up, he muttered, "Took you long enough."

"Humph," Moses snorted. "Someone had to remember his manners. Mama Lee would be furious had she seen the way her boy acted."

"But he let the Indians take Anastasia," Jonah flung back.

"No… No, he didn't. He offered his protection and she refused. Don't forget Anastasia is a grown woman. She had to realize the danger she put herself in by refusing the general. These are hard and troubled times, Jonah. I know you're hurting. We've been together too long for me not to feel some of your pain. But you can't blame General Cass. Don't forget he lost three of his soldier boys, one of whom was watching over Anastasia's house. You don't want to hear it, and I don't like saying it, but its Anastasia's fault she got taken. Now, it's time to stop brooding and let's see if we can find a trail."

Jonah mounted his horse and headed toward Anastasia's house without speaking. Moses found the supply sergeant. General Cass had already ordered the sergeant to take care of the president's man. A pack mule was provided, and the packs were loaded with bacon, salt, flour, coffee, a smoked ham, and a small sack of sugar.

"I'd give you more," the sergeant apologized, "but we are almost out of supplies ourselves."

In addition to the food, Moses packed extra powder and shot, extra pants, woolen socks, and tight-knitted wool shirts to wear beneath the buckskins they had to travel in. The sergeant also had fishing line, hooks, and two razor-sharp sheath knives. As Moses cinched up the pack he turned and found the sergeant had a few gifts for them.

"Here's a sack of tobacco and a jug. There's also a bundle of cigars, but I'd rather you keep them in the saddle bags until you're out-of-town."

Moses couldn't help but smile. There was little doubt where the cigars had come from. The gesture from the sergeant was heartfelt.

"We all liked the lady, Moses. She was something like a favorite to the men after Jonah run that spy through with his sword. She also smiled and spoke kindly to the men and even wrote a few letters for them that wanted to send one home. The men called her Ana, not Anastasia, just Ana. She seemed to like that. The men all took it hard when we found she was missing; not just the general, but every mother's son in the outfit."

"Thank you, Sergeant," Moses replied. He could sense the sergeant felt that maybe they were somehow responsible for Ana's disappearance.

"Good luck, and may the Lord be with you," the sergeant spoke again, breaking the momentary silence.

Moses tapped his hat and mounted his horse. Taking the pack mule's lead rope, he rode off to find Jonah and begin the search.

FOR DAYS, THE TWO followed a cold trail, now and then coming up on someone who'd heard of a Shawnee raiding party with captive whites. "Nobody tried to stop them?" Jonah asked one man.

"What's a man and a half-grown boy gonna do to a raiding party, Mister? Are yedaft?" the man snorted.

"My apologies, sir," Jonah replied. "One of the captives is my fiancé."

"Then I'm sorry, friend, I truly am for the both of you."

Crossing the Detroit River almost ended the search before it started. The ford below Sandwich was half frozen and bitter cold. It proved to be a treacherous undertaking for the men and animals alike. Ice formed on the animals' coats and the men's leggings by the time they left the water. Reaching the Michigan side, they quickly found a site previously used by Colonel Johnson's regiment. While Jonah gathered wood and built a fire, Moses stripped the saddles and packs from the shivering animals and then dried them as best he could. A roaring blaze soon helped both the men and animals. As Jonah added frozen wood to the blaze, it hissed and little vapors of steam rose. A pot of coffee was soon boiling. The strong black liquid helped revive the men; standing next to the fire, they dried their boots, leggings and clothes.

"We can't cross any more rivers in this kind of weather," Jonah said, surprising Moses. "Killing us and the animals is not going to bring Anastasia back."

Feeling the need to comfort his friend, Moses told Jonah what the sergeant had said about how the soldiers felt back at Sandwich and how they had taken to calling Anastasia Ana.

"I like that," Jonah responded. "My Ana. Is she lost forever, Moses… will I see her again?"

Moses let the question hang in the air. He didn't have an answer, no one did.

After another cup of the black coffee, this time laced with a dab of brew from the jug, the men saddled up and moved on. Later that evening, tired and near frozen, with both the men and horses nearly played out, they decided to make camp at a deserted cabin. There was a large hole in the roof in one corner of the cabin, shutters were missing from the two open windows, and the door was sagging. They did have a solid wall that helped with the wind, and the space was big enough for the men and animals. The men kicked around and found a bucket that didn't leak too badly. Jonah got a fire going in the corner where the hole in the roof would allow the smoke to rise up and out. Rats, birds, and other small animals had made their nests in the cabin so Jonah had plenty of starter to use to get the fire going. He also used some of the rotten wood from the roof to add to the starter. Whoever had used the cabin last had left a fair sized pile of wood in one corner. This too was mostly rotten, but it would do until they could get more. Moses entered with a dripping bucket. It was only a short distance to a fast running stream that had yet to freeze over. As Jonah was stripping the animals, Moses poured water in the coffee pot and then took the rest of the bucket over to water the horses and mules.

"Better go get another bucket tonight." Moses volunteered. "In case the stream is iced over tomorrow."

After hanging their saddle blankets over the windows and propping the sagging door closed, the little cabin warmed up. Finishing the last of the coffee and eating the last few crumbs of fried cornbread, a gift from the farmer outside of Sandwich, the men settled down.

Reluctantly, Moses asked, "Which direction tomorrow?"

Jonah didn't answer for moment. Taking a final draw from one of their meager supply of cigars, he thought to himself for a moment. He had cut the cigars in half to share with Moses, so it was not much more than a nub when he tossed it into the fire. Finally, he answered, "South to Maguaga."

"The Wyandot village," Moses said, raising his eyebrow skeptically.

"They have supposedly become very peaceful according to Captain White back at Sandwich. After Tecumseh's death, all the Indians have reportedly become very peaceful."

"Not all of them," Moses quickly brought up. "Otherwise, we'd be back at Sandwich or headed home with Ana."

Chapter Three

THE WYANDOT VILLAGE WAS larger than either Moses or Jonah expected. Bravely, the two rode into the village. Because of the cold, most of the villagers were inside, out of the weather, but after a few shouts of alarm, Indians full of suspicions left the warmth of their dwellings to see what these strangers wanted. Moses, particularly, held their attention as none had ever seen a black man before. Several of the Indians could speak English, and Jonah asked to speak to the chief. They were told to follow a fierce looking brave.

Entering one of the larger dwellings - a council house, Jonah decided, they found several men sitting around a small fire. Jonah and Moses were greeted, not warmly, but there was no outward display of hostility either. Jonah explained that the war was over for him and Moses. The Redcoats had been defeated, and he and Moses had fought against Tecumseh and had seen him fall. An honorable enemy, a fierce battle, but now the war was over. Having returned to Sandwich, they had discovered a raiding party, men without honor, had raided the settlement and taken his woman. He now searched for her. He looked about as he spoke and didn't miss the look of resentment from several of the warriors when he'd called the raiding party men without honor.

Jonah continued after pausing to look directly at each of the men. Directness and bravery was one thing they understood and respected, even in an enemy. "I have no wish to harm any of the braves," Jonah explained. "But I will fight if I must to get my woman back."

The chief then stood, "There are words of steel in the white man's tongue. We have heard of the dark one who fights alongside his white brother. It is good to meet you. We do not have the white women. The Shawnee have passed through and they have two white women. This has been many moons ago. They will sell the women if they can. If not, when they tire of them…" The sentence was left unfinished. When the Indians grew tired of the women, they'd either be killed or set free. There was no way of telling. "You are welcome to rest in our village," the chief offered but Jonah declined, stating they still had daylight left to continue the search. Giving the chief a cigar, Jonah thanked him and they rode out.

IN BROWNTOWN, SEVERAL PEOPLE had heard of a party of Shawnee with white women, but no one could actually say they'd seen them. At Frenchtown, it was different. It had been a hard ride from Browntown; snow had fallen constantly so that the trail and woods on each side were covered in a thick blanket of snow. It was almost sundown when the two stopped at a small tavern on the outskirts of Frenchtown. A teenage boy greeted the men as they rode up. He didn't even ask if they were staying over, he just said, "Go on in and warm-up, I'll care for the horses and mule." All of the animals were looking gaunt. Travel had been hard on man and beast alike.

As the men dismounted, Jonah caught the boy staring at Moses, who pretended not to notice. The tavern was pleasant. The gathering room was full of clamor and bustle as soldiers and volunteers released from their units headed home. It reminded Jonah of the tavern where he and Moses had met Captain Clay Gesslin and his men. A roaring fire made the room bright and warm. Finding a small spot in the corner, Moses and Jonah took a chair after removing their hats and coats. The owner made his way over carrying two tankards and set them on the table. He then took a poker, red-hot from the fireplace, and plunged it into the tankards of cider to mull it. As soon as he left, a woman brought over a large tray; on it was a pot of beans, a plate full of hot bread, and butter that looked like it was straight from the churn, a plate piled high with sliced ham, and a relish dish of onions and cucumbers. A bread pudding with a thick sweet cream was also put down. There was hardly room on the small table to put all of the dishes. When the tankards were empty, the proprietor offered the choice of more cider, small beer, or rum. Both men took the cider.

As the evening grew, a few local folks who'd only stopped to eat cleared out. Moses and Jonah were amazed to see how quickly the floor was swept and straw filled bags were laid out for those not desiring to spend the extra for a private room. After the cold trail, Jonah was more than willing. A dark staircase with only a single wall candle to light the way up led to the four guest rooms that filled the top floor.

A crowing rooster woke Jonah the next morning. He'd slept hard and now his bladder felt like it was about to bust. He was looking around the room for the chamber pot when Moses said, "Next to the chest, between the chest and the wall." Jonah let out a sigh of relief and Moses couldn't help but chuckle. Not an hour earlier he had been thinking of raising the window to relieve himself when by chance he'd noticed the chamber pot. Smelling the odor of fresh coffee, the men dressed quickly. Making their way down the narrow stairs, Jonah saw a large yellow cat lying next to the hearth.

"Got him for a mouser," the proprietor volunteered. "But my daughter's spoiled him so much he ain't worth killing." His daughter glared at the man as she carried two steaming hot cups of coffee to a table by the window. Jonah and Moses followed her and took a seat.

A militia captain opened the door and stepped inside. "Snow has stopped and the sun is out. Better day to travel," he declared. As he looked around the room, he noticed Jonah and recognized him at once. "Jonah! It's me, Captain Lucas." Lucas had been on duty when Jonah and Moses first rode into General Harrison's camp. "Headed home, are you?" the captain asked. Jonah nodded as he swallowed a sip of coffee that almost scalded his tongue. "I've been released, as well," Lucas said. "Not much fighting left 'cept that little run-in with a bunch of Shawnee down at Fort Meigs."

Jonah was suddenly attentive, but the tavern owner was speaking. "Heard about that. A bunch of flatboat men ran into a group of Red Devils who had a couple of white women held captive. Well, a girl and a woman, was the way I heard it. The river men killed all the savages and one of the captives got shot. Heard she was taken to Fort Meigs. Don't recall anybody saying if she made it or not."

"How long ago was this?" Jonah managed to ask.

"It was three, maybe four weeks ago now. Why do you ask?"

"One of those women is my fiancé," Jonah managed to say.

T HE EASIEST ROUTE TO Fort Meigs was not easy at all. The road, which was really no more than a wide path, was treacherous. It had long been a succession of potholes and mud bogs but now it was made worse by the snow, which was melting in the presence of a bright sun and warm day. The constant travel of fighting men headed home only worsened it. Had the underbrush not been so thick, Jonah and Moses would have taken to the woods. The further south they traveled, the more populated the area became. By the time they arrived at Fort Meigs, they were more tired than they were when they had reached Frenchtown.

Feeling he was being put off by the officer of the guard, Jonah for once was quick to pull out his letter from the president and demand to see the commanding officer. General Clay remembered Jonah and was cordial. He summoned the post surgeon, who sadly stated the girl the Indians had captured had succumbed to her wounds.

Moses, who was listening intently, spoke, "You say the girl died, sir. Was it a girl or a woman? We heard there was one of each."

"I would say girl in this instance," the surgeon replied. "She looked to be sixteen or so, blonde hair. She never regained consciousness, so I have no way of knowing her name or who to contact about her death."

Saddened by the girl's death, yet happy it was not his Ana, Jonah asked about the men who'd fought the Shawnee.

"We don't have much of an answer there, I'm afraid," the general admitted. "River men...men on a flatboat, I was told. They could have headed anywhere, but I'd guess they took the flatboat down the Maumee toward Fort Defiance."

J ONAH AND MOSES HAD served as scouts with General Mad Anthony Wayne when Fort Defiance had been built in August, 1794. Jonah recalled the fort was named Defiance after Charles Scott, who commanded a band of Kentucky militia declared, "I defy the English, Indians, and all the devils of hell to take it."

The commanding officer at Fort Defiance was of no help. Flatboats and barges were constantly going up and down the rivers. Therefore, unless attention was brought to some particular event, he'd have no reason to know about it. He did recall a Jonah Lee, who was a scout for General Wayne when the fort was built. When asked if he was related to that man, Jonah nodded but didn't answer.

The fort had been built where the Auglaize and Maumee Rivers came together. From there, numerous waterways connected, some going to Ohio and others going to Indiana. Some even could be followed north to Michigan. It was the end of the trail. Ana was lost. Moses was saddened by Jonah's gloom. He'd liked Ana and felt she would have made Jonah a good wife. Now it was time to head home. Georgia would be much warmer. Maybe that would help a bit. It couldn't hurt. Moses was tired of the bone penetrating cold. A warm day and a cane pole on a sunny creek, that's what he longed for. One of Mr. Lee's wenches or a Creek squaw thrown in wouldn't hurt his feelings any either.

PART II

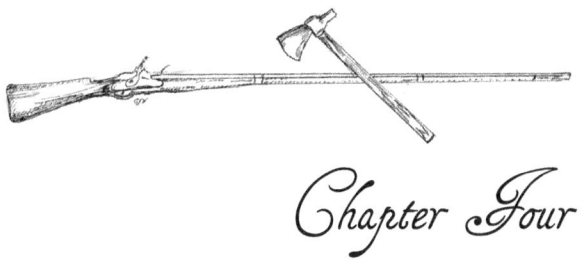

Chapter Four

A CROWD HAD GATHERED AROUND the small table at the Thunder Tavern and was watching the two men compete in the manly art of arm wrestling. Two men may have been an over statement; one of the men was in his prime, while the other one was a nineteen year old lad, full of piss and vinegar. The crowd was shouting encouragement to the youth as he put forth a gallant effort. The tavern's owner, a veteran of America's first war for independence, did not mind the crowd. It was good for business, not a single man watching the duel of willpower and strength did so without a tankard of ale, beer, or cider in his hand.

The front and back doors had been opened as smoke from the cigars and pipes started to build up. Opening the doors created a breeze, and after only a few minutes the smoke had cleared considerably. Old Colonel Lee, who was head of the local area's militia back in 1775 until the end of the war, leaned on the bar next to his son, Jonah, who was watching his nephew, Keaton Lee, take on Moses. This had been an annual battle since the boy turned sixteen. It was a little late this year due to Jonah and Moses having been away with General Harrison's forces at the northern frontier.

The men had only returned a few days ago. While both were physically worn out from the war and travel, Colonel Lee, as he was usually addressed, knew there was more going on than physical fatigue. Standing at the bar, sharing a tankard and smoke, Jonah had explained his melancholy.

Trying to think of a bit of wisdom to quote, the colonel said, "Time alone will heal Jonah, and nothing I can say will change that...time and possibly another woman." The woman must surely have been something indeed for Jonah to act so, the colonel decided.

Many a lass had set her sights on his son. He'd courted, attended socials, dances and such with a few, but when it looked like a girl was getting too serious or controlling, Jonah suddenly had the desire to go on a long hunting trip or adventure. He and Moses would pack up and be gone long enough to send the message that he was not ready to be tied down, and then they'd return.

The colonel had plans for his son to take over the plantation in a few years. He had no doubt he would, after the war was over.

At the table, Keaton was tiring. His arm trembled as he took a breath, and with his last bit of strength gave it all he had. Moses didn't budge and finally the youth gave up. The crowd cheered. The boy had gone at it with the best arm wrestler in Thunderbolt.

"You didn't even build up a sweat," Keaton swore, his hand and head perspiring profusely. He took a bar towel from a serving girl and wiped his face.

Moses smiled and patted the boy on the back and salved the boy's feelings somewhat when he said, "You're a lot stronger than last year."

"Well, just wait until next year," the boy declared. "Now you can buy me a tankard of ale." Moses just raised his eyebrows. "Well, a tankard of cider anyway," Keaton continued. Moses nodded and the girl went to fetch their tankards.

"Good show," Jonah and the colonel said as they seated themselves at the table where the combat had taken place. Some of the men who'd been watching stopped by to say a word or two before moving on.

"I've got news for you," Keaton blurted out, about to bust with excitement. "I'm going to join the militia. My friends have all joined. I'm the last one."

"What have your parents said to that?" Jonah asked.

"You know what they said," the youth replied. "William and John both joined when they were eighteen," he said, trying to justify his decision. The boys he was speaking of were his cousins.

"And William is dead," the colonel snapped. Seeing the shock on Jonah and Moses' faces, he added, "I'm sorry, you didn't know. You were both gone and mail is slow. We'll talk more about it later. Now drink up, it's getting late and your mother will be expecting us for supper."

"Lord help us if we're late," Moses said. "Mama Lee will have our scalps." And then gazing at the colonel's balding pate, he threw in, "Well, some of us anyway."

"Don't get too big for your britches, boy, this isn't Keaton you're playing with," the colonel scolded with a smile.

A FTER TWO WEEKS AT home, Jonah was back to his old self physically and his periods of morose seemed less frequent. He had sent a letter to John Armstrong, the Secretary of War, that was a summary of what he had seen and believed to be the British threat in the northwest. To Jonah's way of thinking, his service to Armstrong and the president was over, it had ended with the Battle of the Thames. It was a complete surprise when a stable boy arrived and cried out "A sojer from Washington is heah." Breathing hard, the boy paused to catch his breath. He'd run all the way from the front of the house, around the side porch and down to the stables. "The colonel said for you to come up to the house."

Jonah and Moses had been looking over their fishing nets and crab traps because Moses had a hankering for a low country boil. This was a type of meal that once eaten would never be forgotten, and it had been over a year since they'd had their taste buds satisfied. They were now ready to lay on a feast and to their way of thinking nothing else but a low country boil would suffice.

Colonel Lee had been reminiscing how he'd first tasted low country boil as a little boy. Slaves would hide small amounts of cargo from ships they were unloading and then go back that evening and get it. Items like crab, shrimp, crawfish, sausage, potatoes, and corn. When they got back to their quarters, they'd take pots and fill them with the ingredients and water, add some spices and boil it. After it was boiled, it would then be poured out over a table or couple of large planks and allowed to cool, and then the whole family would dig in.

Soon, after sampling the concoction, the plantation owners were having it prepared in the kitchen by their cooks. Their meals usually had, in addition to the low country boil, crisp deep fried cornbread, fried shrimp and fried oysters. Duck, quail, and marsh hens were frequently added to the meal as well. If anybody had room left, various desserts were offered, often cakes and puddings. But Jonah's favorite was a crispy, deep fried apple tart.

Laying down their work, the men quickly washed their hands in a watering trough and headed to the house.

"Who is the guest, James?" Jonah asked the boy.

"I don't know, sir, but he's got on a sojer's suit. I heard the colonel say sumthin' like, 'Come in Cap'n, you had a long trip from Washington'."

"Probably headed to Fort Jackson," Moses said as the two walked to the house.

Walking in the kitchen door, they were accosted by Aunt Fannie, the cook, "Stop right there and go clean dem boots off. Just cause you been gone awhile don't mean you can forget yo' upbringing. Now go back outside and clean off dem boots. I got better things to do side sweeping up floors where two good for nothin's done tracked it up. Stay outta dat cornbread too, Moses, I see ya. I swear ya'll act like I ain't got nothin' to do but look after you all day."

After cleaning off their boots and quickly devouring pilfered pieces of hot cornbread, the two wiped their mouths to remove any tell-tell crumbs and then, after wiping their hands on the legs of their buckskin pants, they went back in to meet this captain. The colonel had provided a refreshment for the guest while he waited.

"Sorry to take so long," Jonah apologized. "We had to wash up a bit."

The officer rose up with an outstretched hand and ready smile. "It's good to meet you, sir. My name is Captain Stephen Lieupo. I was not certain you'd be home from the frontier yet or not. I had planned to stop by and ask that word be sent to me once you were home."

"How can I help you?" Jonah asked, coming straight to the point.

"I come from the war department, sir. Secretary Armstrong sent me. I...ah...serve in much the same capacity as Captain Hampton. I have a dispatch for you, sir." With that, Captain Lieupo pulled a large letter from a leather pouch.

"When did you leave Washington?" Jonah asked.

"Shortly after we got your dispatches about the victory over the British, sir. I believe you mentioned you would make your way home in the dispatch. I'm sure the secretary knew the likelihood of catching you on the trail was remote, so he sent me directly here. I was allowed a few days personal time, which I spent in Charles Town."

"I see. Do you know what's in this?" Jonah asked, holding up the letter.

"Not word for word, sir, but it has to do with the Indian uprisings in Alabama."

"I heard about the Battle at Burnt Corn and the massacre at Fort Mims down at the tavern," Jonah admitted. "Well, Captain, it's only three days till Christmas. I'm not going anywhere until after that, but right now Moses and I are going fishing and see if we can pick-up a bit of fowl if we're lucky enough to come across any. Do you have any clothes other than your uniform?"

"Not suitable for hunting, sir."

"Well, come with me, we're about the same size. I'll see if we can't fit you out."

"You are most generous, sir."

Jonah stopped and faced Lieupo, "You can stop calling me sir. It's Jonah."

Lieupo smiled and replied, "And I'm Steve. My father was Stephen, so I'm just Steve."

"All right, Steve. This ugly brute is Moses. He's more like a brother. We grew up together and have never been apart. He's my absolute closest friend. I tell you this so that you'll know anything you have to say to me you can say in front of him. It'll save time, actually, as I will tell him anyway."

Lieupo nodded, "Thanks for setting things straight to start with. Now that we are alone, I can tell you that Mr. Armstrong wants you to keep an eye on Andy Jackson. He's been given overall command of dealing with the Indian problem in Alabama."

"I thought he was a fire eater," Jonah responded.

"Oh, he is, sir. You'll not have to push Jackson. No sir, you may have to bridle him and hope he doesn't get the bit in his teeth."

"Why didn't they put someone else in charge?"

"Who? Jackson is the only choice and John Coffee is an able second in command, but he's not the leader Jackson is. No sir, Jackson was the only choice but it might prove distasteful at times."

"So, Mr. Armstrong wants me to be his keeper."

"Actually, sir, I think it was President Madison."

Chapter Five

CHRISTMAS CAME AND WENT. Captain Steve Lieupo was a guest at the Lee home for the holidays. Jonah and Moses quickly established a solid friendship with the man from the southern part of the state. Lieupo was of French descent but, as Steve put it, it was so far back it didn't show.

Jonah read the two letters in the package, one from John Armstrong and the other from the president. In talking the matter over with his father, he asked, "How can I turn down the president?"

"You can't," Colonel Lee answered.

However, Mama Lee, who had overheard, had an entirely different response. "It's easy, just say 'no'. The men in this family have done enough. Your father fought in the War for Independence, you with that mad man, General Wayne, and now you just got back from traipsing all over the north with those soldiers. Ask me, you've done enough. It's time you settle down, take a wife and have me some grandchildren."

Colonel Lee winced at the mention of taking a wife. Mother did not know the entire story of Anastasia. "Let the boy be," the colonel said to his wife. "He'll settle down with the right woman when the time comes."

A HORSE GALLOPED UP TO the Lee house, its rider jumping out of the saddle before the horse had come to a stop. The rider threw the reins somewhat carelessly over the hitching rail and ran inside. The stable boy was lucky to intercept the horse and tie the reins more securely just as the animal had pulled loose.

Keaton Lee burst into the house excitedly. "I've been commissioned as a second lieutenant in the low country militia. At first, I will be at Fort Jackson learning about artillery, but when our unit marches I will be with them."

"Slow down," the colonel said, then turning to his wife, he smiled and asked, "Mama, can you have Aunt Fannie fetch us a glass of lemonade to cool this young man down, as you can see he is about to burst."

Of course, the colonel already knew about the commission and about the boy being assigned to the relatively safe Fort Jackson. In fact, he, along with Jonah, Moses, and Captain Lieupo, had arranged the whole thing.

"The fort was named for James Jackson," Colonel Lee pointed out to Captain Lieupo, "Not old Andy. Colonel James Jackson was from Britain but fought on the Colonial side. At age twenty-five, he accepted the surrender of the British in Savannah."

The fort had been manned continuously since 1812 when the war had begun. Situated on a bluff as it was, facing the Savannah River, the fort's guns had easily defended American ships from British warships and privateers raiding the area. Lieupo had joked about the thunder from Thunderbolt. This comment led to a discussion as to how the town's name came to be.

Jonah said that as a child his father had sworn a large rock had been shattered by a thunderbolt, causing a spring to gush from the ground. General James Oglethorpe built a settlement and a fort there, naming it Thunderbolt.

"I'm not surprised he built a settlement around a spring," Lieupo responded.

"You ain't smelled it," Moses chided. "It doesn't taste too bad but it smells to high heaven."

Talk then went to the rumors that during the 'first war,' Thunderbolt was a seat for the rebellion against the British. Compared to its neighbor, Savannah, the town was almost all rebels, at least according to the British.

This then led to discussing the McIntosh-Gwinnett duel. While both were staunch supporters of the American cause, they differed politically.

"McIntosh called Gwinnett a 'scoundrel and lying rascal' on the floor of the Georgia Assembly. Father was there listening and was shocked at the tirade. Of course, Gwinnett demanded an apology, which McIntosh refused to give. Our neighbor is James Wright." Jonah continued, "It was in one of his fields that the two met for a duel."

"The colonel was there and seen it all," Moses added.

Nodding, Jonah started again, "Father said they walked off twelve paces, turned, aimed and fired at almost the same time. Both were hit, Gwinnett in the thigh and McIntosh lower in the leg."

"Makes you wonder if they really meant to kill each other," Lieupo said. "That, or they were poor shots."

"Well, Gwinnett died three days later. General Washington was so afraid some of Gwinnett's people would take revenge on McIntosh, even though he was acquitted at a trial, that he had McIntosh carted off to Valley Forge."

Chuckling, Moses added, "Not only was he shot, he had his arse frozen off for his troubles."

"Well, that's better than the opposite," Lieupo said.

Word about Fort Mims was still a topic of conversation, but just as the men were about ready to pack up and pull out, word came that Jackson's army had fought a battle on November third at a place called Tallushatchee, and then six days later another battle was fought at Talladega. Jackson's army seemed to be taking the battle to the Creeks. The next day a scout rode into Fort Jackson with news of the battle they were calling the 'canoe fight'. This involved men from Claiborne's army and was on the twelfth day of November. But that was not all. On December twenty-third, two days before Christmas, a battle was fought that was now being called the Battle of Holy Ground, or as it was called by the Creeks, Econochaca. This area had the largest concentration of Red Stick warriors thus far. It was also a staging area for food and supplies. William Weatherford, also known as Red Eagle, had planned the attack on Fort Mims. It was said it was called Econochaca because the Creek prophets performed ceremonies to establish a spiritual barrier or protection that they believed would have the power to destroy any white man who passed through it, so the name actually meant Holy Ground in the white man's tongue.

The Creek women and children had been evacuated before the battle when Red Eagle learned of the approaching army. Claiborne's army of one thousand men was divided in two groups. One led by Colonel Gilbert Russell and the other one by Major Joseph Carson. When the army breached the sacred spiritual barrier unharmed, many of the Red Sticks fled as they believed the Americans had 'big medicine.'

The warriors that stayed and fought were aided by a large force of former slaves. After an hour, the Red Sticks began to fall back under the overwhelming American force. Once at the river, the Red Sticks found a hole in the American line and many escaped. The war chief, Red Eagle, was one of those who escaped. Surrounded, he rode his horse over a fifteen-foot bluff and into the Alabama River. The battle was not much of a victory other than capturing the needed supplies, but Red Eagle's daring was greatly admired and was now being called 'Weatherford's leap.'

Upon hearing of these battles, Moses voiced what was on everyone's mind. "Do you think there's any need in us going? Sounds like them soldier boys got everything under control."

"Most of those soldiers are sixty-day militiamen," Lieupo replied. "Most of them will have expired enlistments soon. Then we will see who has the upper hand."

Chapter Six

THE GEORGIA SUN WAS already blazing hot in a cloudless sky. It was a warm day for January, a very warm day. Colonel Lee had given his sons (he looked upon Moses as a son) each a fine horse for Christmas. He intended that they ride off to war well mounted. He would have given the boys, as he called Jonah and Moses, stallions, but felt geldings were better suited. Stallions would try to prove their dominance and Lord help it if somebody had a mare whose time was ripe. No, geldings were what were needed. The horses now stood at the hitching rail, pulling on the reins trying to get at some small turf that was less brown than the dead grass surrounding it. James had just brought two pack mules around, already loaded down and ready to go. Jonah's horse was a dapple gray and Moses had a buckskin. The mules were so black they looked almost blue in the sun.

Moses, Jonah, and Lieupo had accompanied the colonel down to the river earlier that morning. The river was used mostly by fishermen, but it was also used by various and sundry merchants and planters. The water level was high from the daily afternoon showers that they'd been having recently. The sky would cloud up and darken, then came the wind with thunder and lightning. For the next hour or so the heavens would open and the rain would fall. The river now had a muddy brown tint as it rapidly flowed toward the bay. The rain had not come today and maybe it would be clear all day, but Moses wouldn't bet on it.

Several black slaves were busy unloading a barge. Casks of tobacco, kegs of brandy, and barrels marked with merchants' names on them were all being unloaded. Sweat dripped from the blacks as they unloaded the supplies, more than one cutting his eyes at Moses, wondering how he came to be so well dressed and mixing right in with the white folks. Moses had long since quit worrying about what others might think of his relationship with the Lee family. It was what it was.

Colonel Lee had found the man he wanted and purchased a cask of tobacco and a keg of rum. Once they were loaded in the wagon, they headed home. "I couldn't let you get on the trail without some decent tobacco and a small keg of rum that will prove its weight in gold. It's not just for swilling," the colonel said, smiling as he did so and causing his eyes to squint, accentuating the crow's feet at the corners.

A few older men loitering around the wharf spoke to the colonel or threw up their hands to wave. Some had been in the colonel's unit back in '76.

As the men climbed into their saddles, a last farewell was given. Mama Lee had hugged them all, including Lieupo, but stood on the porch while Colonel Lee walked them down the steps and to their mounts.

"Got your maps?" he asked, feeling the need to speak to his boys, yet trying to think of something to say that wouldn't betray the emotions he felt. Mama Lee was already dabbing her eyes with a handkerchief.

Tugging on the pack mules' lines, the group trotted out of the yard, scattering chickens and barking dogs. The trail would take them to Woodville and on west to Milledgeville. At Milledgeville, they were to meet up with a group of Georgia militia at Fort Hawkins. From there on it would be rough going with only a few trading posts and settlements until they got to Fort Strother. At Fort Strother, Jonah was to show General Jackson his letter and, with or without his consent, attach himself much as he had with General Harrison, only this time he was to try to keep Jackson in check and not make promises or commitments the government couldn't keep. More importantly, he was to keep Jackson from starting a shooting war with the Spanish.

JAGGED STREAKS OF LIGHTNING pierced the night sky as thunder rumbled in the distance. The horses were wild-eyed and stomped about. The rain had come that evening as it had every evening for several weeks. The only difference was that it came later and lasted longer. The group had a wet camp.

"I had hoped that we'd missed the rain," Lieupo said as a stream of water ran off his hat, spattering the campfire and causing a sizzle.

The rain had just started to fall when they found a leaky lean-to that had been built some years ago. The lean-to leaned far more than it was meant to and let water drip through, but it did knock off some of the wind. They tied a rope between two trees and tied the horses and mules to it. They took extra precaution and hobbled the animals as well. The packs were placed toward the back of the lean-to where it leaked less. A fire pit was left over from some previous visitor, probably a hunter, who had also left a small pile of wood. The men were appreciative of their unknown host. Soon they had a fire blazing and the smell of strong coffee filled the wet air. The wagon trail had been slippery, just as slippery as bear grease; Moses had sworn when one of the mules slipped down and the lead rope jerked him around. That was when they spied the lean-to and decided to call it a night. The heat from the fire helped, but the men ached with the weariness that comes with the wet and cold after being soaked through to the skin.

"Where is that hot Georgia sun now?" Lieupo complained.

"I wish I knew," Jonah moaned, as a gust of wind drove a gush of rain into the lean-to. "Anybody want to cut the cards to see who sleeps at the back of the lean-to?"

"Not with your deck," Moses snorted.

Another flash of lightning lit up the sky and a boom of thunder was heard close by. As Jonah turned toward the back of the lean-to, Moses barked, "Where are you going?"

"To broach a keg," Jonah answered. "If this night doesn't call for a little swilling then I don't know what does."

"I believe you're right," Moses replied. "It ought to warm up the coffee just fine."

Chapter Seven

FORT HAWKINS WAS ONE of several forts built along Georgia's frontier to protect its settlers. Originally, it was manned by troops from Fort Wilkinson at Milledgeville some thirty miles away. At one point, Jackson had one thousand Tennessee volunteers located at the fort along with hundreds of Georgia militiamen.

As Jonah, Moses, and Lieupo approached the fort, Lieupo commented, "Looks like a town is sprouting out of the wilderness."

"Macon," Jonah replied. "It's been here for a while, long before it was so populated. It was once nothing more than a trading post. Being on the Ocmulgee River, folks just seem to settle down."

"Lots of Indians about?" Lieupo asked, with concern obvious in his voice.

"Friendly Creeks, maybe a few Cherokee," Moses responded.

The gates to the fort were open but two sentries stood at the heavy wooden gates. The fort's walls were solid and much stronger than most, which were often little more than just a log palisade. The fort had barracks, storage buildings, two blockhouses, and a hospital. Its strength made it an unlikely target for attack.

"A lot different than Fort Mims," Jonah said as he waved at the sentry who allowed the group to pass.

"That was easy," Lieupo said.

"That's because we look friendly," Jonah replied, and then glancing at Moses added jokingly, "Well, some of us anyway." When his friend didn't reply, and in fact was looking toward a small Indian village, Jonah asked, "What are you looking at?"

"A squaw or two, who may benefit from my protection when two such unfriendly strangers are around," Moses remarked.

G ENERAL McINTOSH WILL SEE you now, sir," the sergeant said in a formal military manner. Jonah and Captain Stephen Lieupo entered through the door being held open by the sergeant, who gave a crisp salute and departed.

Lieupo, being in uniform, saluted the general, who more or less returned it. "So you're headed to join up with Jackson," the general growled. Neither Jonah nor Lieupo was sure who he was addressing.

"I'm actually being assigned to the thirty-ninth," Lieupo volunteered, after a brief silence.

"Good man, Colonel Williams," the general stated. "I don't understand why General Pinckney assigned the thirty-ninth to Jackson. General Flournoy needs them in New Orleans. Of course, Pinckney feels it will take Colonel Williams and the thirty-ninth infantry to make short work of those Red Sticks. You know, Jackson is only a general of militia."

Jonah started to respond that regardless of Jackson's military status, the secretary of war had placed him in overall command of the forces fighting the Indians. But thinking some things were better left unsaid, he didn't speak his mind. Not everybody was a Jackson supporter, not even John Armstrong, for that matter.

The general was speaking again, addressing Captain Lieupo, and ignoring the president's man. "You are in luck, gentlemen, we have a small unit of Georgia militia from Augusta. They will be led by Henry Parrish, who knows the frontier as well as anybody. He was at Fort Mims when Weatherford's butchers attacked. He was able to get out alive with a little girl, Amy Stuart. She saw her folks butchered and mutilated. Henry saved her life and took her to Milledgeville to an aunt. The little girl cried when Henry had to leave her. Of course, in her eyes, he's her savior, crude as he can be. Get your horses rested and be ready to pull out at first light. Listen to Henry and you'll probably keep your hair. The militia has already drawn supplies but if there's anything you might need, just see the sergeant." Turning his attention back to a stack of papers on his desk, the general had effectively dismissed the two men.

Once outside the building, Jonah said, "He don't care much for Jackson, does he?"

"Naw," Lieupo responded, "a lot of regular army officers got their noses twisted when Jackson was given command."

"You don't seem to mind," Jonah said.

"I am not regular army," said Lieupo with a smile on his face, making Jonah think again of his friend, Captain Hampton.

"Are you really being attached to the thirty-ninth?"

"More or less," Lieupo said.

Damn, Jonah thought, *you rarely get a straight answer when talking to these damn spies.* Hearing a familiar voice followed by female laughter, Jonah saw Moses in conversation with a group of squaws. "Well, he won't be of any use to us today," Jonah snorted.

"Making medicine, is he?" Lieupo joked.

"I don't know if you could call it medicine, but I guess a release of humours could be considered balm for the soul, as well as physically beneficial."

Henry Parrish sat under a stoop in front of the trading post smoking a pipe that was crafted by some Indian, from the look of the design. A jug sat next to him, uncorked. His buckskins were stained, and he had gray whiskers that looked to be about a week's growth.

"Have a good ride from the coast, did ya?" Parrish asked.

"Wasn't no trouble," Jonah answered.

"Well, you best be looking out for trouble soon. Them murdering heathens." It was obvious Henry felt an intense hate for the Red Stick after what happened at Fort Mims. "They murdered folks they had known all their life," he said, when Lieupo mentioned Amy and her parents. "Shucks, Peter McQueen had hunted with little Amy's daddy, even ate off their table. How can you eat a woman's fixings one week, and then bash in her head the next week."

"Do you know McQueen did it?" Jonah asked the scout.

"Makes no difference, he did it or allowed some other brave to do it, it was did just the same. Five hundred of God's children kilt. Weatherford was there as well. Seen him wid my own eyes shooting Major Beasley. Of course, that weren't any loss. I did lose a good mule, though," Parrish said as he appeared to be recalling the massacre, all the while holding his pipe in one hand and holding the jug against his leg with the other hand. "I took Weatherford hunting and fishing when he was a boy. I knew his uncle, his mama and his daddy. Good Scots they are, course his uncle is dead now, old Alexander McGillivray. Creeks called him emperor. He ruled over thousands of the buggers, lived in a fine plantation house. His sister, Schoya, had married a Scot named Charles Weatherford. William's, or as he calls himself now, Red Eagle's father, was given a huge plantation as a wedding gift from old Alexander. The boy had all anyone could want with an uncle rich as old King George himself and a daddy rich as all get out. The boy then went and turned Injun."

"I thought he was an Indian," Lieupo said.

"Only a tad, about an eighth, I heard. Regardless, half the folks he murdered he knew as friends. Some even had family connections and such to a lot of those devils. Of course, I do hold the Redcoats and Dons at fault, as well."

"Dons?" Lieupo asked.

Henry nodded, "Yep, them Spaniards in Pensacola got a little blood on their hands to my way of thinking." Rising stiffly, Parrish yawned. It was just getting dark so the man shouldn't have been that tired and sleepy. Maybe the contents, or lack thereof, in the jug caused Henry to yawn. "Get yore possible together and see to yore animals, then get some shut eye. I aim to leave early to meet up with old Andy. We got us a heap of killin' to do," Henry said, stifling another yawn as he ambled off.

"I wouldn't want to be on his bad side," Lieupo whispered.

"Me neither," Jonah answered. "Let's keep Moses close until Henry gets to know him."

"Should we go look for him now?" Lieupo asked.

"Not if you want to keep your hair," Jonah answered, smiling.

Chapter Eight

F OR A WEEK THE small group of riders rode steadily toward the Alabama border. Each night, Henry held a captive audience with his tales of living with the Creeks. One night he was asked by a young corporal with the group of Georgia militia why the Creeks were called Red Sticks.

Henry eyed the young man for a moment and then, taking his pipe from his mouth, he bumped it against the sole of his boot, knocking the cold burnt ash from it. He picked up his cup that was sitting on the ground beside him and reached out toward the coffee pot. The corporal grabbed the pot and quickly filled the grizzled old scout's cup. "They ain't all called Red Stick," Henry said, as he blew on the hot coffee before taking a timid sip. "The hostiles are called Red Sticks. Red Eagle, Menawa, and Peter McQueen's group; they are Red Sticks. Got that moniker from the war clubs they carry. The friendly Creeks are called White Sticks, by some."

"Did you know Tecumseh?" another young militiaman asked.

"I see'd him, heard him talk, didn't know him. He was looked at as big medicine by some until these here fellows filled his carcass with lead."

The talk then went to the Battle of the Thames. After a brief summary, the corporal asked why Tecumseh was so all set to side with the Redcoats.

"Land, son," was Henry's short answer. "We keep growing as a nation. As we grow, we push the Indians off the land they've lived on for hundreds of years. Tecumseh felt the only way to save the civilized tribes was to join King George. The Redcoats promised to keep the Indians on their land." Shaking his head, Henry repacked his pipe and, taking a burning stick from the fire, lit it.

Moses gently nudged Jonah. The Georgia boys appeared mesmerized by Henry, waiting patiently for him to light his pipe. Once a good glow could be seen in the bowl, Henry exhaled a cloud of smoke and gave a sigh.

"If it weren't for the massacre at Fort Mims, I might have been camping with old Menawa's bunch."

"Why?" someone asked.

"Well, young sir, they always seem to get the worse of it. They fought with the French and lost. They fought with the Redcoats in 1776 and lost, and now we're set to whoop 'em again."

"You'd think they'd have learned," the corporal said.

"No...no, they know their way of life is changing. We keep pushing and pushing. It's the only chance they got to keep their sacred land."

"What did you mean by civilized tribes?" This time it was Captain Stephen Lieupo.

Henry eyed the captain and replied, "I thought you were a learnt man."

"Not in the ways of our noble Redman, I'm afraid."

Henry nodded and said, "I see, at least you admit to your shortcomings. There are some that don't." Draining the little remaining coffee, Henry leaned over and sat the cup on a rock next to the fire. "I don't rightly know about any of those northern tribes, but in the southeast the Creeks, Chickasaw, Cherokee, Choctaw, and Seminoles are all considered civilized. Most live better than white folks. They got vast sums of land, good farmland it is, and a bunch of 'em got slaves to work their fields. Until this war and old Tecumseh stirred them up so, they was plumb friendly. There were lots of interracial marriages, and lots of little half-breeds running around."

"One last question, Henry," asked the corporal. "Have we done well? The Georgia militia, I mean."

Jonah could sense the boy's apprehension. The desire to measure up, maybe afraid he'd fail. Looking at the old scout, Jonah could tell he recognized the young man's apprehension also.

"Georgia has held its own, son. I don't know if you've heard of General John Floyd. He had a force of about a thousand Georgia volunteers and three to four hundred friendly Creeks. They attacked the Red Sticks at a stronghold on Calibee Creek called Autossee. It happened on the same day as Jackson's men fought the Red Sticks at the Holy Ground. Kilt two hundred or so, I'm told, and didn't lose a dozen men. Of course, there was a sight of wounded, including General Floyd. A bunch of the Red Sticks got away, including Red Eagle, who jumped his horse off a bluff into the river. You ask me, son, I'd say the good men from Georgia have done themselves proud." This seemed to satisfy the young soldier. "We best be getting some shut-eye," Henry said as he stiffly rose up from the stump he'd been sitting on. He gave an exaggerated stretch and yawned. Knocking the ash out of his pipe on the heel of his hand he spoke to Jonah, "We are getting close to Fort Armstrong now. Could be we will run into hostiles without meaning to. I 'spect it wouldn't be a bad idea if we decided to share in the watch standing at night. I know them fellas mean well, but to tell the truth, I'd hate to trust my hair on their keeping watch." Henry looked about to see if anyone was listening and then leaned in toward Jonah and whispered, "Man my age don't hold his water like a young pup. I always have to get up once, sometimes twice a night. Time has come in the last few days I was up, did my business, and was back in my snoggins and none of them the wiser. Could tell by you and Moses' breathing that you had heard. Had I been a Red Stick I'd have at least one fresh scalp and a hoss or two to impress some little squaw. Might even be enough to get her in the mood to share a blanket."

Jonah nodded and said he'd speak with Moses and Captain Lieupo. Henry nodded, "I'll be up before dawn so I'll take that watch. Figure we need to be on the trail come sun-up."

Taking a last pull on his cigar, Jonah slowly looked it over, trying to decide if it was worth saving. Deciding not, he threw it into the campfire, sending sparks and small embers up into the air. *Fleeting,* he thought. The air quickly put the flying sparks out. *Is that how it would be with Ana? A fleeting spark. Will I ever find her and will it be the same if I did?* He had written his friend, Captain Hampton, who'd promised in his answer that he'd put out feelers and see if he could come up with anything. If anyone had a chance, Jonah decided, it would be Hampton. His network in the northwest had been vast, so there was no reason to think he didn't have spies everywhere east of the Mississippi.

Chapter Nine

THE SUN ROSE HIGH and it was hot early on. "Too blame hot for January," Henry snarled, wiping sweat from his brow with his shirt sleeve. The men had had a cold breakfast, water, dried biscuit, and jerky. A fleeting deer was seen as the men rounded a bend. The deer had been standing alert at the edge of a small stream where it had been drinking. Seeing the column, the deer bounded away and then suddenly stopped, blew, and changed direction.

Speaking softly to Henry, Jonah said, "See that."

"Umm, huh."

Moses let the column close up and whispered for them to be very watchful. The narrow trail widened once across the stream. A fire in recent years had cleaned out the underbrush on both sides of the trail. The woods were not as thick as they had been, and one could see about a hundred yards deep into the forest. A rider suddenly appeared in the woods riding parallel to Jonah's group. Jonah noticed the rider had a red plume.

"He ain't no friendly," Henry whispered as he used his thumb to bring the hammer of his long rifle back.

Three more Creeks rode into view. Their lean, nearly nude bodies were painted red as they followed along behind the first brave. Behind Jonah, he could hear the nervous chatter of the young militiamen as he thought of Keaton and was glad he was back at Thunderbolt. Jonah could hear Moses speaking in a hushed tone and the chatter stopped. The Indians' ponies suddenly picked up their pace and trotted out of sight.

"Small party," Henry volunteered, as the group stopped and milled about, relief plain on the young men's faces.

"I thought sure we were fixing to kill a mess of Red Sticks," the corporal said.

Henry looked at the young man and firmly said, "Don't you go starting a shooting 'thout seeing me shoot. And then you load and shoot quick as you can. But if you see me run, boy, you fall in behind and you run like hell." Moses cut his eyes toward Jonah and a tiny smile creased his face.

"Good advice," Captain Lieupo said.

"Tonight we camp close up," Henry said. "Keep the horses and mules close up. Otherwise, we liable to be minus a few of them come daybreak."

Each of the men understood well what Parrish meant.

THE MEN RODE THE rest of the day without spotting another Indian. Just at dusk they came upon a creek where the land jutted out so that the creek was on three sides.

"Let's camp here," Jonah said. "The creek will make it hard for someone to sneak up on us. We can pull a couple of downed trees closer to help make the place better defensively."

Henry merely nodded. Moses and Jonah started unpacking the animals as Henry went about gathering wood for the campfire. Lieupo had the militiamen snaking deadfalls across the front of the camp. Moses and a couple of the militiamen broke out fishing line and soon had a mess of bream on the bank. The fish made a tasty meal, better than the cold breakfast they'd had.

"Catfish would have been better," Moses said.

Henry agreed, but Jonah said, "Both would have been better with corn fritters and grits."

"Well, I wouldn't have turned down either," Lieupo said, "but if I had my druthers, it would have been a big juicy steak like Aunt Fannie fixed that last night before we hit the trail. Steak with hot biscuits and those baked sweet potatoes with brown sugar and cinnamon. Yes, sir, I would trade all the fish in that creek for a good steak and glass of cider."

Jonah tossed a fish tail at Lieupo and said, "Shut up or you'll make the rest of the trip without Moses and me."

THE MEN HAD TURNED in early. The sun had been warm that morning but there was a definite chill in the night air. One of the young militiamen, Giles, whispered to Jonah, who was standing watch with the boys, "It's awful quiet. I don't even hear a cricket or a frog. Just the creek running."

Jonah nodded, "It's too damn quiet. I know it's cold, but don't look into the fire. And stand back from it. Keep your back to the fire and your face toward the creek. You'll see better that way."

The moon was full and bright. Shining down on the creek, it made the water shine. The mules and horses seemed nervous; the big gelding was pawing and looking about. Not liking it, Jonah casually walked by Moses and then Henry, nudging them with the toe of his boot. Moses was instantly wide awake. He rolled over as if he was turning in his sleep but took hold of the stock of his long rifle and gently prodded Lieupo. The captain opened his eyes but didn't move.

On the creek, the shine on the water seemed to change. Dark spots appeared and they were moving. The drowsy Giles rubbed his eyes and then looked again. "Mr. Jonah," he called.

A war whoop broke the silence followed by the sound of musket fire and running feet. The predawn was filled with stabbing flames as muskets cracked. Alarmed men rose from their blankets, their muskets ready, searching for a target. War whoops mixed with shouts of alarm and panic from the young militiamen were followed by cries of pain. It all seemed to come from every direction at once. Indians and horses jumped over the log barricade. Henry shot one of the braves and then clubbed another. Jonah and Moses were reloading their weapons. Lieupo, seeing another mounted brave hacking at the rope holding the horses, jumped on the back of the Indian's horse, pulling the brave to the ground. Using his spent pistol as a club, Lieupo bashed his foe in the head. Jonah lined up on a brave pulling back his bowstring to fire an arrow. In a hurry, he fired too quickly and instead of hitting the Indian in the chest, he blew his jaw away, scattering teeth as the bullet passed through the jawbone. Indians were now charging from the creek.

One swinging a red-handled war ax attacked Giles. The young man was fighting for his very life, struggling with the wet, slippery brave. Moses quickly grabbed his tomahawk and gave it a throw. The sharp steel blade buried itself in the Indian's back, severing his spine and dropping him instantly. Giles, with his face bloody, was alive and trying to reload his musket. The militiamen had been trained well in the art of loading, finding a target, firing and reloading again.

Like a nightmare, the men kept up a punishing fire, shooting at anything that moved. The mad rush was over. It ended as quickly as it had started. Besides Giles, two other militiamen were wounded, but not seriously. All would live to fight another day.

"Six," Lieupo said, "I count six dead Indians inside our perimeter."

"That's all?" Giles asked. "I'd have sworn we killed a hundred."

This caused Jonah and Moses to laugh. Henry just shook his head, "God Almighty, boy, who taught you Injun fighting?"

"Nobody, sir."

"Humph, that's what I thought," Henry said. "'bout what I thought."

PART III

Chapter Ten

THE SUN WAS SINKING low and a slight change in temperature was noticeable as the day grew late. Jonah was beginning to wonder if maybe they shouldn't have already met up with General Jackson. They'd met up with a small patrol earlier in the day, who said they should catch up with old Andy before sundown. Maybe his reckoning had been off or with the three wounded militiamen they'd traveled slower than they had realized.

They had traveled a day and a half since the skirmish without further incident. A time or two Indians could be seen, but it was Henry's feeling that "there's no harm in looking, so let 'em be." Jonah and Moses were of the same accord, so they rode...cautiously, but they rode. They had not gone more than another mile when a loud boom filled the otherwise quiet forest.

"We are close now," Henry said through clenched teeth. It amazed Jonah how the old scout could clench the stem of his pipe on one side of his mouth and talk out of the other side without losing his pipe.

Lieupo sidled up to Henry. Noticing no alarm, he asked, "Was that a cannon?"

"Yep, old Andy lets them fire off one or two before they make camp every evening just to let them know we're about."

"You don't think they know?" Lieupo asked.

"Sure they do, most of the time," Henry answered. "He just wants them to know he knows."

Moses looked at Jonah and cut his eyes, not sure if that had any-thing to do with it at all. "Most likely, it is just to let the men practice, would be my guess," Moses said.

"Well, thar's that too," Henry admitted.

The group had not gone more than a couple hundred yards when a buckskin-clad figure stepped out into the trail as they rounded a bend.

"Whoa," Jonah said, as he and Moses pulled hard on the reins to check their mounts.

"You liable to get trampled that way, Davy. You ought to know better than stepping out like that." Turning to his fellow travelers, Henry introduced them. "Men, this varmint here is Davy Crockett. He came down with a passel of boys from Tennessee to help Andy rid us of the pestering Red Sticks."

Crockett stood before them, leaning on his long rifle and grinning from ear to ear. After a few words of good-natured bickering, Davy said, "Ya'll follow me and I'll take you to old Andy's camp." With that he loped off.

As Jonah's group urged their horses forward, Henry took his pipe from his mouth, spat, and said not too quietly, "Don't believe anything Crockett tells you. Biggest liar ever walked the hills of Tennessee. That is, unless he's talking Red Stick trouble, and then believe everything he says. He's a natural scrapper that one is."

"Why does he lie?" Lieupo asked in a sincere voice.

"For the fun of it," Henry replied with a chuckle. "Purely for the fun of it. Gets so tickled by his tales sometimes, he gets bull yearlings in his eyes."

Seeing that Lieupo was lost at the term bull yearlings, Moses added, "Tears, big tears."

Henry continued, "Like as not, tonight he'll have the camp believ-ing he scared us half to death. Of course, they will know he'll be lying but they laugh just the same. I heard General Coffee say it was good for the men to laugh, like medicine for the soul."

"Well, it sounds like he's full of manure," Lieupo said.

"I doubt he'd disagree with you, Captain, but like I said, he's a scrapper."

THE MEN RODE INTO camp as everyone was getting ready for the evening meal. "Looks like we got more fixins than they do," Moss muttered.

"They ain't having no feast," Henry agreed. "It's been that way from the get go. Short supplies, wore out men and wore out horses. But still Andy keeps pushing. There ain't any back-up in Andy by God Jackson." The men trailed behind Henry to an area that was less crowded.

"Captain Lieupo," Jonah said formally, "maybe we should go report in to General Jackson. You come along as well, Moses." Jonah had spotted a few slaves in camp and he wanted to establish Moses as his own man from the start. Not that he couldn't set the record straight on his own, but by doing it this way it might prevent trouble down the road. As the three men approached the command tent, Jonah stopped suddenly, almost causing Lieupo to run into his back. "Sorry," Jonah muttered as he started again.

Jackson stooped as he ducked from under the tent opening, wincing as he brushed his arm against the flap. Jonah had heard he'd been wounded in a duel. It must still be bothering him, Jonah thought. As Jackson stood erect it was apparent he was taller than the average man, well over six feet, Jonah guessed. He appeared to be very thin and frail, without an ounce of fat on his lean body. His face was long and his jaw looked like it was chiseled from granite. His hair was unruly and prematurely gray. Hadn't seen a comb in weeks, Jonah would guess. He had a very obvious and prominent scar on his cheek. Was that from a duel as well, Jonah wondered? His nose reminded Jonah of an eagle or hawk's beak. He wore a pair of baggy brown pants, and his blue coat hung over his shoulders like sack cloth. Only his eyes gave away the true nature of the man. They were blue but had a fiery piercing quality to them. They were set under bushy brows, the likes of which Jonah had never seen. Yes, it was the eyes that identified the man for what he was. Andy Jackson was a warrior. There was no doubt in Jonah's mind the stories he'd heard about the man were true. Very few men caused Jonah to feel in awe, but this one did. There was little doubt the man possessed the courage of a bear. He would be ferocious and relentless in his pursuit of the enemy, and God help any man who got in his way.

No wonder the president felt Jackson needed a strong hand to subdue the man on occasion. His relentless will would not tolerate weakness, neither in his men or himself. The Almighty might be able to exert a controlling force on Jackson, but Jonah doubted he could. Clearing his throat, Jonah stepped forward, reaching out his hand in greeting.

"General, I'm Jonah Lee, and this is Moses. We grew up as brothers. This is Captain Stephen Lieupo. We just arrived with a small party of Georgia militiamen." He had rushed through the introductions. Jonah noted the general did little more than raise his eyes toward Moses when Jonah had introduced him.

Jackson shook hands with the men vigorously. "It's always a pleasure to gain volunteers," Jackson said smiling, "no matter how few." They all chuckled at this.

"I have a letter of introduction, sir," Jonah said, pulling the paper from its leather case. Better to get everything in the open from the start, he decided.

Seeing the seal on the envelope, Jackson cleared his throat, "From the president...humph. I didn't realize we aroused such attention."

Thinking he might as well join in, Lieupo said, "And here are my orders, General. I will be ah...attached to the thirty-ninth, I believe."

"Well, we'll see about that when the thirty-ninth arrives. Captain," Jackson called, and a man in a uniform similar to Jackson's but in better shape appeared. "This is Captain John Reid," he said, introducing his aide. "Make these men comfortable while I read these...letters. I'm sorry we have so little to offer other than coffee or water, gentlemen, but we have been short on rations. I have hunters out now. Hopefully, when we return to Fort Strother tomorrow, men and supplies will have arrived. I hope there's mention in your letter from the president, Mr. Lee, how a commander is supposed to keep his forces in the field without the basics. By that, I mean the basics – men, ammunition, and food."

Jonah, Moses, and Lieupo all looked at each other. Neither of them failed to notice Jackson had placed food at the bottom of his list. Accepting a cup of lukewarm, watered-down coffee, the men settled down to wait until...until.

Chapter Eleven

JONAH, MOSES, AND CAPTAIN Lieupo were all somewhat surprised when Jackson did not make another appearance or send for them that evening. Not long after the three found Henry and started making their camp, a shout of joy rang out and men rushed to the opposite side of the campsite.

Jackson had hinted at his lack of supplies, but Henry snorted and said, "Supplies?...ain't been any supplies. We have been living off the land for the most part. Stealing and looting Indian villages and hunting, that's how we have kept from starving." Shaking his head, Henry said, "Son, we've been plagued, purely plagued, by supply shortages since the start of this mess."

Neither Jonah, Moses, nor Lieupo knew who Henry was speaking to with the term son. However, it was Lieupo who responded, "I thought the secretary of war authorized Governor Blunt to furnish supplies."

"They was promised shore nuff but I'll give you a bit of advice, soldier boy. The gov'ment is noted for being long on promise and short on delivering. I tell you something else. An empty belly makes a man quarrelsome. Discipline is lax at best. Don't reckon anybody other than our Andy could keep the men handy. Of course, he ain't like most generals, what's got their own vittles. Andy eats what the men eats. Iffen they don't eat, he don't neither. That's why the men follow him. You hear that, soldier boy? That hooting and hollering means the hunters Andy sent out accomplished two things. They kept their hair and at the same time were able to bring in some camp meat."

Following Henry to the center of the camp, it was apparent the hunters had been lucky. Jackson was standing with the hunters admiring their kill. A small wagon was loaded down with several turkey and three deer. One of the deer was small enough that Moses wondered if that was milk on its lips, but starving men took no such notice. Ten or twelve squirrels lay in a heap and, to everyone's joy, a large gang of wild hogs.

Jokingly, Jackson questioned his men, "You didn't raid some settlers' hog pens, did you, men?"

"Shucks, Andy," one of the men responded. "You know there ain't any settlement here abouts. Kilt them with my bow so's not to make a racket. The hard part was dragging the critters up the bank and out of the bog they were in."

Jonah noted with interest how the men addressed Jackson as Andy and not general. He'd stick with the General, at least for now. By the time it was dark, cook fires were burning bright. Pots of squirrel stew were simmering; a hog and a deer were hung over a hastily made spit, and men were drooling over the promise of full bellies. Jackson ordered General Coffee to send out a good string of scouts to alert them should the Red Sticks decide this was the perfect opportunity to attack. Having been in the position in years past, Jonah volunteered his and Moses' service to take a watch.

"You both look well fed," Coffee commented and readily accepted the offer. Henry volunteered as well.

"Thank you, gentlemen," Jonah turned to see Jackson had walked up and heard the conversation. "Maybe you will be of use to us yet." Hearing this, Henry winked at Jonah and Moses.

"Where's Captain Lieupo?" Jonah asked.

Taking his pipe in hand, Henry chuckled, "Crockett has done got him treed." This caused Jackson to laugh.

Damn, Jonah thought, *he is human.*

⧉

THE MEN BROKE CAMP at first light and headed to Fort Strother. The trail was in good shape and they made good time. Coffee and a man named Russell rode at the general's side. Soon, another man rode up and joined the group.

Seeing Jonah's interest in the group that was obviously Jackson's inner circle, Henry spoke, "Feller in the buckskin shirt is William Russell. He's in charge of what some call Jackson's spies. They are just a good group of scouts actually. Imagine that's who I'll be assigned to once we get back to the fort. Wouldn't hurt none if you and Moses were to tie in with his bunch. You would learn a lot more about the goings on than you would hanging around the fort." This had Moses' attention and Jonah could tell if given a choice, this would be his. "The other feller in the homespun shirt," Henry continued, "is George Mayfield. He is Jackson's interpreter. He hangs close to Andy most of the time. He's from Tennessee like Jackson. When he was just a boy, his daddy, Southerland Mayfield, had him a nice homestead at the edge of the frontier and the Creek's lands. One day a dozen or so braves attacked the farm and kilt all the males 'cepting George and his younger brother. For the next ten years or so, George lived with the Creeks. It got so he couldn't even speak English. He had to be learnt all over again."

"What happened to the women?" Moses asked.

"They survived and settled in Nashville. Soon as George found out they was alive, he became a white again. He's one I can't figure," Henry admitted. "He doesn't seem to hate all the Creeks but the ones that he does, he is pure murder on. He returns to his savage ways at times. I kind of keep my distance from him…can't rightly say why, only I do."

Fort Strother was like most of the hastily built forts that Jonah and Moses had been to in the Northwest. It was named after Jackson's topographical engineer, Captain John Strother. The fort had been built in November the previous year, close to the Coosa River at a spot known locally as Ten Islands. The fort would be Jackson's primary base of operations and main supply base. Supplies received overland could be loaded on flatboats and floated down the Coosa River.

"Yep!" It'd be an easy chore to float supplies," Henry snorted, "were there any supplies to be had."

It would be easy to smile at the old scout's comments if they were not so true. The fort was rather large. A tall and long log palisade, with four blockhouses located at the corners, provided security for the inhabitants. The fort was built to hold several thousand men. Jonah was surprised to see so many people there as they rode in, remembering Henry had said most of the Tennessee militia had gone home. He had figured there would be no more than one-hundred-fifty men at the fort plus another three hundred or so friendlies. By friendlies, he meant Indian allies, mostly Cherokee but some Creeks. The friendlies all wore white feathers or white deer tails to distinguish themselves from the hostiles.

"Old Andy ought to be tickled," Henry declared as they swung down from their horses. "Looks like the gov'ment finally got around to filling some of their promise."

Jonah estimated one thousand men plus the Indians were inside the fort, along with a line of supply wagons.

"Damn, this is a big fort," Lieupo spoke for the first time, appraising the fort with a military eye. "Blockhouses, three large parade grounds, three... no, four, separate camps. Looking around I see infantry, cavalry, and Indians. Jackson has got the makings of a sizable force."

"Better look again," Henry responded. "Half them fellers are raw recruits, some of which ain't never shaved."

Moses clapped Henry on the shoulder saying, "Well, they can't all be old he-coons like you, Henry." This caused a chuckle from Jonah and Lieupo.

"Yer right. And a passel of them boys ain't never gonna be, either," Henry replied knowingly.

Chapter Twelve

THE EVENING MEAL WAS the heartiest Jackson's men had eaten in days. With their bellies full, the contented men broke out their pipes, cigars, and chewing tobacco as they gathered in little groups, some passing jugs of corn squeezing. One group was much larger than the others.

"That's Crockett spitting out one of his tales," Henry snorted, walking toward the circle of men. Smiling at Henry's comments, Jonah, Moses, and Lieupo followed him.

Crockett saw the group walk up and paused in his tale. "Make some room, boys. These men are notables. Mr. Jonah Lee there has the president's paper. Lem...Lemuel Smith, don't hog that jug. There are others that have got a thirst besides you." The smallish man looked a little sheepish but passed the jug.

Crockett naturally reached out, taking the jug he took a long pull. Shaking his head, he wiped his lips with the back of his grimy hand, and then passed the jug to Moses. "Where was I?" Crockett said. "Oh yeah, we were building Fort Strother when me and a couple other scouts captured some Creek warriors. Their leader was a breed named Bob Catala. We continued to scout around and found a hostile Creek village about eight miles to our east. We took our prisoners and reported back to Andy as quick as we could. He ordered General Coffee to destroy the village." Crockett paused just long enough to intercept the jug of corn squeezing. He held it up to his ear and shook it. "About as I figured," he snorted and drained the last of the liquid from the jug.

"See if we can round up another one," Crockett said, tossing the empty jug to a group of men. Smacking his lips, he continued, "It was early in the morning on November third, a chilly morning with frost crunching under foot when we made it to the village without being spied. General Coffee sent Captain Hammond's rangers to the left and I went with his group. We hadn't gotten far when a Creek warrior doing his early morning nature call saw us and let out a yell. Hostiles came pouring out of the village to meet us. General Coffee ordered his men to fire and they let 'er rip. Injuns were down and kicking but them that survived returned our fire. Men were down, cussing and hollering, but Coffee kept up the advance and soon we had closed formation around the village so nobody could escape. I guess the Red Devils knew it was hopeless, so most of them surrendered. However, a group of Red Sticks, about fifty I'd say, ran into a house. Once the warriors were inside, a Creek woman picked up a bow and since it was a strong bow, she used her feet to pull it back and let fly an arrow. Poor old Lieutenant Moore didn't know what hit him. He was the first person I ever seen kilt by an arrow. This made the men see fire. Enraged, a group shot the woman. At least twenty balls blew through her. After that, the massacre was on. There wasn't no stopping the men. Somebody, one of the soldiers, set fire to the house and burned it down. Forty-six bodies counted. I saw a young boy, about twelve years old, crawling on the ground with a broken arm and leg. He was so near the burning house the grease was spewing out of his skin, making him beg for mercy. Somebody obliged the young boy and shot him."

Jonah wondered if Crockett had been the somebody but didn't ask. "By the end of things," Crockett was saying, "we killed one hundred and eighty-six warriors. I hate to admit it, but eighty-four women and children got killed as well." Shaking his head, Crockett sadly whispered, "We didn't set out to harm no women and children, it just couldn't be helped. They fought as hard as the braves. We lost five soldiers, and twenty to forty were wounded. When Andy heard about the battle from General Coffee, he wrote to the governor of Tennessee, Mr. Willie Blount, declaring 'We have retaliated for the destruction of Fort Mims.'"

Realizing the tale was over, men began to hoot and cheer. More than half-drunk, Crockett stood up slowly and took a bow.

"Told you he was a windbag," Henry stated, "ought to be a politician. But his story was as near the truth as could be. I heard it from several men. They all tell the same tale."

"No need to lie when the truth is that exciting," Lieupo added.

H EARING FOOTSTEPS, JONAH TURNED and came face to face with a young army officer. His uniform was clean and near immaculate. Jonah realized this was one of the new officers who had just reported to the fort. The man was younger than Jonah had thought at first glance. He seemed to scowl and that made him appear older.

"I'm Ensign Houston, sir, Sam Houston. I have been sent to make sure you have found a billet."

Jonah looked at the tall, dark, young officer. "We have not been assigned a specific billet, but we unloaded our packs with Henry's here. I believe this is the camp for Russell's scouts. Is that all right?"

"Yes sir," Houston replied smiling. "We're not fussy around here. The general just wants to know where you're at. I'm to tell you there will be an officer's call first thing in the morning. The general said for the three of you to be there."

Jonah didn't know which of the four had been left out but assumed it was Henry since himself, Moses, and Captain Lieupo had arrived and reported together. "Thank you..."

"Sam," the young officer filled in. "Call me Sam, if you like that, or Houston. I'm used to either."

Shaking hands, Jonah promised Houston they'd be present in the morning. As Houston took his leave, he paused and talked with an Indian, speaking in the Indian's native tongue.

"That's Sequoia," Henry offered. "He's the chief of the Cherokee."

"What was that name he called Houston?" Lieupo asked.

Moses, who had been mostly quiet, listening, and taking everything in answered Lieupo's question, "Colonneh! Colonneh means the raven."

Watching Houston fall into step with Sequoia after an embrace and then follow the chief to the Cherokee camp, Lieupo said, "I'll be damned. It's hard to know who's who in this war. At least, when you're fighting the British, they have on red coats." The men couldn't help but laugh.

"Just remember red and white," Henry advised. "Red, you're dead, white feather or armband they're friend."

"Humph...I'm not sure I'll take the time to check for feathers or armbands when I'm about to part with my scalp." The men all laughed again as they made for their camp.

Chapter Thirteen

SEVERAL OFFICERS WERE PILED into Jackson's quarters waiting on the general. Jonah, Moses, and Lieupo were officially introduced to several men, including General Coffee and Captain William Russell, whom Jonah and Moses had more or less attached themselves with since Henry was part of the captain's unit.

"A company of spies is what they really are, not scouts," Lieupo whispered.

"I know." Jonah didn't doubt his friend.

George Mayfield was introduced to Jonah, as was John Carroll. The men didn't have to wait long. Jackson's aide, Captain John Reid, entered and laid several documents on a rough-hewn table that had only one chair. Jackson entered the room and General Coffee pulled the chair out for his friend. Jackson looked pale this morning and Jonah wondered if he'd had a restless night. Turning sideways, it was obvious Jackson was shielding his shoulder.

That's it, Jonah realized. He'd heard the Tennessee men talk about Jackson's duel and wound. The wound was certainly giving the man trouble. What was it Henry had said? 'They ain't no backup in the man.' *Well, he was right,* Jonah decided. Those were not empty words and Jonah found himself admiring the man even more.

Seating himself, Jackson hunched over a crude map. When the officers crowded in, Jackson pointed his forefinger at a spot on the paper. "This, Captain Russell tells me, is the Creek village of Emuckfaw. There is a large band of Red Sticks here. I intend to march to that village on the morrow. We will march from Ten Islands, or as young Houston would say, 'Oti Palin.'" This caused a grin to spread across Houston's face and Jonah realized that the two men must be friends and not just comrades in arms.

Focusing his thoughts back to the general, Jonah heard him say, "We'll push down south and southeast. Captain Russell will lead an advance party. It is my aim, gentlemen, to burn the Red Sticks' town. We will kill every hostile Creek we find, with no quarter given."

Jonah looked at Moses when the statement was made. But it was Houston, whose face looked drawn with a deep scowl. Friends he might be with Jackson, but it was obvious he didn't agree with him on everything.

"We will not saddle ourselves with prisoners," Jackson was saying. "Is that understood?"

The officers muttered their understanding, and then some brave soul from the back, Jonah couldn't see who, asked what was probably on everyone's mind. "General, do you think with these raw recruits a forced march through difficult terrain and the threat of a numerically superior force of hostiles is advised?"

"Fool," Lieupo whispered in Jonah's ear.

Jackson's face became livid. "Who asked that?" he bellowed.

Like the parting of the Red Sea in biblical days, the men opened a gap. A colonel Jonah hadn't met was standing there, looking very pale.

"Our men have sixty day enlistments, Colonel," Jackson said, gaining control of his rage. "They volunteered to fight. Would you have me wait until their enlistment is nearly up, our new supplies consumed and more settlers put to death before we march, sir?"

"No, sir," the colonel managed in a trembling voice.

"Good," Jackson snapped, slamming his hand down on the table. "Prepare your men to march at first light." With that, Jackson stood and made his way out, his step somewhat quicker than when he entered, the pain having been replaced by rage.

AT DAWN THE FOLLOWING day, Jonah and Moses rode out with Henry and Captain Russell's scouts. It was January 17, 1814. Jonah had halfway expected Captain Lieupo to accompany them, but he had been summoned to the general's quarters where he apparently had been assigned to Jackson's staff, at least for the time being.

Russell's group was made up of experienced backwoods men. Unlike the raw recruits, these men were tough, seasoned veterans, not a man of whom couldn't sneak into a hostile camp and slit a man's throat before he even knew he was dying.

Russell had briefly talked with Jonah and Moses after the meeting with Jackson the previous day. "Henry tells me that you were a scout and fought with 'Mad' Anthony Wayne." Jonah nodded while wondering where Henry had picked this up as neither he nor Moses had mentioned it. "I also hear you fought at the Battle of the Thames and helped take down Tecumseh."

"We were there," Jonah admitted.

"He's the Indian that started this whole mess, him and his prophets with all their signs and such," Russell said. "Cost many a good man on both sides his life. I wish that I'd been there. I'd love to have had the red devil in my sights. I'd have blown him clear to the great spirits." Jonah couldn't help but smile at the captain's contempt for a dead man.

For the next three days the men silently made their way through the heavy forest. Twice they came upon Indians but were so quiet they were never discovered. Once, an Indian astride his horse walked right past the scout, Lemuel, without knowing how close to death he'd been. Each day at dusk Russell would send a scout to report to Jackson. Each morning the scout would return with a bag full of food.

Noticing the men wiping their hands in the dirt and on tree leaves, Jonah discussed it with Moses. "The food has the smell of the soldiers," Moses reminded his friend. "That Creek warrior would surely have smelled Lemuel had he not done so after eating. I've even seen a few chewing on tree bark to get the smell from their breath." Jonah realized his friend was right.

THE EVENING OF THE twenty-first, the scouts closed with the Emuckfaw village. Making a quick reconnaissance of the village, the scouts faded into the darkness and made their way back to the general's camp some twelve miles away. Little did Russell or Jackson know, their main army had been spotted by a Red Stick hunting party who had camped not three miles from where Jackson's men were encamped.

Chapter Fourteen

IT WAS DAWN, AND the men were beginning to stir about on this cool morning. Moses woke up and was instantly alarmed. It was not the men who'd already left their blankets, it was something more. He moved his foot from beneath his blanket and nudged Jonah with the toe of his moccasin. Jonah was already awake. He slowly pulled his long rifle to him and then reached for his tomahawk. The movement, slight as it was, woke Lieupo. He reached beneath his saddle and pulled his pistols to him.

A shrill scream shattered the early morning stillness. Muskets barked from the undergrowth, spewing lead into the sentries and men who'd already gotten up. After the first volley, the Red Sticks charged.

"Weatherford," Henry cussed and shot at a running warrior clad only in a loin cloth.

War whoops rang out amid the curses and screams of the soldiers. Captain Reid was shouting for the men to form around the command tent. The flash of weapons lit up the early morning with stabs of flames gushing from musket and pistol barrels. Moses fired, hitting a dashing brave, and quickly ducked to reload. This gave Jonah the opportunity to line his sights on another warrior. The impact of the lead ball slamming into the Indian's chest knocked him backwards. Jonah didn't look but could hear Lieupo firing first one pistol and then the other. Henry was in the process of reloading when a Red Stick darted toward him. With the ramrod still in the barrel, Henry pointed the long rifle at his foe and pulled the trigger. It was point blank range. The ramrod impaled the brave just below the sternum; when he hit the ground a good portion of the rod was sticking out his back. Moses found another target and cut him down.

The Red Sticks were now inside the camp and there was no time to reload. Jonah fired one last shot that hit a brave in the shoulder, spinning him around. Moses threw his tomahawk, hitting an Indian in the back with a sickening thud. It buried itself deep, severing the warrior's spine and dropping him. The battle had reached its crescendo. Lieupo was fighting an Indian hand to hand. Knife blades were locked together. Wrestling his one hand free and making a desperate swing with his fist, Lieupo broke the brave's jaw and then stabbed him, spilling the warrior's innards as the sharp blade sliced open his gut.

Moses was also fighting hand to hand with a brave, while another was circling with a knife looking for an opening. Jonah clubbed the second one with his long rifle and then used the butt plate to smash his foe's skull. Officers could be heard barking orders to the men. The element of surprise gone, the Indians began to retreat.

"Pour it on," Jackson was shouting.

A few targets remained but they were fleeing and then it was over. Thirty minutes...the battle had lasted only thirty minutes. It had seemed a lot longer. Lieupo had a cut on his arm from the knife fight but was otherwise unhurt. Jonah, Moses, and Henry were bruised but had not been wounded.

"There goes our surprise attack," Jonah declared.

"Yeah, and there goes my ramrod." Henry had pulled the bloody and bent rod from the dead Indian. "Would you just look at that?"

Seeing the scattered weapons, Moses said, "I bet you can find another." Henry grunted and started looking about until he found a rod that suited him.

Sam Houston trotted up, his face black and grimy from the spent gunpowder, "The general wants to strike while we got the Red Sticks on the run. He's sending out Coffee with half the men to attack the village. Hammond's rangers and Russell's men are going as well."

Picking up a canteen that was draped over a dead soldier, Henry said after taking a long swig, "You don't think they'll be waiting on us?" Houston shrugged his shoulders and then hurried back to the command tent.

Crockett was with the men forming up. He had a large dark spot on his buckskin shirt. Seeing Jonah's look, he grinned and said, "Don't worry, Jonah, it ain't my blood." Jonah had come to like the loud boisterous man and was glad he was not hurt. "You boys coming along on this little adventure?" Crockett asked.

"We can't let you have all the fun to yourself," Moses threw back.

I N LESS THAN AN hour after the battle, Coffee's men had closed with the Emuckfaw encampment. He sent out Russell's men to scout the place before they attacked. Jonah and Moses went with Henry. They were within hearing distance of the camp when Henry pulled up behind a huge pine tree and ducked down. Peering around the tree, he quickly ducked down again. "We need more men," he said in a whisper. "There's over a thousand braves there. I spotted Menawa, Weatherford, and Peter McQueen."

"McQueen," Jonah repeated in a whisper. "Is he a white man?"

"Half-breed," Henry answered. "His daddy was a Scot. Let's back out of here," he advised the men. "I've seen enough. I don't mind a proper fight but attacking this would be suicide."

Jonah and Moses were of the same mindset, so they backed out and high-tailed it back to General Coffee to report. Other scouts had returned with the same report so Coffee turned his men around and headed back to Jackson's camp. When he reported, he could tell Jackson was disappointed but knew it was better to back off and live to fight another day.

"You did what you thought best, John," Jackson said, resting his hand on his friend's shoulder.

A cry went up from the edge of the camp. A couple of Russell's scouts came running in, sounding the alarm, "Here comes the Red Devils again."

"Arm yourselves and take cover," Jackson ordered. "Hold off till I give the word, men," he shouted his last order. "Let them get close and then blow 'em to hell."

"That's Andy," Crockett said as he scooted down next to Jonah and Moses.

In spite of the coolness, sweat trickled down from Jonah's brow. A horse whinnied and stomped its foot. A mule brayed, and then they came, charging out of the trees as arrows filled the air from archers hidden in the brush. The anxious raw recruits didn't wait for the command. A nervous finger pulled a trigger, closely followed by others. Rifles spat forth a deadly swarm of lead balls at the charging Indians.

"By twos," Jonah barked to the men beside him. He and Moses let go with their long rifles and then ducked down as Lieupo and Henry found targets and fired. From the command tent, Jonah watched as a sword glinted in the sun. Down came the arm and the men at the command tent fired. *At least some of the men waited on Jackson's command,* he thought. A crashing volley emptied saddles but the charge continued. Men feverishly worked with their powder horns and ramrods as weapons were reloaded. The Creek horsemen, four and six abreast, charged the center. They were upon the command tent when another volley rang out and more saddles were emptied. Another volley ripped out at a bunch of warriors charging on foot. The swath of lead balls cut down a number of the warriors, but still they came.

Jonah could barely see through the battle smoke. The near naked braves showed no fear as their scarlet painted bodies continued the attack. The sky was darkened by another cloud of arrows fired from the cover. The sound of war whoops mingled with cries of pain and death. The two forces were now upon each other and there was no time to reload. Indians jumped over crates and barrels, hacking at the soldiers. Muskets were turned into clubs, and the soldiers rushed to meet the fearless Red Sticks. One man lunged at a brave, his bayonet piercing the Indian's throat, but before he could retract his weapon, he was cut down by a war ax.

Jonah's group had pulled their tomahawks and knives when Coffee hollered, "To me! They're trying to flank us."

Seeing an Indian aim his bow at Houston, Lieupo fired his remaining pistol. Houston touched his brow in salute. Hurrying, they closed with Coffee as he charged the Indians. The attack was now almost to the rear of the camp. Many of the men hurrying to turn the flank attack brought their muskets. Quickly, Coffee put the men in two lines. The front line fired and then knelt while the second line fired. This stopped the advance.

Crockett gave his tomahawk a throw and down went a warrior with a red plume in his headband. "You might be protected from our rifle but that blade sent your soul to hell," he shouted. Jonah realized the man must have been a Red Stick prophet.

The grass was high and brown from the cold frost. Jonah spotted a bit of movement, watched for a second as the tall grass parted, and then flung his tomahawk. He was rewarded with a cry of pain. Two more volleys tore into the grass and underbrush. More yelps of pain, and then the remaining Indians popped up and ran. A few scattered shots could still be heard back in the camp.

Jonah felt a hand grab his shoulder. Turning, it was Moses who motioned with his head. Lying on the ground, with a huge dark place spreading across his shirt, lay Coffee. The man was alive but severely wounded. His face was ghastly pale. Jonah ordered two men to return to camp and get a surgeon. It was not long before the men were back with the surgeon and a stretcher. Jackson was with them. He reached down and took Coffee's hand.

"You saved us, John, you turned the attack. Rest now, and the surgeon will take care of you or I'll have him shot for incompetence."

Coffee smiled and the surgeon winced. Jonah was sure it was meant as a joke. He was just as sure that with Jackson there was no telling. One thing was sure: his comment didn't help the surgeon's confidence a bit. He caught Lieupo's eye. The man felt the same way. They walked off following the stretcher barrier, wondering when the next attack would come.

Chapter Fifteen

IT WAS A SUBDUED army of survivors that hugged the campfires that evening. Maybe the men felt a sense of security from the flickering flames that lit up the early evening and would burn through the night. Watches were relieved every two hours. The surgeon and his helpers were busy trying to save as many of the wounded as possible. Captain Reid left General Coffee's tent to inform Jackson that his friend was alive and would surely survive. A breeze picked up and blew at the flap of Jackson's tent. Several officers were gathered there.

Looking over the camp, Reid wrinkled his nose and spoke to Jonah, "The place reeks, Mr. Lee."

Reek it does, but not unlike other battlefields, Jonah thought. Charred wood from burnt crates and barrels mixed with the sickening smell of burnt flesh. Blood, urine, and dung, all seeped together to fill the air with a putrid stench. Death, the unmistakable smell of death, be it man or animal, hung on the evening air. All woven together to produce the reeking smell of a battlefield.

Sometimes it took days to clear your nostrils... sometimes it never did. The smell of death seemed to linger, an omen to what the future may hold. Hearing a cry from one of the wounded being jostled, Jonah could only imagine the fear some of these men had felt that afternoon. Having faced not one, but two attacks and knowing another could be launched at any moment. Men who'd laughed at death while passing the jug with Crockett not many nights ago now thankfully ate their cold biscuits in silence as they huddled together, heads hanging down, some tired, some praying. Would they be next to lay beside some friend or neighbor who had already been killed in battle, or would their body be dragged off by savages and mutilated beyond recognition? Thoughts that never came to bear a few nights ago now weighed heavily on more than one man's mind. Seeing his friend was not paying attention, Moses nudged Jonah breaking his reverie.

Jackson was saying he intended to move at first light. He'd been going over several possible routes back to Fort Strother with Captain Russell. He had decided to take one that, while longer, should be safer. Jackson then dismissed the officers to get the men ready to march with the morning light. "A moment, Mr. Lee," he had called as Jonah was leaving the tent.

Returning back inside, Jackson's servant offered a cup of weak, warm coffee and cold bread. Seeing Jackson dunk the bread in the coffee before placing it into his mouth, Jonah followed suit.

"The men today, how do you think they did?" Jackson asked after finishing his biscuit.

Without taking time to think, Jonah responded quickly, "For raw recruits without the benefit of training, I thought they did very well."

"Do you think I was wrong to rush these men into action?" Jackson asked very bluntly.

"Time, sir, is a commodity circumstance seldom allows. You have the men...all volunteers I might add. You have an enemy who is highly trained; indeed, warfare has been bred into him. It's something he eats, sleeps, and breathes. That enemy will murder, rape and mutilate countless innocent settlers if he is not brought to task and quickly. He has already done so. No, sir, General, I do not fault you and I certainly don't judge you."

Jackson stood and bending over the table held out his hand, "Thank you, Mr. Lee, that was well said."

After shaking Jonah's hand, Jackson turned and walked out. In that moment, that one moment, the General had been vulnerable. A powerful hard man...but a man.

CRCS

THE SUN ROSE AND the men seemed to be in better spirits. They were alive and had survived the night without further attack. Jonah, Lieupo, and Moses discussed the situation.

"We expected them and they knew it," Moses stated. "Weatherford, or Red Eagle, whatever he's called, is a patient man, a war chief. He will attack when we are least prepared and the odds are in his favor. It's a long way to Fort Strother," he added.

The army marched out in a long column. As the sun rose, the morning chill evaporated with the dew. The men found traveling over the rough terrain tiring. When a halt was called, some just flopped down where they stopped. Officers and sergeants bawled out the stragglers, some cursing to high heaven.

"Some of those cursing were doing a lot of praying last night," Lieupo commented. "Some soon forget until they need help again," Moses replied, disgust in his voice.

Up ahead, Jackson could be heard sending an advance guard out. Henry was riding down the column and stopped when he saw Jonah's group.

"Enotachopoo Creek just ahead," Henry said. "Andy's sending out his forward guard. I was told to tell the colonel to hurry this bunch along."

Looking back and seeing two colonels, Jonah wondered who was supposed to do the hurrying. One was the colonel who'd questioned Jackson about attacking the enemy with raw recruits. He's staying out of sight, Jonah decided. By the time the three had gotten to the creek, the artillery was being sent across. Falling in beside the artillery major, Jonah, Moses, and Lieupo were midstream when a blood-curdling death whoop struck fear in the retreating stragglers. The underbrush next to the creek bank was suddenly a dense cloud of smoke as numerous muskets fired. Red Stick horsemen bounded out into the creek, cutting down the straggling soldiers left and right.

Hearing the war whoops, the two colonels spurred their horses forward and refused to stop when the artillery major shouted at them. "Cowards, damn cowards, they've deserted their men."

The drivers for the artillery wagons cracked their whips, urging the horses across the creek, trying to save the cannons. The last few soldiers were in a full run as they rushed into the creek. Some were shot, while others slipped and went under the cold water, soaking powder and shot. Another volley from the shore sent more men to a watery grave. The Red Sticks were firing from the underbrush, from up in the trees, and a group on horseback milled about the creek bank making easy pickings of the retreating soldiers. Using their horses for cover, Jonah, Moses, Lieupo, and the artillery major were returning fire. Henry tried in vain to halt the running troops. He finally gave up and joined Jonah's group. With the colonels running, there was nothing one man could do to stop the panic.

Balls plucked into the creek about Jonah and his group, sending up small spouts of water. The gunfire had made the horses nervous and wild-eyed. It was difficult to control the horses and return fire at the same time. Jackson could be heard from the far shore shouting orders and encouragement. A counterattack was being put together. The bullet and arrow riddled bodies of dead soldiers floated face down in the shallow creek. As Jackson's men re-crossed the creek to meet the hostiles, some of the bodies had to be pushed aside.

A ball plucked Lieupo's sleeve. Looking for his assailant, he shouted, "Damn this." Then sighting an Indian lowering his musket, Lieupo aimed and fired. Watching the brave hit the water, Lieupo said, "You might not have been the one who ruined my shirt, but somebody had to pay and you was the first I seen."

Hearing Lieupo, the other nearby men burst out laughing causing others to wonder, 'why in God's name are those idiots laughing while we're getting our arses shot off?'. Colonel John Carroll and a group of men were now riding past Jonah's group so they remounted and raced to meet the hostiles. The surprise was now over and the soldiers were getting the upper hand. Moses sighted a brave firing his bow from a tree. He took quick aim and shot. The warrior grabbed his face with both hands and toppled out of the tree to the water below. So many muskets and pistols had been fired, spent powder smoke hung heavy along the creek bank and over the water. The Red Sticks made a final wild rush. It was hand to hand, hack, cut and thrust. Blades bit into muscle and bone. A few more bangs were heard as men were cut down cursing, shrieking, hollering, and crying out in pain.

Finally, a last war whoop was heard, the gurgle of a punctured lung gave way to the chilled coldness of death, the creek's waters ran red and it was dotted with bodies. The soldiers on the creek bank opened up a space as the men on horseback returned. A cheer went up from men glad to be alive. Jackson personally thanked the men who'd turned the battle with the counterattack. He then spotted the two colonels who ran, deserting their men at the creek bank. Lieupo happened to be the closest officer to Jackson when he spotted the colonels.

"Captain Lieupo."

"Sir."

"Arrest those two. They will be held for court martial once we reach Fort Strother." Without another word, Jackson turned and rode away.

Henry, who'd heard Jackson's orders, as did most everyone else, sidled his horse up next to Lieupo. Taking his pipe from his mouth he spat and said, "Lucky, damn lucky they are. It's a wonder Andy didn't just up and shoot 'em down his own self. Save time wid a court martial, it'd seem."

Chapter Sixteen

THE RETURN TRIP TO Fort Strother was without further event. "I don't understand it," Captain Lieupo said as the army halted at sundown. "I doubt we could have driven off another attack."

"Jackson's medicine is big," Moses said. "The Red Sticks have attacked three times. While we lost some men and more were wounded, the Red Sticks have suffered significant losses as well. They thought that they had us at the creek."

"And they almost did," Henry interjected. "Well, the surprise was theirs, but we turned the rout and they lost heavily. I saw as many Indians floating in the creek as I did soldiers."

"Can't deny that," Lieupo replied.

"Where's your charges?" Jonah asked Lieupo, realizing the two colonels were not present.

"Jackson had Captain Reid take charge of them," Lieupo replied.

"What do you think will happen to them, Henry?"

"I don't know, Jonah. Andy has been known to order a man shot, but two colonels. They may be cowards but they didn't become colonels without backing from somebody. Andy ain't dumb, he's got political ambition if you ask me. Shooting two colonels ain't gonna help him none, and he knows that. I 'spect they'll be sent home with the full understanding they got off easy and they likely need to find another profession."

"Well, everyone isn't cut out to be soldiers," Jonah said.

"Naw, they ain't," Henry agreed. "They ain't the first to run from an Indian attack either."

❦

THE ARMY STARTED ON the trail at first light the next morning. A fine mist hung in the air, and when the sun was fully up, the sky was gray. Leaves had fallen from the hardwood trees, creating a carpet of sorts across the trail. Wounded men cried out in pain when they hit bumps in the trail, bouncing the wagons or travois on which they lay. General Coffee made the trip in silence, gritting his teeth and grimacing rather than crying out. Just before noon, the army halted and buried two more men. After the quick burials, the men ate cold biscuits, jerky, and drank water.

"Not much of a meal for a marching army," Jonah said.

"Been this way since the onset; supplies always short in coming and when they do arrive, generally it ain't enough," Henry said. "I've said it before; it's hard to get a man to fight on an empty stomach."

"This weather don't help the misery none either," Moses added, flexing his knee trying to get the ache and stiffness out.

The mist turned into a drizzle in the early afternoon. The wind picked up and pine trees began to sway. A whispering sound came from the swaying pines. They made camp an hour earlier than usual. Jonah watched Jackson stiffly dismount his horse and stumble when his feet touched the ground. He was rubbing his shoulder and his face was pale. The man was obviously in pain yet he didn't utter a sound.

Tents were pitched for the wounded and the general. Campfires were started with what little dry wood could be found. When wet wood was added, a sizzling sound could be heard and steam rose up. Soon, however, several large fires were going. Henry, Crockett, Lemuel, and a few others struck out to find some game. At dark, the three returned with two deer. Not a feast, as there were so many to feed, but it did help. A broth made for the wounded seemed to perk them up some.

Jackson visited with the wounded, "Hold on men. We will be at the fort tomorrow and you can fill your belly with a hot meal and sleep on a real cot." It was amazing how much effect the general's positive words had on the men.

THE RAIN WAS GONE the next morning and while it was cool, the sky was clear and there was very little wind. The last of the biscuits were served as breakfast. Henry had been saving the coffee grounds. This was the third time they'd been used, so the coffee was little more than colored water, but it was warm. Crockett had a bag with a couple teaspoons left of ground up chicory in it.

"This might help a tad," he said as he tossed the bag to Moses. Dumping the chicory into the boiling water, Moses thanked Crockett and said, "It can't hurt."

The chicory coffee was much stronger with a slight bitter taste. Taking a sip of the hot brew, Henry looked up at Crockett, "Much obliged, Davy. I'll stand you a tankard when we get to the fort."

"I'll hold you to it," Crockett replied, "but it better be quick. I heard Russell will be sending out patrols in a day or two."

"Do tell," Henry snorted. "What are we going to be looking for? We know where the damn Red Sticks are. We left a trail of graves to mark the way."

Crockett just shrugged and then looked at Jonah. "Captain Russell says you and Moses are to look him up once we get back to the fort, Jonah. Seems Andy sets store by you and wants you present for a meeting." Jonah nodded and saluted Crockett with his cup of chicory.

"More than likely wants us out of his hair," Moses volunteered.

"I don't think so," Jonah answered. "Unlike with General Harrison, I think Jackson really welcomes us."

Seeing the question on Henry's face, Moses explained, "General Harrison didn't like the president sending a man to push him against the British up in the northwest and Canada."

"If Harrison and Jonah hadn't served together under General Wayne, Harrison would probably have sent Jonah packing," Lieupo said.

Now how does he know that? Jonah thought for a second and then remembered Lieupo's connection to Captain Hampton. *Spies,* he thought to himself. *Was that what he and Moses were turning into... spies?*

SUPPLIES AND NEW RATIONS had arrived at Fort Strother during their absence. Jackson ordered a large meal for all the men. The wounded were taken to the hospital where the surgeons busied themselves. Wounds were cleaned and redressed. A few arms and legs had to be removed. By nightfall the rest of the men were well sated. Good food, rest, and contraband corn squeezing did a lot to restore the men's spirits. Crockett even had a crowd gathered around listening to his lies and tales of derring-do.

Jonah, Moses, and Lieupo met up with Captain Russell and accompanied him to General Jackson's quarters. Upon entering, each man was offered a cup of coffee. Either Jackson didn't imbibe or there were no spirits to be had...other than the contraband.

"Come in," Jackson said, greeting the men. As soon as the men were seated, Jackson asked, "What do you make of our recent action? Would you call it a defeat?"

Russell seem to hesitate before he answered, giving Jonah the chance to speak. "I think the answer would depend on the objective in which the march was undertaken, General. If the objective was to wipe out the Red Sticks, we failed. However, I doubt that was our objective. If it was to take raw recruits and turn them into soldiers, we succeeded. If the objective was to meet the enemy and bring them to action, we succeeded. If it was to test our firepower against the enemy's weapons, we succeeded. We were attacked by superior numbers three times. We drove the enemy off three times. The men have been bloodied and seasoned. You have found your strength and weaknesses in both the men and officers. You have answered a lot of questions. I would say you have a tactical victory, sir."

Jackson smiled. "Do you agree, Captain Russell?"

"In all aspects, General."

"Thank you, men. Now let's get down to why I requested your presence. We have a group of settlers that need a scout to accompany them to Fort Armstrong. I'm sure you have someone who will serve, Captain Russell."

"Yes sir, Henry Parrish knows the trail well. I can send him."

Jackson nodded as he sipped on his coffee. Setting the cup down, he cleared his throat and spoke again. "I'm expecting the U.S. 39th Infantry any day. When they arrive I intend to mount an offensive to end the Red Stick problem. Until the 39th arrives, I need to know what's happening, to be kept aware of the Indians' movements and actions."

"We can handle that," Russell said. Jackson nodded again.

"I'd like to accompany the captain, if I may, sir?" Jonah asked.

Jackson nodded once more, a smile on his face. "I was sure you would, Mr. Lee." Turning his head toward Lieupo, he added, "and you may go as well, Captain."

"Thank you, sir."

Once outside the general's quarters, Moses punched Jonah in the arm. "All these willing maidens waiting on me and you go volunteering us to hit the trail again. I tell you, Jonah, sometimes I question your common sense."

"Amen to that," Lieupo added. "You didn't have to volunteer."

Jonah said defensively, "Yeah! If I hadn't, what would I have looked like? Well, you two have the night," Jonah responded with a smile.

"Well, let's don't be wasting it," Lieupo said. "Come on, Moses, lead the way." With that, the two marched off toward the gate.

"Deserted you, didn't they?"

Turning, Jonah was face to face with Jackson. "They'll be back in the morning."

"Well, since you have lost your comrades, come in," Jackson replied. "Reid has confiscated a jug we should uncork and try."

"By all means, General," Jonah replied and followed the general back into his quarters.

Chapter Seventeen

HENRY HAD BEEN ABSOLUTELY right about Crockett. The loud, boisterous man in camp was a consummate woodsman. Russell had sent out several scouting parties of four men each. Henry snorted and grumbled about being saddled with a bunch of pilgrims, but in the end he did as he was told. Jonah had always considered himself a good woodsman, not as good as Moses, but better than most. So it was with infinite wisdom he decided Crockett was not only good, he was better than Jonah and near as good as Moses.

The men had been on the trail for four days. They followed the Coosa River and had taken the precaution of cooking only one meal a day. After they cooked, they covered the signs as well as possible and moved on, never tarrying long at the cook site. They were nearing Fort Williams when the smell of wood smoke alerted them. Turning west away from the river, the men followed a cut in the forest.

Crockett halted suddenly then turned south. The four had not gone far when Crockett held up his hand for the men to halt again. He had a scowl on his face and his nostrils seemed to flare. Jonah immediately picked up the scent. The sickly smell of burnt flesh and death filled the air. Long rifles were cocked and ready as the men warily picked their way through the forest toward the stench. Noises could be heard: whites and Indians, screams and laughter. Crockett suddenly ducked down with the rest of the men following suit. A group of Red Stick warriors thundered past, whooping and hollering. Each of the riders had fresh scalps, dripping blood as they swung back and forth on the lances they were tied to. The warriors were all naked except for loin cloths, their skin painted red and spattered with blood.

Once the horsemen were out of sight, the men hit the trail again. A dead cow was lying across the trail, a tomahawk still embedded in her head, blood oozed from her nostrils. Flies already were buzzing around the pool of blood. Leaping over the cow, Crockett followed a bend in the trail where he halted so quickly, the other men almost collided with him. A boy lay on the ground. He looked to be about twelve.

"He was probably bringing the cow in," Crockett whispered.

The boy had been scalped and horribly mutilated. Stepping over the boy, the men quickly came to the edge of a clearing. A man lay beside a well. Like the boy, he'd been scalped but he'd also been emasculated. Sticks protruded from empty eye sockets. Just past him lay another boy about eight or ten years old. Beside the boy lay a woman. In addition to being scalped, their arms and legs had been broken and lay at odd angles.

"They do like to play, don't they?" Crockett hissed.

"I hope they were dead first," Lieupo said.

"Me too," Moses responded and then added, "But I wouldn't count on it."

Over by the porch a dog lay. The poor animal had so many arrows in him he looked like a porcupine. Jonah felt his throat tighten and felt clogged up. He needed a drink of water. The cabin had partly burned.

"They must have had water inside to put out the fire," Lieupo said.

Jonah nodded, "Maybe the three at the well were trying to get more water."

Hearing a noise, the men looked up. A figure stood in the doorway of the ruined cabin…a naked teenage girl. From the blood around her midsection it was obvious that she had been raped. Her arms were outstretched where they had been tied to a limb. Someone had jabbed an arrow across and through her buttocks. Little sticks had been stuck under her eyelids to prop them open.

"Help me," the girl begged. Her lips were swollen and bloody. "Help me," her voice hardly more than a whisper.

Jonah spoke softly, "You're safe now. We will not let any more harm come to you. Steve," He said using Lieupo's first name, "see if you can find some brandy or liquor. Moses, if you'll help me, we'll see if we can help this lady."

Crockett looked pale. He swallowed and said, "I'll keep a lookout."

Leaving the girl's arms tied as so to keep her from flailing about, Moses broke the head off the arrow and jerked the shaft from the girl's buttocks. They had calmly explained to the girl what they intended beforehand. She nodded her understanding. When the arrow was pulled free, she only gave a little cry. Blood flowed freely, which Jonah thought was a good thing.

"Helps wash away the poison," he whispered to Moses.

With the arrow out, the men laid the girl down. Using his canteen, Jonah washed the girl's eyes out. He had to talk to the girl in a soothing manner, continuing to explain what he and Moses were doing. After washing out her eyes, the men took out the sticks holding the eyelids open. Jonah pulled down on the lower lid while Moses pulled up on the upper lid. With his free hand, Jonah removed the sharpened stick from her eye. After washing the eye out again, they repeated the process for the other eye. The girl blinked her eyes several times and tears began to fall. Sitting the girl up, they cut the ropes that held her arms outstretched.

Lieupo was soon back. "I found this in the barn," he said. The jug was half full. Passing the jug to the girl, she took a long, deep pull causing the men to look at each other. Coughing, the girl brought the jug down, with tears running down her face she said, "I wish I could stay drunk forever."

Moses reached for the jug and poured some of the fiery liquid over the arrow wounds on the girl's buttocks.

"Damn," the girl hissed, causing the men to look at each other again. "I need to get some clothes," she said as she looked down at her bruised breasts and realized she had nothing on.

"I'll get you something," Lieupo volunteered.

"No, I'll do it. I need to ah...look down there." They immediately understood.

The girl stood, and as she made her way in the cabin door, she stopped. Motioning with her sore arms, she spoke to Jonah, "You come, I might need some help."

The two were gone for several minutes before Jonah returned. He picked up the near empty jug and then disappeared again. From inside the cabin, a yelp of pain was heard followed by another damn. After hearing rumbling around in the cabin, Jonah and the girl returned. She was wearing a shirt that was tight and pants that were a little too large. Her brother's, Moses figured. Finding a battered hat, the girl put it on. Jonah had brushed the girl's hair as well as he could with a broken brush, but it still looked out of sorts. The hat would cover it some and make the girl feel better. At least she was covered.

"Gentlemen," Jonah said as the men gathered about. "This is Mary. Mary, this is Moses, Captain Stephen Lieupo and Davy Crockett."

"Pleased to meet you," the girl humbly whispered. "Thank you for helping me."

"Well, where to?" Crockett asked sensing the need to change the subject before the girl broke down.

"She has family at Fort Williams," Jonah said. "How close is it?"

"Closer than Fort Strother," Crockett replied.

"Well, let's be on our way," Lieupo said.

Moving out, the men picked up the trail toward the fort. Keeping the river to their right, the men made good time, but thinking of the girl, they did not push it. Taking a chance, they built a fire at dusk and cooked a mess of fish that Lieupo and Moses caught. Keeping to their habit after eating, the group moved out. After another thirty minutes on the trail, they found a good site and made camp. The group was again on the trail before the sun rose. They made it to Fort Williams by mid-morning.

Mary's people were there as expected, and it was a bittersweet reunion. After making a detailed report to the fort's commanding officer, the men ate a big meal and decided to layover until the next morning. Jonah stopped by and checked on Mary before they turned in for the evening. The girl wept as she thanked Jonah for all they had done. "I'll see you off in the morning," she promised.

"No, you rest," Jonah said.

Finally, the girl agreed to rest. However, as the men left the next morning she was standing at the gate. She hugged each of the men and again thanked them. As they made their way out the gate, she called out, "You be careful, Jonah Lee, you be careful."

Moses started to chide his friend, but seeing the look on his face he change his mind. Mary might be thinking about Jonah, but Jonah's thoughts were on Ana.

Chapter Eighteen

THE MEN SPOKE VERY little on the return trip to Fort Strother. They had seen plenty of signs that the Red Sticks were not slowing down in their aggressive actions to wipe out the settlers in what they considered their lands. Mary's homestead was just the latest. She had admitted that one of the braves had spoken up for her and that was probably the only reason she was still alive. Her family had come across the Indian when he was a boy, and he'd fallen and busted his leg. They had splinted the leg, and Mary had hand-carried food and water to him. Now he was a brave, a warrior and had taken part in the raiding party. Mary was not sure if he'd killed anyone. He'd shown up when another brave had just jammed the arrow in her buttocks. They were fondling her breasts and poking them with another arrow. Her fear was they were going to pierce her breasts like they had her other end. But the brave her family had helped showed up. He roughly pulled the Indian with the arrow away and after a heated conversation, the Indians mounted up and rode away. The young brave who had intervened paused only long enough to look Mary's way, nod slightly and ride away following the others.

"I don't understand it," Lieupo said. "How can you so casually mistreat and murder people you have known for years. It's hard to fathom."

"Well," Crockett said, pausing to take a drink of water from his canteen. "It ain't all one-sided."

"You mean we are guilty of similar acts?" Lieupo asked, not believing Crockett.

"That's exactly what I mean," Crockett said. "Of course, you don't have to believe me. You can ask old Henry. He'll tell you. He was at Talladega same as me."

When Crockett didn't continue, Lieupo called him, "That's it, Davy? You tell me we are guilty of the same type of mayhem and then you just drop it."

Crockett lowered his long rifle to the ground. After standing silent for a minute and looking about, Crockett lifted his rifle and pointed. "It's late and that little clearing behind those rocks will make a good camp." He still hadn't answered Lieupo's question.

Lieupo took a step toward Crockett to pursue the subject. Sensing that Crockett didn't want to speak of that time, Jonah laid a hand on his friend's shoulder and shook his head no. Lieupo shrugged but let it drop.

M OSES HAD HOOKED UP with the cook back at Fort Williams. The cook had parted with a bag of crackling bread: cornbread fried with cut up pork skins in the batter. He also had given Moses what was left of a shoulder of smoked ham. Unknowingly, he had also parted with a sack of chicory coffee and a bag of salt. This had been taken when the cook went to fetch the smoked ham. Moses had not been the only scrounger. Crockett had confiscated an extra canteen, which he'd filled with corn squeezing. He'd not opened the canteen all day. After the men had their meal and laid out their blankets, Crockett reached for the canteen.

Pulling the cork free, he passed it to Moses saying, "It'll help take away the chill." Each of the men took a swig and then passed the canteen back to Crockett. He took a swig, and then as an afterthought, took one more. He wiped his mouth with the back of his hand. He then offered the canteen to Moses who shook his head no. Crockett corked the canteen and with his back propped against a boulder, he pulled his blanket over his legs. He laid his rifle so it was within easy reach and then shuffled his back, back and forth, against the rock until he was comfortable.

"He was there, Henry was, same as me. He'll tell you." Crockett had spoken when it was least expected. Maybe he'd had to gather his thoughts. Jonah wasn't sure, but they let Crockett tell his tale without interruption. "A friendly Creek heard the Red Sticks making plans to attack Leslie's fort. So he skedaddled out of there and hit the trail to Fort Strother. There he told what he'd heard. Andy quickly gathered up a force to protect Fort Leslie from the raid. Henry and I were sent out as scouts. We left Fort Strother at midnight to cut down on any movement being reported to Menawa or Red Eagle. We forded the Coosa River at a place that was about six hundred yards across. To cut down on the time it took to ford the river, each of the cavalry-men carried a foot soldier. Riding double like this, the crossing didn't take much time at all. We marched all that day through some rough country, fighting underbrush, deadfalls, vines, and skeeters. That evening, we made a cold camp. Henry and I set out to find the Red Sticks' camp. We hadn't gone five or six miles and there it was...a big camp. Henry pointed out Weatherford...Red Eagle is his Indian name. It was all I could do to keep the old he-coon from putting a ball through the Indian right then and there. Menawa was there, as were some of his prophets, all making big medicine. We watched for awhile but Peter McQueen, the half-breed, kept looking our way. I knew he couldn't see us but it made me nervous, so I pulled on old Henry and we got out of there. We took a roundabout way back to the main camp. 'They're there,' Henry said to Andy, 'Upwards a thousand of the Red Devils at Talladega town, not six miles from where we stand right now.' Excited, Andy called his officers together and planned our attack. We broke camp at four a.m. on the ninth. I know what time it was because Andy told Captain Reid to make a note of the time. We had a good size army at that time. Twelve hundred foot soldiers and eight hundred horse soldiers. How we made it without getting spotted is a mystery...a pure mystery. We made our way to Leslie's fort. Russell had his scouts out, which Henry and I was part of. We came upon a mess of the Indians sliding through the woods getting ready to carry out their attack, still unaware we were about. When all the scouts came back and reported, Andy figured there was somewhere between ten and eleven hundred Red Sticks. Andy divided his forces so as to make a circle around the heathens. He then told Captain Russell to bring on the battle. Once we got everyone in place, we poured it on. Henry looked everywhere for Red Eagle but couldn't find him. Once we cut loose, those Red Sticks came charging. They were painted red as scarlet and naked as the day they were born. When they rushed, it reminded me of a cloud of Egyptian locust you read about in the bible. They were screaming like the devils of hell had all been turned loose and the head devil himself was there in the lead. Of course, we were pouring it into them as fast as we could shoot, reload, and shoot again. We must have dropped a hundred of them right off the start. After another volley, one of their prophets fell. I don't know if it was because he fell or what, but the charge broke. Then like a gang of steers, the Red Sticks ran toward the other line. All the while they were constantly under a heavy fire. We had killed upward of four hundred of the devils in no time at all. They fought with guns, bows and arrows but didn't have a chance. I thought we'd kill them all before it was over. And then to old Andy's dismay, a band of drafted militiamen misunderstood orders and retreated. This left a hole in our lines which was quickly discovered and seven hundred or so Red Sticks high-tailed it out of there through that opening."

Crockett paused and let out a sigh. "If those militiamen had held their ground, we'd have ended the war right then and there. The poor devils didn't have a chance. I fired old Betsy here," he said, patting the long rifle at his side, "until the barrel was so hot it burned my hand. We lost seventeen to death that day, and maybe seventy-five to eighty-five wounded. That was the second battle in six days where we killed over six hundred Indians, many of them women and children."

Pausing a minute, Crockett picked up the corn liquor canteen and took another swig, a long swig. He corked the canteen without offering to share it. It was obvious that he was in deep thought, his mind elsewhere. In a minute, he looked toward his companions and said, "It ain't something you care to dwell on."

Chapter Nineteen

S AM HOUSTON GREETED THE group soon after they had returned to the fort. "The Cherokees are having a feast tonight," Houston said. "Sequoia has extended an invitation to you."

"To us?" Jonah asked, not sure why they would be invited.

"Well, it's mostly to Moses," Houston admitted, "but courtesy requires since you are friends that you all be invited."

Smiling, Jonah suddenly understood. Moses had spent his free time in the Cherokee camp just outside the fort. More than likely, one of the chief's daughters had set her mind on his friend. Several fires were roaring in the Cherokee camp, and hot coals from the fire were being raked into a pit over which venison hung from a spit, roasting. Seeing Jonah looking at and sniffing the meat, the Indian squaw cooking the meat picked up a wicked looking knife and ran the blade through the smoking meat. She laid the slice on a slab of wood and then she reached into a bag sitting on a rock and sprinkled a few pinches of what looked like salt over the meat and handed it to Jonah.

Jonah took his own knife from its scabbard. He cut off a small piece and stabbed it with the point of his blade. He sniffed the meat and then popped it into his mouth. He closed his eyes as the flavor lit up his taste buds. This was the best meat he'd eaten since Christmas.

Houston walked up and said, "Not bad, is it?"

"Humm…" Jonah moaned. He chewed the meat and swallowed, and then answered, "No, it's not bad, at all. Fact is it's the best I've eaten since we left home."

"Here's a little something to wash it down," Houston said and handed him a bottle.

Taking a quick slug, Jonah lowered the bottle coughing and tears in his eyes. "Rum...," he said between coughs.

Smiling, Houston said, "I thought you'd like it." Jonah ceased coughing and then took a small swallow, handing the bottle back to Houston, muttering thanks. Taking the bottle, Houston tipped it back, his Adam's apple bobbing as he drank down a long swallow. He let the bottle down and grinned, his permanent scowl softening some. "Damned if that won't put a fire in your gut." He then asked, "Where's Moses?"

"I am not sure," Jonah admitted. "I smelled the meat and stopped at the cook fire. Moses and Lieupo kept going."

Handing the bottle to Jonah, Houston picked up a clean slab of wood and held it out toward the squaw. As with Jonah, the squaw sliced off a hunk of meat and sprinkled a pinch of salt over it.

"Collonneh like?" she asked. Houston nodded and patted his belly. The squaw seemed to swell with pride. Seeing Jonah's stare, Houston shrugged. "Women love me. White women, squaws...they all love me."

"Humph..." Jonah snorted. "That rum's gone to your head."

The two men walked on toward the center of the camp where a drum had started to beat. Several braves already sat in a circle. Jonah and Houston found an open spot and sat on the ground. Across the circle sat Moses and Lieupo. Two squaws sat with them. The young woman next to Moses was tall, slender and her skin was the color of copper. Her black hair hung in two braids. As Jonah looked about, he noticed a few older women grinning and pointing at the two.

"Moses don't know it," Houston said, "but he's fixing to find out he has a Cherokee wife."

Startled, Jonah turned toward Houston. "You think he knows this?"

"I'm not sure, but sitting at Moses' side like she has, she's declared herself to him, and that's why the children and old women are grinning. Love is in the air. Among women it's the same in any language. He might not know it yet," Houston said again, smiling as he spoke, "but he'll find out soon enough. He's lucky though, that's one of Sequoia's daughters. She won't be cheap but Sequoia will be fair in his price."

Damn, Jonah thought. He'd never considered Moses getting married. When it came to women, Moses had always gravitated to his Indian heritage and not his black side. *Was this due to his grandfather's influence as a warrior or because most of the blacks they knew were slaves or servants?*

Moses was nobody's servant. Since he'd been found by Colonel Lee, he'd been raised as a free man. Not a black, and not an Indian, but a free person and a brother to Jonah.

Mama Lee! Lord, what would Mama Lee say when Moses brought home a squaw. It would take a bit of getting used to but she'd embrace it. It would not be Moses bringing home a Cherokee bride, it would just be one of her boys had brought home a wife. Jonah's thoughts then took a detour. *Would Moses' woman want to go home? Woman*...Jonah didn't even know her name. *Would she follow Moses or demand he stay with her tribe*? Jonah knew most Indian women who married outside the tribe followed the husband if he didn't stay. *What would she do?* Jonah couldn't see any woman making too hard a demand on Moses. *But love was something all together different. They'd have to see.*

After stuffing his belly with succulent vittles and rum, Jonah soon became lethargic and decided to call it a night. Houston mumbled his good-by when Jonah said he was leaving. Houston had his eyes locked on a young maiden. Walking back to the fort, Jonah wondered how Mary was handling her recent ordeal. She had been strong while she was with her rescuers, but Jonah knew all the emotions would come tumbling down at some point. Probably in the wee hours when she lay wide awake, trying to sleep but it wouldn't come. Hopefully, she'd have someone there to comfort her. Did Ana have someone to help her through her ordeal? Did she find comfort in one of the riverboat men who had taken her from the Indians? Had one of them taken his place, Jonah wondered. He'd given her all his private information. She knew his family lived in Thunderbolt. Hopefully, she would get word to him there. Would her rescuers let her, Jonah suddenly wondered. Was she still a captive? Jonah's body shook with an involuntary shudder. *Damn*, he thought, *I'm letting my mind get away from me.*

Grabbing a post and pulling himself up on the wooden walkway in front of his quarters, Jonah saw newly promoted Major Russell. He'd just gotten used to calling him captain and now he was a major. Russell was talking to Henry. Jonah only caught a few words of the conversation, but it seemed Lemuel had been expected back a day or so ago and still hadn't showed up. Shaking his head, Jonah knew this didn't bode well for the scout. Thinking back, Jonah was sure Lemuel had left on the same day his group departed. They'd added an extra day...day and a half taking Mary to Fort Williams. Not good, Jonah decided. Hopefully, his scalp wasn't hanging from some Red Stick's lance or war ax.

Undressing, Jonah climbed into his rack. Even with a full belly and a snout full of rum, sleep was elusive. His mind kept going back and forth from Lemuel to Mary to Ana. At some point, he drifted off to sleep. It seemed like it had only been a few minutes when Moses was standing over and shaking him.

"Get up, get up, Jonah. Mama Lee would have a fit thinking her boy had slept this late."

It took a minute for Jonah to clear the fog and get his eyes to focus. When he finally was able to sit up, he looked at Moses and remembered the beautiful maiden from last night. Feeling devilish, he asked, "You married yet?"

Chapter Twenty

L EMUEL HAD NOT RETURNED by officer's call the following day. Henry had asked Major Russell to allow him and a few volunteers to go search for him.

"I'm not going to lose another man looking for someone who is most likely dead already." The major's words were very blunt, truthful but blunt.

Jackson felt the same way but also needed the information Lemuel would have brought back. After a bit of pacing back and forth, Jackson stopped at the end of the table where his officers were sitting. The officers had grown accustomed to their general's ways. He'd enter the room, take a seat and then stand and pace. When he stopped pacing, a decision had been made. "Major!"

"Yes, sir."

"Send out another party, three or four men. If they find Lemuel, good, but what I need to know is how many Red Sticks are still able to fight, and if any of the other tribes appear to be joining them. If they join as some of our leaders think they might, we'll have to pull men from fighting the damn Redcoats to deal with the savages. That might cost us the war." Jackson paused and then said, "And if you find any Redcoat, I want you to take him alive and bring him back to me."

T HE DAY WAS COOL. A mild wind blew and the sky was clear. The men rode out of the fort without haste. They had a bag full of smoked meat, dried venison jerky, biscuits and coffee. Henry had taken Crockett's place but otherwise it was the same group, Jonah, Moses, and Lieupo.

"Might be the last excursion I get to take before the thirty-ninth gets here," Lieupo said, explaining why he'd volunteered to ride along.

"I'd have figured you'd want to stay close by the fort," Henry said. "With Moses on the trail, your only competition for them pretty little squaws is Houston."

Lieupo cleared his throat and spit. "Humph, Houston ain't no competition. I figured I'd just let them, meaning the Cherokee maidens, rest up a bit so they'd be ready to take care of business when I get back." This brought a chuckle from the group.

The men rode on through the woods. Jonah couldn't help but admire God's creation; the rolling hills full of timber, a mixture of hardwoods and pines, and streams running fast and clear. Once, when they paused to let the horses drink, they could see a school of fat trout scurry away. Magnolias grew wild, reminding Jonah of the two huge magnolia trees outside their dining room window back at Thunderbolt. His mother would stand at the window and stare at the huge flowers when they bloomed.

Seeing Jonah's gaze, Moses spoke, "Makes you think of home, doesn't it?" Jonah nodded but didn't speak.

Crossing a small creek, they spooked a small herd of deer coming down to drink. "Did you see that big boy?" Lieupo asked excitedly. "He was massive."

"A twelve point," Jonah added.

"The rut must be over," Moses said, joining the conversation. "Otherwise, he wouldn't be traveling along so peaceful with those does."

The men continued on and just at dusk heard horses on the trail up ahead. Leading the way, Henry left the trail and moved into the woods. They dismounted, and with hands over their horses' nostrils and mouths, watched as a group of braves rode by in single file. At the end of the file a pack horse was being led. The animal was loaded down with game, turkey and deer hung over the animal's back. One of the braves was very animated, and from his gestures it seemed he was bragging about the shot he made with his bow. The other braves were doing their best to ignore him.

Once the Indians were out of sight, Henry seemed to exhale. "Choctaws," he said, "hunting party."

"Aren't they friendly?" Lieupo asked.

"Back at the fort," Henry replied. "Out here, who knows? But friendly or not, if they didn't see us they can't tell anyone we're here."

Seeing the logic in the old scout's words, Jonah said, "That's true."

The men made camp that night and Henry pulled out his pipe. "Last chance to enjoy a bowl. We'll be getting close tomorrow and can't risk the smell being detected."

The next morning, Henry broke a limb off a small pine tree and rubbed himself down well. Seeing the question on Lieupo's face, Moses said, "It helps with the scent. Jonah and I do it all the time when we go hunting." Nodding his understanding, Lieupo broke a small limb and followed suit.

BY NOON THAT DAY Henry called a halt. "Let's let the horses drink," he said, pointing to a small stream. "Then let's take them off the trail and tie them up. They should be safe, and we'll go a ways on foot."

"That close, are we?" Jonah asked.

"Close enough I can smell 'em," Henry replied. Jonah doubted this but didn't argue the point.

It was dusk when the group closed with the village. Menawa was quickly spotted; it seemed a council was taking place. The atmosphere was gloomy and uneasy. The scouts had arrived at the end of the meeting. The warriors suddenly stood and drifted off, some alone and others in small groups. One group sat at a campfire close to where the scouts were hiding.

"That man is named Durant and next to him is Peter McQueen," Henry whispered. "They're cussing General White and General Cook. If he'd followed Andy's orders and left Hillabee Town alone, Menawa would not have taken up the red club of war. But because the generals disobeyed orders and then wiped out a whole town of friendlies, Menawa, who is the Creek Emperor, had to declare war. They don't have the confidence in him as they do Lumhe-Chati." Realizing Jonah didn't know who he meant, Henry added, "Lumhe-Chati is Creek for Red Eagle. Weatherford, Red Eagle, and Lumhe-Chati, they're all the same person."

Jonah listened quietly to the braves, who continued their grumbling. He only understood a few words here and there, but Henry was taking the conversation all in. Finally McQueen rose. He was obviously disgusted when he spoke, "Come Durant," he said. "Let's go get drunk."

As the two warriors ambled off, Henry made a motion to the men for them to back out. They quickly made their way back to the horses without speaking. Once back at the horses, the men looked about to make sure the horses hadn't been discovered and an ambush lay in wait. When all was decided to be safe, Henry paused to catch his breath, "Did you understand what McQueen and Durant were so riled up about?"

"I only picked up a few words," Jonah admitted, "but it seems they're not happy with Menawa's leadership and would rather have Weatherford leading them."

"That's part of it," Henry said, "but what has got their blood up is Menawa has decided to fort up at Cholocco-Litabixee. That's the Creek word for Horseshoe Bend. Some Redcoat has said they can build a barricade across the front to keep that crazy old Jackson away. They will have the river at the back which will prevent Jackson from attacking from the rear."

"Why does that rile them?" Lieupo asked.

Moses, who'd kept his silence, finally spoke, "Because Weatherford says it's a foolish idea, a deathtrap worse than at the Holy ground. He says the prophets and British are foolish. The barricade will not protect the Red Sticks, it will be their ruin. He says they've lost too many braves to place all that remain behind some wall…trapped. We lost too many warriors at the Holy ground to make the same mistake again, he argued. He said between the Holy ground, Talladega, and Tallaschatchee, they have lost half their warriors. Why would they risk the rest in a death trap?"

"Will his influence change things?" Lieupo asked.

"I doubt it," Henry said. "Now let's get out of here and report back to old Andy."

Chapter Twenty-One

THE HORSES PICKED THEIR way across the small creek, taking a moment to take a quick gulp of the cool water. Moses was suddenly uneasy. He brought his horse up alongside Jonah, and without speaking, nudged him with the barrel of his long rifle. Jonah didn't speak or turn. The nudge was enough. A whoosh was heard, followed by a cry of pain. An arrow protruded from Lieupo's hip. Another struck his horse in the hind quarters. It had missed Lieupo, as he'd had the sense to lean forward over the horse's neck, making himself a smaller target. He and Henry had been in the lead. Henry jumped off his horse looking for a target.

"There," Jonah shouted, "six or eight of them."

One was aiming his bow, the arrow pulled back till the feather touched his cheek. Jonah shot him just as he let go of the arrow. Two more shots crashed out. Moses and Henry had obviously found targets. One of the warriors shrilled out the death cry of the Red Sticks while the remaining warriors crashed into the creek. The charging horses sent up a shower of water. One of the warriors, his tomahawk waving in the air, was almost on Lieupo. Jonah rammed his ball home and was removing the rod from the barrel when a shot fired. Lieupo had managed to pull out one of his pistols and shoot the charging Indian square in the chest. The impact of the ball knocked the brave backward, his legs rising in the air as he toppled off the rear of the horse and splashed limp into the cold creek water.

Another Indian was almost on top of Henry when Jonah took quick aim and fired. Moses fired at another warrior, striking him as he leapt from his horse. His rifle, now useless, fell from Jonah's hands into the creek as he grabbed his tomahawk. Another brave was trying to line up his arrow on Jonah. Jonah quickly ducked beneath his horse and grasping the Indian's leg, jerked him from his horse. The Indian dropped his bow and grabbed at his horse's mane to no avail. Catching his balance, he kicked out at Jonah, who dodged and struck with his tomahawk, the steel blade burying itself in the Indian's brow and face. Jonah felt a sudden sharp, burning pain in his left upper arm. Pain like he'd been stuck by a hot poker. He'd been shot but had never heard the report. He whipped out his long knife with his right hand but it was over. The remaining two Indians had no more fight in them and bolted away.

Moses helped Jonah find his long rifle at the bottom of the shallow creek. The once clear water was now a mixture of blood and mud. Handing Jonah his rifle, Moses yanked the tomahawk from the dead Indian and rinsed it off in the creek. He wiped the blade on his buckskin pants and then handed it to Jonah. "Let's get on the bank so we can look at your arm and check on Steve." Grimacing in pain, Jonah nodded and started walking.

Henry was beside Lieupo, who was still leaning over the neck of his horse. "You alright, Steve?"

"Well, I ain't about to go dancing, but I don't 'spect I'm about to die. I do have a terrible pain that runs from my hip to my arse though."

Moving into a small clearing in a thicket about a hundred yards from the creek, Moses tied Jonah's arm up after a quick look. "Ball cut a notch or a furrow in your arm. We get back to the fort, the surgeon can put some salve on it, but that ought to stop the bleeding."

Moses then moved over to where Henry was tending to Lieupo, who still sat astride his horse. Henry asked, "Jonah alright?"

"He'll mend," Moses replied.

Henry and Moses helped Lieupo down while Jonah held the horse steady. The arrow was buried deep, right in Lieupo's hip. "Feels like it's grinding bone when I move my leg," Lieupo gasped.

"Got to try to take it out," Moses said, "ain't no way around it. It's going to hurt to high heaven. Still, it has to be done." Washing his hands with water from a canteen, Moses took out his knife. "Steve," he spoke to his friend, who seemed to be drifting in and out of consciousness due to the pain. "I saw the surgeon take an arrow out of a man's back when we were at the Thames River. He stuck the knife in so the arrow's head wouldn't get hung up coming out." Lieupo managed a nod. His face was pale and clammy with sweat dripping from his skin.

"Shouldn't we run the blade through a fire first?" Jonah asked.

"I'd be feared to take the chance of building a fire," Henry said.

"Just get her done," Lieupo grimaced.

"Here is a biting stick," Henry said putting a trimmed twig in the wounded man's mouth.

Splitting Lieupo's pants and finding where the arrow went in, Moses made a quick probe with his finger. He then quickly and deftly pushed the knife blade in along the arrow shaft. This caused Lieupo to cry out and then he mercifully passed out.

"Quick, while he's out," Jonah advised.

Moses held the blade in place while Henry grabbed the arrow shaft with both hands and yanked...nothing. "It must be stuck in the bone," Henry said.

"Give it another try," Moses said.

Grabbing the arrow again, Henry yanked with all his strength. He yanked so hard he pulled Lieupo off the ground causing the man to scream out.

"One more time," Moses said. "I think I felt it give." Henry gave a doubtful look.

"Wait a minute," Jonah said. He lay across Lieupo and nodded he was ready. Henry yanked again and this time the arrow came free, causing Henry to lose his balance and bust his butt on the ground. Looking at the arrow in his hand, Henry cursed, "Damn, the points broke off."

Inspecting the arrowhead in the dim light that remained, Moses said, "Couldn't be much. Still most of its out so we can travel now."

"What about the bleeding? I always heard cobwebs were good for it. With all the granddaddy long legs we've come across, it shouldn't be hard to find a web here about."

Henry set out looking and was back in fifteen minutes or so. He had a thick wad of webs wrapped around the end of a stick. Seeing Henry's look, Jonah asked, "What's the matter?"

"I found Lemuel," Henry said sadly.

"That's bad," Moses said.

Henry nodded, "The butchering savages. They tortured him good. They cut out several ribs and tied wet leather around him. He was scalped and they cut off his privates. He was stretched between two trees. Varmints have been at his feet. He didn't die quickly. You wait, there's gonna be some payback for this."

Jonah knew no amount of words would comfort his friend. Then he thought of Crockett's words, 'It ain't all one-sided.' Well, it wasn't, but it sure as hell seemed one-sided. They seemed to take morbid pleasure in torturing and mutilating. Could this be excused by saying if the whites hadn't tried to move in on their lands it wouldn't have happened? Did the president fear Jackson's retaliation would be worse? It would be hard to control a man who has seen his soldiers so mistreated. Too many questions, Jonah decided.

Now the only important question was: could they get Steve Lieupo back to Fort Strother safely? Would the broken tip of the arrow cause infection? All questions only time could answer.

"Let's get going," Jonah said. "I've had enough of this place."

Chapter Twenty-Two

IT TOOK THREE DAYS of careful travel to reach Fort Strother. The men gave a collective sigh of relief when the fort's palisade came into view. Jonah's arm was red and swollen. It was also very tender and warm to the touch. Jonah had mostly ignored his arm out of concern for Stephen Lieupo. As bad as Jonah's arm looked, Lieupo's hip looked worse. Jonah's arm wept some, but a bloody pus-mixed drainage had started flowing from Lieupo's hip the previous day and had not stopped. Lieupo was feverish and at times his pain was so great he passed out. The group waved at the sentry at the gate and nodded when they passed Jackson talking to an army officer outside the general's quarters. Jackson paused his conversation and watched as the scouts stopped at the fort's hospital.

The surgeon must have seen them coming, as he rushed out to help in lifting Lieupo off his horse. The surgeon was a young, tall, clean-cut man who carried an air of authority. Jonah liked the professional manner in which the surgeon carried himself but couldn't help but wonder if he wasn't a mite young to be a surgeon.

"I'm Doctor Bridges," the surgeon said, introducing himself. *He's from the south, probably from Georgia,* Jonah thought, recognizing the accent.

While the attendants were cutting away Lieupo's pants and remov-ing his boots, the surgeon called to Jonah. He had seen the bloody bandage. Slitting the shirt sleeve and cutting away the bandage to examine the wound, the surgeon clucked to himself. Jonah couldn't help but wince at the man's ministrations. Jonah's bandage had stuck to the wound and hurt like everything when it was pulled loose.

"Damn," Jonah muttered.

"It will feel better when it quits hurting," the surgeon said with a chuckle. He then surprised Jonah by leaning forward and sniffing the wound. Satisfied, he had the attendant clean up the wound.

The attendant did this by washing the wound with warm water. He then poured whiskey over the wound, causing Jonah to wince and curse under his breath. After the whiskey, he applied a salve and a clean dressing.

Seeing Jonah's questioning look, the surgeon said, "That's an old Cherokee remedy I learned about. It seems to work better than anything I have, even if it smells awful." Smiling, Bridges said, "Probably scares off the ill humor and stings a bit too, after a while."

This caused Moses to smile, "Not for a tough man like Jonah."

"Damn you," Jonah snorted, starting to feel the sting.

"Let me see you again tomorrow," the surgeon said as he made his way to where Lieupo lay.

"His name is Lieupo," Jonah said, speaking to the surgeon. "Captain Stephen Lieupo."

"Well, be off with you," Bridges threw over his shoulder, "while I see if we can help Captain Stephen Lieupo."

G LANCING OVER THE PARADE ground, Jonah and Moses took in all the unusual activity. There was a lot more men walking about. More tents had been pitched and the stables were full to almost overflowing.

"Best Moses and me take care of these horses while you go report to Andy," Henry recommended. "He saw us ride in, and he's bound to be curious."

Jonah nodded and handed his reins to Moses and made for the general's command post. He was intercepted by Sam Houston just before he got there.

"Trouble?" Houston questioned.

"Some. Captain Lieupo is in a bad way. Arrow in his hip, never thought we'd get it out," Jonah replied.

"Damn," Houston swore. "I like Steve. Hope he doesn't lose his leg...or worse."

"Don't talk like that," Jonah responded. By that time, they had reached the stoop outside the general's office. Grabbing a pole and pulling himself onto the plank porch, Jonah paused and said, "The Red Sticks are forting up for a battle at Horseshoe Bend. They had a big council over the choice. Weatherford thinks it's a fool notion, but Menawa and his prophets are preaching big medicine and feel they can defeat us there."

Shaking his head no, Houston said, "Not anymore. The thirty-ninth rode in yesterday. Jackson now has close to five thousand men under his command. I'm sure you saw all those soldiers in uniform."

"I did," Jonah admitted.

"Well, if Menawa holds with his plans, Weatherford was right. It will be their death trap. This war will be over soon. I already heard Major Montgomery say the thirty-ninth swung by here to help out before going on down to New Orleans to fight the British."

This caused Jonah to pause and think. The door to the general's quarters squeaked open. Houston quickly said, "I'll see you tonight," and then hurried off.

C HOLOCCO-LITABIXEE," JACKSON SNARLED.

"Means Horseshoe Bend," Major Russell said. "It's a place where the Tallapoosa River loops out and then swings back again. It forms a peninsula of sorts. The widest part is about one thousand feet wide. There are several high points that rise up about seventy-five feet; makes good lookout points," Russell added.

"Is it thick woods or has it been cleared?" Jackson asked.

"I'm not sure, sir, maybe Henry will know."

"Well, Parrish?" Jackson asked.

"A good deal had been cleared the last time I was over that way. But there's a high ridge that still had a good stand of pines and hardwoods. However, there are thick woods all about on both sides of the river. There's a small village close by that was used by hunting parties. Stayed there once," Henry added, "before the hostilities."

Jonah had made his initial report to Jackson earlier that day. Jackson had then called in his officers, including a couple of officers from the newly arrived thirty-ninth. Major Montgomery was at the meeting but the colonel commanding the regiment was conspicuous in his absence. Did a colonel in the regular army dislike being under the command of a militia officer, even when he was a major general? *He'd better get used to it*, Jonah thought, *or Jackson will send him packing like he did those other two colonels.*

Chapter Twenty-Three

MOSES SAT ON A barrel enjoying the warming rays of the sun. He whittled at a stick while waiting on Jonah to have his arm looked at. Henry sat on a crate next to Moses, puffing away at his pipe. A little cloud of sweet smelling smoke hung in the air, causing men to sniff as they walked past. It was getting on toward the noon meal and, unlike when they had first arrived, Jackson's army now had plenty to eat. Fully supplied and men all raring to get this war over with. Moses was sure they'd be marching soon...but not too soon.

Jackson was a brave man but also a cautious man. He wanted to make sure everything was as it was supposed to be. He didn't want to march into a surprise. He also didn't want a draw, he wanted a victory...a resounding victory. He wanted to defeat the Red Sticks once and for all.

Jonah walked up. "How's the arm?" Moses asked. While Jonah never complained, Moses knew the arm had been very painful. Had they not gotten to the surgeon when they did, he might have lost it.

"Doing better," Jonah said, extending his wounded arm rotating it.

"Did you talk with Lieupo?" Henry asked.

"No...Doctor Bridges had given him some laudanum, so he was out of it."

"Is he ever going to walk again?"

"Hopefully. Dr. Bridges had to do a lot when he operated. The arrow had broken off a part of what the surgeon called the ball of femur. That and a piece of the arrowhead had to be taken out and the wound cleaned up. There were also parts of Steve's pants driven into the wound."

"Reckon they'll amputate?" Henry asked.

"I asked that same question," Jonah replied. "Doctor Bridges says there's nothing to amputate. Steve will get well or die."

"I will be praying for him," Moses said solemnly.

"I guess we'd all best be doing it," Henry said.

THE FORT HAD ALMOST turned into a city. Settlers in wagons and makeshift cabins and tents now camped on the opposite side of the fort from the Cherokees. Farmers, trappers, boatmen, and army personnel all mingled about.

"Place keeps growing like this, we'll be seeing lawyers next," Henry joked.

"Well, they won't find any business," Sam Houston said. He'd walked up on the conversation. "Around here, 'Andy by God Jackson' is the law and the only law." This caused the men to chuckle. "Let's go over to Widow Hayes and see if she's fixed dinner yet."

The Widow Hayes was one of the few survivors from Fort Mims. She'd gone to stay with kin, and then as luck would have it, they'd been wiped out. She'd set up a kitchen of sorts outside the fort. Men tired of army cooking and having the money to spare frequently found a hearty meal at her place. Crockett and a few others would provide fresh game in order to get a free home-cooked meal. She'd sew on a button, mend your clothes or provide a little corn squeezing for the right price.

Sitting down at a slab table, Moses wrinkled his nose. "I wish she had hot baths." The men sitting at the next table smelled to high heaven: a combination of sweat, tobacco, and liquor.

One of the men heard Moses. "You talking about us?"

Never one to start trouble, Moses never ran from it either. "I was making a general comment," he said, "but I don't think a bath would be amiss."

"Listen to that," the man snarled, his rotten breath contributing to his overall stench.

"Sit down, Lige," said another man at the table.

"Sit down, I ain't sitting down. Where'd you learn to talk like that?" Lige asked Moses. "Amiss, I ain't never heard no nigger speak so, not even no red nigger."

Jonah and Henry were both on their feet. "Enough," Jonah hissed.

"You his keeper?" Lige asked. "You shouldn't even bring him in here."

"Maybe you'd like to step outside," Jonah threw back.

Whipping out his long hunting knife, Lige said, "Shore, I'll step outside, but I wanna see if he bleeds red first."

An unmistakable click was heard as a pistol was cocked. Sam Houston held the pistol with the barrel touching Lige's head. "I believe you have been asked to step outside, sir. A gentleman would be accommodating. Now, unless you've no desire to see the sunset, I'd drop the knife and then either apologize or agree to walk outside."

"I ain't got no quarrel with him," Lige whined. "Besides, his arm is bandaged."

"I wasn't talking about Mr. Lee," Houston said. "I was talking about Moses. He's the one you slighted. Now apologize or walk outside."

"Apologize, Lige," the man's companion said. "Apologize and let's be on our way. Besides, we do stink."

"I ah...I apologize."

"I apologize, sir," Houston said, emphasizing his words with a nudge of his pistol.

"I apologize, sir."

"We both do," Lige's friend said. "You'll get no more trouble from Lige, I promise. We head back up river tomorrow at first light."

As the men left, Widow Hayes came over, "Pay him no mind, Moses. He tried to start something with Crockett yesterday, called him a lying, loud mouth braggart." This made everyone at the table smile.

"What did Crockett say?" Jonah asked.

"I don't recall his exact words, but it had something to do with Lige's heritage and how old Betsy would be glad to rectify it so that it wouldn't be passed on to poor helpless children." Everyone knew Crockett called his long rifle Betsy.

After they'd eaten, Henry broke out his pipe again. He then passed his sack of tobacco around to the others to fill their pipes.

"Care to walk over to the village?" Houston asked Moses. "Leave these old coons to the comfort of their tobacco while we comfort a maiden or two."

"I believe a stroll in that direction might be good for digestion," Moses replied.

Watching as the two men walked away, Henry asked Jonah, "Does Moses have to put up with that kind of thing very often?"

Jonah thought a minute. He reached for his wooden cup filled with cider and took a sip. "That's the first time in a year or two, as I recall. Usually, Moses handles it himself, but because we're here, attached to Jackson's command as we are, I thought it best if I intervened."

"What could Andy do?" Henry commented. "You're the president's man."

"Well, it's a long way to Washington."

"Yep, there is that," Henry admitted. "You two are really close," he added.

"Closer than brothers," Jonah said.

"You've both been educated," Henry continued. "Fact is, Moses is more educated than most white men I know."

"Well, that's because Mama Lee wouldn't have it any other way." Then, for the next hour, Henry found out how Moses came to be with the Lees and all about a proper upbringing according to the gospel of

Mama Lee. She was a strong woman of deep abiding faith, who rarely put her foot down, but when she did even the colonel would stop and bend to her wishes.

Slaves were plentiful in coastal Georgia. At one time, the Lee family had slaves just like all the other planters and families of substance. However, after Moses came along, Mama Lee had a talk with the Lord and decided the institution of slavery was against God's holy word. A lot of back and forth went on when the colonel wouldn't just up and free his slaves all at once. The economics would have ruined the family, he argued, not to mention the Lees suddenly becoming outcast to the whole community by such an act. But as a compromise, each slave had become an indentured servant, and after seven years of loyal service and attaining the adult age, the slaves would be freed.

"I bet a lot of them took off," Henry said.

"A few," Jonah admitted. "But for the most part they all stayed and worked for wages, room and board."

"Did your mama name Moses?" Henry asked.

"Yep, she sure did. When we were little she'd read to us about Moses in the bible and how he led his people out of bondage. Little Moses would play and imagine himself like the biblical Moses. To this day, he can tell you more about the scriptures than most preachers. Then, one day it happened. One of the men off a boat called Moses a little no-account, half-breed nigger and shoved him in the dirt. Moses had noted the man's foot on the edge of the scales when he was weighing up grain. Not only was Moses smart about the bible, but Mama Lee educated us well. Eyeing the bag, Moses knew right off there was not near enough grain in the bag to equal the weight that was claimed. Moses picked himself up, dusted himself off and told the man he was a cheat. The fool clubbed Moses with a whip handle, cutting him over the eye."

"You didn't help?" Henry asked incredulously.

"Oh, I tried. But I was younger, and all I got was a slap upside the head for my efforts. We went home to tell papa – that's the colonel, but he wasn't there. Mama Lee was, however. Seeing us dirty and Moses bleeding from his eyebrow, she made us tell her the entire story. She got mad as a wet sitting hen. She had the wagon hitched up and off we went. Those mules had never pulled the wagon so fast. When we got there, I pointed the man out. Mama walked right up to him and said, 'Are you the heathen that struck my child?' The man opened his mouth but never had a chance to speak. Mama had a buggy whip in her hand. Faster than a striking rattler, she lashed out and she kept lashing out, chasing the lout around the weighing scales, around the wagon and all about. The man was begging her to stop. 'Please stop, Madame,' he cried, all the while the whip kept lashing out. Mama Lee was yelling and telling him with each lash, he'd think twice before he struck a Lee child again. A crowd had gathered around laughing their heads off but not lifting a hand to help the poor sod. Finally, papa rode up and got the whip from mama. I remember his words to this day, 'That's enough, mama, I 'spect he's seen the error of his ways and repented.' I hoped he had, because mama sure beat the devil out of him. Moses whispered to me on the way home, 'We better not tell Mama Lee anything bad again, she's liable to kill someone.' Well, the need to never come up again. We were grown boys before anyone ever made a similar comment again. Being a strong man, Moses just turned the other cheek, so to speak. I didn't always, but he did. He'd say, 'They the ones gotta answer to the Lord, not me.'"

"I will bet you one thang," Henry said draining his tankard, "word got out what to expect from your mama and most ain't foolish enough to tempt a woman with a temper."

Jonah laughed until he cried. "You are a smart man, Henry Parrish...a smart man."

Chapter Twenty-Four

IT WAS ALMOST DAWN. Of the four men sleeping in the cots on the frigid second floor of the Wilderness Tavern, not a single one had done more than stick his head out from under the covers. Outside the window situated next to Jonah's cot, a tree limb cracked like a musket shot as it broke from the freezing cold and fell to the frozen ground. Jonah shuddered. He had to go...go badly. Normally the call of nature was met with acceptance; he'd get up and relieve himself. However, today was anything but normal. The landscape was solid white. A late winter snow storm had brought everything to a halt. It was cold, a hard, bone chilling, and joint aching cold. 'A great cold,' Moses had called it. For three days now the temperature had not risen above zero. A hailstorm had caught Jonah, Moses, Crockett, and Houston twenty miles or so north of Fort Strother on the trail to Fort Deposit. The hail was followed by howling winds and snow. It snowed until huge drifts blocked the wagon road. The thought was to turn south and return to Fort Strother, but Houston remembered the Raccoon Mountain Trading Post.

"Think it's still there?" a doubtful Jonah had asked.

"Yeah," Houston replied. "The man that runs it is kin to Peter McQueen. It'll be there. We might not be the most welcome guests, but they won't turn us out, not with gold in our pockets anyway."

"What about McQueen, Weatherford or some of their bunch?"

"I don't know," Houston had admitted. "But I would rather chance it, seeing how the weather is getting worse, and it's a sight closer than either Fort Strother or Fort Deposit."

That had been four days ago. Footsteps could be heard on the first floor. Good, somebody was stirring about. A door slammed and angry curses were heard. It was more-than-likely Madison's slaves. They should soon have a fire going in the big fireplace. The heat would rise and help thaw out the room.

"Damn," Crockett swore. "I gotta go bad, but I'm afraid it'll freeze and break off if I get out of these covers."

"No big loss," Moses muttered.

"Maybe not for you," Crockett returned. "But there's a heap of women that would be devastated should such a tragedy occur."

The floor groaned as Jonah jumped out of bed. He bent over, looking under the beds. "Anybody seen the slop bucket?" he asked.

"By the chest," Moses answered.

By the time Jonah was finished, it felt like his nose and ears were frozen. *You'd think they would have a slave minding the fire at night,* he thought.

They heard a knock at the door and then it creaked open. The glow of a candle lit up the room. Jonah quickly jumped back in his cot. It was one of Madison's house servants. She'd shown an interest in Moses that first night when they had ridden in. Each morning she'd come in and light the lamps in the room so the men would have light to get dressed by. Today, though, nobody seemed anxious to leave the warmth of his bed. "Biscuits in the oven," she said as she left the room. Anxious or not, it was time to get up.

"Oh hell," came from under Crockett's blanket. He'd stood it as long as he could but finally had to get up and empty his bladder.

Madison was part Scots. He'd built the trading post nearly twenty years ago. When the trading post was hit by a party of Chickasaw warriors, he'd cleared the land around the building and built a stockade. The stockade was square and looked to be fifty to sixty yards wide and just as long. Jonah was not sure how much protection the stockade really afforded. The night that they had ridden in, there was no sentry or guard at the open gate. The hinges looked so rusty that it was questionable if they worked. They were already at the tavern's door before anyone noticed them at all. Madison had done well with his trade with the Indians. He'd treated them fairly and had been left to live and prosper.

Once dressed, Jonah quickly made his way downstairs. There'd be a fire roaring in the fireplace, he was certain. It was warmer in the great room but coolness and dampness still prevailed. The heat from the fireplace was beginning to thaw the ice on the window panes. Watching the ice melt and run down the panes, Jonah could see snowdrifts had piled up and onto the porch. Icicles hung from the eves of the slanted porch.

"Good morning to you," Madison said, entering the room. He had a steaming mug in his hand. From the strong smell, Jonah knew it was coffee. Suddenly his taste buds became very active and cried out for a cup of the brew. "Mama," Madison called to his wife. "Bring Mr. Lee a cup to warm up his innards." Jonah nodded his thanks.

Madison had once been a powerful man, but age and good living was taking its toll, and he was starting to get fat. *Will I get to a point of such contentment that I'll run to fat*, Jonah wondered. His father had gotten thicker but was not fat. Since they'd been forced to hole up at the trading post, Madison had smoked his pipe and drank homemade beer and corn liquor. He had been content to let 'mama' run the business. A good job she did of it too, Jonah decided.

Jonah had just gotten his cup of coffee when they heard the sound of men bounding down the stairs. "Outside," Crockett said, holding his long rifle tightly. Alarmed, Jonah ran to the window. Indians, six or eight of them. They seemed to have a few whites with them, too.

Madison had slowly gotten his body in motion and made it to the window. Looking out, he said nonchalantly, "Weatherford. Now what's he out in the cold for?" Without hesitating, Madison opened the door and called to the Indians. "Come in here and get out of the cold."

Weatherford seemed anxious but trusted Madison. Leaving the door cracked open, Madison turned to his four guests. "No shenanigans. The weather isn't fit and my post is open to all who are friendly."

Houston took his own, Crockett's, and Moses' rifles and headed back up the steps. Out of sight but not far out of reach. Anxiously, the four waited until Weatherford and his braves walked in...without any firearms. Jonah gave a sigh but didn't let down his guard.

Chapter Twenty-Five

JONAH MOVED FROM THE center of the fireplace allowing the new 'visitors' to get close to the hearth and warm themselves. Jonah was not sure what he'd expected Weatherford to look like, but it was not what he saw. The fearsome Red Stick war chief known by both Red Eagle and William Weatherford was dressed in white man's attire, a wealthy white man's attire. His clothes were of thick wool. His coat, a red plaid mackintosh, was not the type of apparel you'd normally see an Indian or white man wearing. Of course, his grandfather, old Alex McGillivray, was said to have been a man of great means.

He owned a huge plantation and several flatboats, which carried his cargoes to Mobile for trading. Henry Parrish had said McGillivray traded on a grand scale. On one trip south, his shipment would fill several hundred flatboats, keelboats, and barges. McGillivray was the emperor of the Creeks. He was known by the president of the United States and leaders of other nations. Jonah also remembered something his father had said. McGillivray had been a freemason. As emperor, he felt for the Creeks to survive that they would have to emulate the white man. Most of the Creeks wore shirts, trousers, and boots just like the whites. They owned numerous slaves and had large landholdings, often greater than the white settlers, who continued to encroach upon the Creek lands.

McGillivray's daughter was an Indian princess. He had given a huge plantation to Charles Weatherford as a wedding present for marrying his daughter. Why, then, did William Weatherford, Red Eagle, turn his back on his father and grandfather's wealth and way of life?

Did he feel such a calling from his mother's people? Was he tired of seeing jealous white men destroy the Indian way of life? Was he tired of broken treaties and white man laws being made just to steal away what the whites had not already taken? Gazing at the warrior, Jonah recalled something else Henry Parrish had said. Had it not been for the massacre at Fort Mims, he would be siding with Weatherford.

MADISON HAD TO FORCE the door shut against a heavy wind. Once the door was closed, he spoke in Creek to the new guests. He then returned to speaking English. "Gentlemen, this is Lumhe-Chati, or Red Eagle. He is also known as William Weatherford." Mama Lee's training in manners caused Jonah to reach out his hand.

"You may call me William, if you like," Weatherford said, grasping the hand in a firm but friendly handshake.

"I'm Jonah Lee, Mr. Weatherford. It's a pleasure to meet such a gallant foe."

"Good words from a man who is known not only as the president's man but a warrior in his own right."

I'll be damned, Jonah thought. *How'd he know that?*

Smiling, Weatherford released Jonah's hand and said, "We should not be enemies on a day such as this. There is no glory in freezing."

This time it was Jonah who smiled. "A truce, then, until the weather clears and a day has passed."

"Agreed," Weatherford replied. Jonah then introduced Moses, Crockett, and Houston. Eyeing Houston, Weatherford said, "You are known as Colonneh – the raven, by the Cherokees."

Houston nodded. Weatherford kept his eyes on Houston for an uncomfortable minute and then spoke again, "I think you are a good man, but I must tell you, the Cherokees have made a mistake backing that crazy old Jackson. He is not the Indian's friend. One day, he will steal their lands like he is doing ours. Mark my words, Colonneh, they will one day regret their decision."

Houston was silent for a moment and then said, "Hopefully not."

Weatherford let a faint smile creep across his face. "I see it in your eyes. You know it is true." He then turned to Moses, "You are Lee's brother in blood, if not in skin." Moses nodded.

Before any further conversation could take place, Mama Madison brought in a tray with cups of hot cider. Jonah had noticed two whites with Weatherford when they rode up. However, once they entered the tavern's great room, they went straight to the kitchen. Apparently, they were known to the Madisons.

After the cider was passed around and everyone, white man and Indian alike, had taken a swallow of the warm liquid, Weatherford spoke again. "It is said that you and the black warrior are the ones who killed Tecumseh."

"We were there," Jonah admitted. "There was much fighting and many shots were fired. Neither Moses nor myself can say for sure who killed the war chief." This time it was Jonah who found himself under Weatherford's scrutiny.

"It's not fear that keeps you silent," the Indian finally said. "You are not a braggart like some," Weatherford said, casting a glance at Crockett. "No, you are an honorable warrior, Jonah Lee. I will hate to face you on the field of battle, as I would take no pleasure in killing you."

Jonah was moved by the man's words but felt a response was warranted, "Nor I you." A big grin broke out on Weatherford's face.

THE WOMEN HAD COME back into the main room and walked to the fireplace. Their coats had been left someplace but their cheeks and noses were rosy. Thinking of some of the young ladies at home, Jonah knew the color of the women's cheeks was not from rouge but the cold. The wind had caused the older woman's eyes to water and her oval cheeks were streaked with tears. Even half-frozen and with rumpled clothes, it was easy to see this had once been a beautiful woman. The younger female was much like the older woman…daughter or sister? Jonah didn't want to ask, fearing he'd offend someone.

"This is Margaret Vaught and her sister, Mavis," Mama Madison said, introducing the two women. "Their home burnt down, falling in on Mr. Vaught as he was trying to save some valuables. It was lucky for them Red Eagle and his band saw the smoke and chose to investigate. Otherwise, they would have frozen. He took a chance and brought them here to us."

"A gallant act," Jonah said.

"No more than you would do," was Weatherford's dry reply.

THE REMAINDER OF THE day and evening passed in polite conversation. Occasionally, one of the braves would enter the conversation, and the women rarely would make a comment. Weatherford talked about his mother, grandmother, and his Indian heritage. He spoke of meeting Tecumseh and how he was enlightened by his convictions. He spoke once or twice about his grandfather but never once mentioned his father. At the supper table, he ate with the whites while the other braves sat at another table.

Madison entered the conversation talking about the price of skins, hogs, and how the cold was sure to have killed any chance for getting any kind of bargain from Mobile. "Vultures, every last one of them," he swore, speaking of the Mobile merchants.

Cider was served again, and when the sun was down, the Madisons made ready for bed. A pallet was put down in the kitchen for the Vaught women. The Indians found places on the floor around the fireplace, and Jonah's group went back upstairs. Jonah was the last to climb the stairs, not sure why, but not wanting the evening to end.

Finally, he reached out his hand once more, "I have enjoyed our meeting and talks."

Weatherford nodded, "We could be good friends, you and I. If only more were like you, we would not be fighting this lost cause."

Jonah felt sad for the man in front of him. "You know you have no chance of winning?"

"I've known it all along," Weatherford admitted. "We have already lost so much and so many, and still volunteers march to Jackson's camp. We will lose, but it will be a remembered fight."

Jonah nodded. A useless fight, he thought. "I will speak to the President," he said.

"He has the Redcoats to worry about," Weatherford said.

"They will be defeated," Jonah said with all sincerity.

"Their agents think not, and the Spanish think not."

"What do you think?" Jonah asked.

"I think it is better to die in battle with one's pride than to be told where we will live, when we can hunt, and what we can do."

Jonah felt for the warrior in ways he couldn't explain. Finally he said, "It was nice of you to help the Vaught women."

"I am human," Weatherford responded. He paused and then added, "I regret Fort Mims. I had no intention of harming any women or children. I tried to stop it, but how do you stop something once it's started?"

"I understand," Jonah said.

"No, you think you do, but you don't. You have no idea how many Creek women and children have been killed. We have received far worse than the whites received at Fort Mims."

Shaking his head, Jonah said, "There has been too much killing."

"There will be more," Weatherford said matter-of-factly. "Do not join Jackson at Cholocco-Litabixee, Jonah. It will be the death of the Red Sticks, but many whites will die, as every warrior has sworn to fight to the death."

Jonah nodded, "It is not something I can control."

A faint smile and Weatherford replied, "Nor I. Go with care, Jonah Lee. You will be safe until you reach Fort Deposit."

Damn, Jonah thought, he even knows where I'm going. Not revealing his surprise, Jonah said, "And you travel carefully. I pray that God rides with you, friend."

Weatherford nodded and headed to his blanket while Jonah went upstairs. He was amazed at himself for calling Weatherford a friend. Did he mean it or was it polite speech? He wrestled with the thought until sleep finally took him.

Moses shook him awake the next morning. "Biscuits are in the oven."

Jonah yawned, rose up, and looked out the window. The sky was clear and the sun was shining. He turned back to Moses, "Is Weatherford up?"

"Up and gone before daylight," Moses said. "He left you this with Madison."

"What is it?" Jonah said looking at a buckskin pouch.

"It's a medicine pouch," Moses said. "It's supposed to bring you good luck and keep evil spirits away."

Jonah nodded to his friend, realizing he had not just been polite last evening. He had developed a friendship with Weatherford...a friend but a foe. Would he be able to pull the trigger if he had to? That was a question he didn't want to answer.

PART IV

Chapter Twenty-Six

G UNFIRE! JONAH'S GROUP REINED in their horses. "That's coming from the fort," Houston stated. Several more shots rang out.

"Muskets, it sounds like," Crockett volunteered.

The men sat still for a few minutes listening. After the initial eruption of gunfire, everything grew quiet. Off to the left, the sound of horses racing through the woods was heard and then silence again. No sound of pursuit, no shouting or war whoops, nothing.

"It didn't sound like an attack," Moses said.

"No, but I think we need to make sure we approach the fort with caution," Jonah advised. "There's liable to be some with itchy trigger fingers at the gate or on the walls."

"I will lead off," Houston volunteered. Of the four, he was the only one in uniform. "I'm known to the garrison," he added.

"They know me too," Crockett said. "But I ain't wearing no pretty soldier's suit, so you go ahead and get right up front."

While Jonah and Moses chuckled at Crockett's comment, Houston gave Crockett a hard, cold stare. Nobody had missed the implication of Crockett's words. If the guards did have itchy fingers, Houston would be out front and the likely target.

Drifts of snow were still scattered about here and there, more under the shade of the trees. However, the sun had melted most of the snow on the trail and it had turned into muck. The horses' legs and withers were splattered and caked with the muck. The riders' boots looked much the same.

At the edge of the clearing, the riders pulled up and Houston called out. "Hello in the fort, Ensign Houston and a party from Fort Strother."

The guards on the wall at Fort Deposit were primed and ready, but an experienced sergeant laid his hand on a private's shoulder. "Let's not be killing off our own." With that, the sergeant called out, "Be that old he coon with you, Crockett?"

Houston smiled and replied, "Yes, due to misfortune, we were saddled with his ornery carcass."

"Come ahead," the sergeant called and then sent the private to fetch the officer of the guard.

As the four approached the fort, piles of dirt-stained snow were against the palisade. "Looks like they got some of the same storm we did," Moses said.

Jonah nodded and replied, "I'm glad we decided to hole up."

As the men rode through the gate, a cluster of men were gathered at the corner of the fort just below the block house. A lieutenant greeted the group. He addressed Houston as Sam, so it was obvious they were acquainted.

"Trouble?" Houston asked.

"Some," the lieutenant admitted. "I was headed that way," he said, motioning with his head to where the soldiers were gathered.

As they approached the group, the ranking officer, a colonel, said, "You sure it was murder?"

Another man looked at the colonel, and after a brief pause said, "Finding a guard with a bayonet protruding from his chest gives me cause to think it's highly likely the man didn't die from natural causes."

Jonah couldn't help but snicker at the man's comment and knew right off he'd like this fellow.

Hearing the snicker, the colonel glared at Jonah, while the man who had spoken smiled and his eyes seemed to sparkle, finding someone who found his words humorous.

"My apologies," Jonah said. "I meant no disrespect."

Feeling the need to diffuse the situation, Houston spoke up, "Colonel Fleming, this is Jonah Lee. He is here on behalf of the president and has been assigned as an envoy to General Jackson."

"A spy for the president, huh? Well, we got enough spies around," Fleming said, eyeing the man who'd been speaking. "You ought to get along well." And then, after a pause, he added, "Not that I don't think Jackson doesn't need watching. Thinks he has been given a special calling by God himself and he ain't even regular army."

Not a Jackson supporter, Jonah quickly decided.

Looking at the men's dirty boots and legs, the colonel must have decided he didn't want Jonah's group tracking up his quarters. "Lieutenant Seymour," he called to the officer of the guard. "Show these men to suitable quarters so they can get cleaned up and then escort them to my headquarters."

Knowing Houston was an officer, and since Jonah was from the president, he knew he'd be treated as an officer, a high ranking officer, but glancing at Moses and Crockett, the lieutenant was not sure if they were to be included. "All of them, sir?"

The colonel paused in mid stride and turned back to the lieutenant. "They're together aren't they, Seymour?"

"Yes, sir."

"Alright then." The colonel shook his head and muttered about perils of kin being under his command.

"Nephew," the officer who'd called the killing a murder, volunteered.

"Ah," Jonah said. Nepotism, something the military seemed to thrive on.

Reaching up, the officer held out his hand to Jonah, "I'm Gregory Clark. I'm a barrister by trade, but for the duration of the war I work for John Armstrong." So he is a spy, Jonah realized, grasping the extended hand and shaking it. "Where's my friend, Stephen Lieupo?" Clark asked.

"Back at Fort Strother mending from an arrow in his arse," Crockett said.

Looking alarmed, Clark inquired, "Is he going to be all right?"

Jonah dismounted, and after taking his saddlebags, allowed a private who had suddenly materialized to take the reins of his and the others' horses and head toward the stable. Turning to Clark, he said, "It was actually an arrow in the hip that broke off some of the bone. He is on the mend, but the surgeon says he will probably always have a limp."

"I see," Clark responded, concern in his voice. "Lieupo is a good man."

Nodding, Jonah said, "He spent Christmas with Moses and me at our family home in Thunderbolt. We have become very good friends." Jonah then introduced the rest of the group to Clark.

After the introductions, Clark placed his hand on Jonah's shoulder and spoke in a quiet voice. "We have a mutual friend, a Captain Hampton. He asked me to share with you that though we don't have anything definite, we have reason to believe Ana and the river men passed through Memphis and are likely headed to New Orleans." Jonah was suddenly excited. "Don't get your hopes up," Clark cautioned. "Hampton doesn't want you to go traipsing off on some wild goose chase. He has things in order and will keep you posted."

Jonah couldn't help but feel excited. However, he knew Hampton would do as he stated and notify him should the lead prove correct. Looking at Moses, his friend smiled as he placed his hand on Jonah's shoulder. No words were spoken. None were needed.

W HAT ABOUT THIS MURDER?" Houston asked as the men washed the mud and trail grime off and finished dressing.

"British agent we'd captured," Clark said. "That's why I'm here. He was captured after a skirmish with the Red Sticks. His horse was shot and fell on the man's leg, so he couldn't run off. Colonel Fleming's man knew right off the man was British from his heavy accent and clothing. It was like nothing you'd get around here, so they locked him up and I was sent for. After interrogating the man, there was little doubt who he was or is. How he escaped is the question. He must have had some money stashed and bribed a guard, likely the one who had the bayonet in his chest."

"Serves 'im right," Crockett snarled.

"Yes, but he wasn't alone. There was a horse and at least two Red Sticks waiting for him at the edge of the forest. I believe he is here to assist Menawa."

"Maybe he's the one who enticed the Indians to build a barricade and make a stand at Horseshoe Bend," Moses said.

"I think he was likely the engineer," Clarke admitted but didn't know for sure.

Is this what Weatherford had hinted at when he said Horseshoe Bend would prove to be a death trap? Jonah wondered. He'd also said it would be a remembered fight and encouraged Jonah not to be there. Thinking it over, Jonah was sure he was right.

Delivering the dispatches to Colonal Fleming's office, Jonah told of their group being closed up with Weatherford at the tavern. The colonel listened and then said, "Well, with the women there, it was little you could do without endangering them." *He missed the whole point*, Jonah thought. That night Jonah found sleep elusive. The comments about it being a death trap and a remembered fight kept coming back to him, but as sleep finally took him, his last thoughts were on Ana. *Did they have a real chance of locating her? Was she safe?* If only he could know.

Chapter Twenty-Seven

THE BUCK PAWED AT a patch of green that was partially covered by melting snow. A few icicles still hung from the long leaf pines, but they too were melting as the early morning sun grew higher and brighter. Ice still gathered at the edges of a narrow creek, and the frost-covered ground still crunched underfoot in places as the hunter moved as quietly as possible to position himself for a better shot.

Jonah, Moses, Crockett, and Houston had left Fort Deposit the previous day after lunch and had again stopped at the Raccoon Mountain Trading Post. The Madisons seemed truly happy to see the group, as were Margaret and Mavis Vaught. At supper that evening Mama Madison had said she was tired of hog meat. "That's all that is left in the smokehouse," she complained to Mr. Madison.

For his part, Mr. Madison seemed to ignore his wife. He heated up a poker in the fireplace and when the tip was fiery red, he then stuck it in his tankard of cider to mull it. Jonah watched as a tiny blue flame danced at the top of the tankard and the poker was shoved home. As soon as the liquid sizzled, the poker was removed and laid back on the hearth of the fireplace. The mulling left a faint odor that drifted across the room. Waiting on his mulled cider to cool, Madison lit up his pipe. He puffed away and, once he had a cloud of smoke drifting up, leaned over and spat into the fireplace, causing another sharp sizzle.

Settling in his chair and lifting his tankard, he responded, "So, its fresh meat you want, is it, Ma? Well, if Weatherford or some of his bunch come by, I'll make a trade if they have any game."

"It wouldn't hurt you to go hunting, you lazy old coot," Ma had retorted.

"Naw. Naw, it wouldn't," Madison admitted. "And as soon as it warms up I'll do just that."

This caused the Vaughts to giggle and Ma Madison to snort. Crockett grinned like an old sulling opossum, while Jonah, Moses, and Houston did their best not to chuckle.

That night, alone with the others in their party, Crockett said, "I think I'll get up in the morning and see if I can get a deer or a couple of turkeys." The next thing he knew, Moses and Jonah had decided to go hunting as well. Houston had yawned and asked his companions to be as quiet as possible getting up as he intended to sleep in, since they'd be back at Fort Strother the next day and the routine of army life would undoubtedly prevent him from enjoying a peaceful rest for some time.

Jonah knelt beneath a low, overhanging pine limb. He froze, not making a move as the buck lifted his head and twitched his tail. Jonah continued to watch, as he knew he was down wind, so the deer had not smelled him. Had he made a noise or had the deer picked up on his movement? After what seemed like an eternity, the deer's head went back down. Trying to not make a sound, Jonah lifted his rifle and drew a bead on the buck. Jonah cocked the trigger as the deer pawed at the snow. Again the animal's head came up and he seemed to look directly at the hunter. Tail twitching again, it was obvious the buck was nervous. He'd stood all he could. The big buck swung around to flee, but it was too late. Jonah had squeezed the trigger just before the deer moved. The crack of the long rifle was followed by a whomp. Jonah knew before the smoke cleared he'd made a good shot. Now came the dreaded part...field dressing the deer with half frozen hands. Jonah thought briefly about just waiting until he got back to the trading post to gut the deer. But by doing it here, he'd lighten the load by at least a third.

Reloading his weapon before he moved, Jonah picked up movement. Was this what spooked the deer? Easing back under the tree, Jonah intended to circle around and see if he could pick up the movement again. He didn't have far to go, as he backed out from under the tree, he stood up and turned, coming face to face with an Indian woman. She carried no weapon and seemed frightened to be discovered by the white man. Finally she spoke, "Your deer?" Surprised that she had spoken in English, Jonah continued to stare. "Your deer?" the woman asked again.

"Yes," Jonah managed.

"We hunt too," the woman said.

"Any luck?" Jonah asked.

"No, no gun, only bow."

The movement Jonah had first picked up was moving again. It was an Indian boy; twelve, maybe thirteen years old. He carried a bow but no other weapon was visible.

Seeing Jonah eyeing the boy, the woman volunteered, "My son."

Knowing that it was not normal for a boy and his mother to be out hunting, Jonah asked, "Where's your man...the boy's father?"

"Dead, he died fighting that crazy old Jackson." Then realizing she may have said too much, the woman asked, "You Jackson soldier?"

"No. I sometimes ride with Jackson, but I'm not one of his soldiers. I do not make war on women or children," Jonah added.

"I'm no child," the boy snapped.

"I see you're not," Jonah said, not wanting to hurt the boy's feelings. "You help with deer and come to trading post, I will see you are fed," Jonah said.

"No take white man's kill," the boy said.

"You help with deer and then we will share kill," Jonah said. "Maybe we," pointing to the boy and back to himself, "maybe we go hunting again. This time you shoot deer." Now he had the boy's attention.

The woman expertly gutted the deer. Tying the legs over a pole he cut, Jonah handed his rifle to the woman while he and the boy hefted up the pole onto their shoulders. With the woman leading, they made their way back to the trading post. Once there, Madison's slaves took the deer out back where two more hung. Crockett and Moses had been lucky, as well.

The Madisons did not seem surprised that Jonah had returned with guests. Washing up, Jonah quickly told his story to his friends of his meeting. After eating a good noon meal, Jonah had Ma pack a bag with fried cornbread and leftover bacon. He rounded up the boy whose name sounded like Wolf, so that's what Jonah called him. Crockett had passed a small creek with some patches of green and close by was an old oak tree. He said, "Acorns are most likely all frozen but the deer may come looking for a morsel." Finding the spot, Jonah and the boy checked the wind direction and then found a place that provided cover on two sides. About an hour had passed when two does came up. They were close enough that Wolf was able to kill one with his bow. Jonah was cold, stiff, and about ready to call it a hunt when a buck showed up. Wolf had previously told Jonah his father had taught him to shoot. Therefore, when the buck crossed the creek, Jonah handed the gun to the boy. Taking the gun, Wolf drew down on the deer and dropped it in its tracks. Once the deer was down, the boy let go with an excited little whoop. This time they had brought a pack mule along. Loading up their harvest, they headed back to the trading post. All the time, the boy never stopped talking and jabbered through the evening meal. The boy's mother didn't say much, but she gave Jonah a look of gratitude.

Before going to bed that night, Jonah and Moses had a few minutes alone. "I somehow feel reluctant to return to Fort Strother," Jonah confessed. "I don't know that I feel the same way as I did before we left. I think I know…I understand more how Henry Parrish feels now."

Moses nodded, "It's hard to kill a man you don't hate, and it's hard to hate a man once you've come to know him and shared a meal. Did you ever think, Jonah, how easy it could be for us to be having our lands, our way of life taken from us? I don't mean fighting the British. I mean people we'd welcomed and helped who suddenly turned on us." Moses then turned to Jonah, "Can you imagine how I've felt at times looking at people of color or Indians and knowing but for the grace of God and Mama Lee." The mention of Mama Lee made both men chuckle then Moses continued, "I would be in the same boat as many of them had things been different. Being a part of the Lee family has provided me with things some could only dream about. I've been treated as a son and as a brother." Moses said this putting his arm on Jonah's shoulder. "I know how you feel about me. But what if tomorrow I turned on you and tried to take all that the Lees had worked for, for my own. How would you feel then? That's the feeling the Red Sticks are feeling now."

The two men were silent for a while and then Moses spoke again, "Weatherford was right, you know. Once Jackson wins this war and he has no further need for his Indian allies, he will turn his back on them. Sam knows it's true. I know it's true and deep in your heart you know it's true."

Jonah didn't speak but nodded. *What a complicated world we live in,* he thought. *It is being made worse by politicians and greed.*

"It's getting cold," Moses volunteered. "I'm going inside." They'd been sitting on a back porch step. Jonah hadn't really noticed the cold. Was Moses cold or just giving Jonah time to be alone with his thoughts? Sitting on the steps for a while longer, Jonah heard a plank creak as a person stepped on it. Standing and turning toward the porch, Jonah saw Wolf's mother. What happened next was something

Jonah would remember for a long time. Sometimes with fondness, other times with guilt...but remember it he did.

Wolf's mother spoke much as a white woman, "Thank you for being a friend to my son." She then opened the heavy robe she wore and stood naked before him. Jonah was stunned at the beauty this woman possessed; beauty that had been covered by her winter clothing. She pulled him toward her and all the emotions and needs a man could have came flooding forth over Jonah as he felt himself drifting away in the arms of this woman. A woman who sensed the man was about to break and comforted him the only way she knew how. When Jonah woke up the next morning, the boy and woman were gone. No good-byes, no complications, nothing but gratitude, at least on Jonah's part.

Chapter Twenty-Eight

THE TRIP BACK TO Fort Strother had been uneventful. No bad weather, no Indians, and only very few birds. Crockett said it just wasn't natural to make the trip with no bother at all. "Man has got to have a little bother, regular like, to keep him on his toes," he declared. "Otherwise, he is likely to get lazy. Once a man gets too relaxed, his hair ends up on some Indian's lance. No, a man needs a little bother in his life."

Moses grinned at the scout and said, "Well, I wouldn't mind a little bother now and again but it seems mine always comes from a woman."

"Can't disagree with you there," Crockett responded. "I thinks I'd rather deal with blood-thirsty savages everyday than some nagging woman once a week."

"You listening, Sam?" Jonah asked.

"Sure I am," Houston answered. "I was just trying to figure out where this conversation is going. I don't know about Davy, but I ain't yet heard Moses complain about the attention he's been getting."

"That's just it," Crockett jumped on Houston's words. "In the spooning stages it's all they can do to please you. They don't fuss if you go hunting or pull a cork on a jug or anything. But you just wait till they got you treed. Then you'll find those carefree days of being one's own boss is long gone."

"That why you volunteered to join Andy?" Houston asked. Jonah didn't miss the 'Andy'. Out of camp, he'd address the general as others did.

"Well, yeah," Crockett admitted. "She didn't even seem overly glad when I went home for a spell. No joyful reunion, she just sat in nagging about what needed doing whilst I was home." Moses had got the conversation started on this current path but had clammed up.

Houston was not about to let it rest. "What about it, Moses? Is your pretty little squaw still in the pleasing mood or has she got you treed yet?"

"Humph," Moses snorted. "I'm not near as treed as she'd like me to be. Of course, Indians are different."

"Not that I've seen," Crockett threw out. "I don't care what color you are, women are women. Reminds me of a little saying our old neighbor used to say." Pausing a second to get his thoughts right, Crockett recited the saying; "God created earth and rested. God created man and rested. God created woman, and since, neither God nor man has rested." This brought cackles from the group including Crockett who laughed until he cried.

Once he was able to stop laughing, Jonah leaned over and said, "There is one I know who would get a kick out of that."

"He sure would," Moses admitted, knowing Jonah meant his father. After a second, Moses added, "But not in Mama Lee's hearing."

"Definitely not in her hearing," Jonah agreed.

THE GROUP WAS GREETED with hoots and hollers when they rode back into the fort. Fort Strother had been well-manned when they left but now the place seemed to be busting at the seams. General Coffee was up and about, seeming to have fully recovered from his wounds.

When Jonah discussed his meeting with Weatherford, Coffee snorted and said, "I'd have shot him dead right then and there."

"You may have, General," Jonah said not to kindly, "but I pride myself on being a man of honor. When given shelter, I respect a man's property and rules, not to mention giving my word to Weatherford."

Coffee was not satisfied, "Your word to a Red Stick."

Jonah rose up and with clenched jaw said, "My word to any man, General." After a tense moment, he added, "In fact, I had a much more invigorating conversation with this man than you would expect. He's really very educated. His grandfather is well known by the King, Heads of State, and even the President of the United States."

Coffee seemed to settle down but still had to get in one last word. "He's still the enemy."

Determined to stand his ground, Jonah said, "And so is the King, but that doesn't mean you wouldn't call a truce and sit down to talk under the right circumstances."

Jackson must have felt that the banter had gone on long enough. "Quite right you are, Jonah. Now, let's get down to business and discuss our latest scouting reports."

The next hour was spent talking about the breastwork being constructed at Horseshoe Bend and the number of Indians making their way into what was now called the 'stronghold.'

After the meeting, Jonah and Moses went to visit Captain Stephen Lieupo. He was sitting on the side of his bed playing checkers with Henry Parrish. Jonah and Moses had missed the old cuss but figured he was out scouting for Jackson. Lieupo's color was back and he seemed in good spirits. "I ain't ready to straddle no horse yet, but otherwise I'm doing tolerable," he said.

Jonah and Moses told of their trip and all that had taken place. Well, most all, as Jonah didn't divulge his night with Wolf's mother. They then discussed the buildup of Red Sticks at Horseshoe Bend and the construction going on.

"Why does Jackson wait?" Lieupo asked. "He's got a fair number of the Red Sticks there now. Why wait until they've got a wall up and make things that much harder."

"I tell you why," Henry volunteered. "Jackson wants to push south and fight the Redcoats. The fastest way to do that is to do away with the Red Sticks. Andy's going to wait until he's got them all bottled up in a wad and put an end to it once and for all. Wall or no wall, once he's got most of them there, we'll attack."

How wise, Jonah thought. Henry Parrish had more savvy than a lot of men gave him credit for.

THE NEXT WEEK WAS filled with the hurry up and waits of military life. Houston resumed his duties. Jonah and Moses killed time by joining in on a couple of short scouting trips. A few fights broke out, as will happen when men have too much time on their hands. Crockett was back to his tales of derring-do, now made stronger by his face to face encounter with the Red Sticks war chief, Red Eagle. And in case some didn't believe it, Sam Houston, Moses, and Jonah Lee were all there, just ask any one of them, they'd tell you it was the gospel.

At the end of the week, a small patrol rode in from Fort Deposit. To Jonah's surprise and delight, Captain Greg Clark was with the patrol. An officer's call was held immediately. Clark explained about the British agent they'd captured but who had escaped. This was not new, as Jonah and Houston had added this in their reports. However, Clark now had reliable information that this agent was assisting in the design and construction of the defenses at Horseshoe Bend.

"This will not be just some timbers thrown together," Clark advised the general. "This will be a formidable wall. One your cannons will have little effect in hopes of breaching." This was not welcome news, but it was important.

Turning to Major Russell, Jackson said, "I want a series of scouts sent out. I want a man with a fair hand at drawing to go with them. I want as detailed a sketch as we can get. We may have to move sooner than expected. And Major!"

"Yes sir," Russell replied.

"Take any prisoner you can, especially any British prisoner." Russell gave what passed as a salute and left Jackson's quarters.

The meeting lasted a while longer. After the meeting, Clark agreed to dine with his new friends that evening, as they had to return to Fort Deposit on the morrow. He then had to head back to Nashville. But for now, he wanted to visit his friend, Captain Lieupo. On the way over to the fort's hospital, Clark paused and answered Jonah's unasked question. "No, there has been no more news from Captain Hampton in regards to Ana."

F OR THE NEXT SEVERAL weeks, Jackson did all he could to prepare for the final engagement with the Red Sticks. He realized his supply route needed to be shorter than the distance from Fort Strother to Horseshoe Bend. Fort Williams would be the ideal base from which to launch his attack. He sent out a forward force that included engineers to build roads on which wagons and marching men could easily pass. Not wanting his raw recruits to fail him, as had been the case earlier that year, he grudgingly took the time to have his volunteers trained. He also sent out scouts when it was time to march to Fort Williams. He had to know things were as they appeared to be, that the strong-hold at Horseshoe Bend was not just a faint. The scouts would meet up with the main army at Fort Williams.

Chapter Twenty-Nine

FOR TWO DAYS JONAH, Moses and Henry spent more time astride horses than they did in their bedrolls. They zigzagged from Fort Strother south and east toward Cholocco-Litabixee, as the Red Sticks called it. Horseshoe Bend was the white man's name for it. Henry reminded Jonah and Moses that the name Cholocco-Litabixee meant 'horse's flat foot.' Something he'd explained at least three times. Was the scout getting forgetful? Something Jonah doubted.

"More like he's anxious to get this done with," Moses whispered. Jonah agreed with his friend.

Tension was building at the fort. The officers were grumpy and argumentative. The men were stressed and ready to fight at the least little provocation. The scouts could have cut their trip in half, but Jackson had been adamant that they should not make their destination obvious.

"Andy's got a hair crossed if he thinks the Red Stick scouts don't know where we're headed," Henry argued. "It ain't getting there that concerns me as much as the getting back."

This caused his friends to smile. Henry was right as usual. Past Talladega, past the place near Emuckfaw where they'd recently battled the Red Sticks, and continuing southeasterly the men traveled. They'd stop, eat, and move on until they found a suitable spot to layover for the night, one man always on guard. Jonah had noted the woods had seemed to thin out and open up.

"River is close by," Henry said, pulling up on his horse's reins and taking his unlit pipe from his mouth. It had been too dangerous to light up but Henry still kept the worn, old pipe clenched between to-bacco-stained teeth. Swinging down from his horse, Henry handed his reins to Moses. "Be right back," he said and then quietly disappeared over a rise.

Jonah was starting to get nervous about sitting, as they were, out in the open, an easy target. He'd decided it was time to find better cover when Henry returned.

Mounting back up, Henry whispered, "We're close." With that, he turned his horse and rode more easterly. They hadn't traveled but a few hundred yards when Jonah picked up the sound of running water.

Turning in his saddle, Jonah looked at Moses and mouthed the word river. Moses nodded; he had always had excellent hearing. After riding about a mile, Henry turned into the woods. Finding an area that was fairly thick with growth, Henry dismounted and motioned for his companions to do likewise. He led the horses a few more feet and tied the reins to a sapling.

"Not the best place to hide the horses," he said matter-of-factly, "but it's the best we got."

With the noise of the flowing river covering most of their sound, the men headed toward a nearby spot where a dead tree lay by the bank. They squatted down by the dead tree. Recent runoff from the snow and rain caused the river to flow faster than usual.

"She's usually a gentle lady," Henry declared. "Flows soft and gen-tle-like most of the time."

So this is it, Jonah thought as he peered over the downed tree. The Tallapoosa River. Directly across from where they hid was Horseshoe Bend. It did look just like a horseshoe, Jonah decided. The river made a large loop in the direction they were hiding. The loop created a pen-insula. A rather large peninsula, eight hundred to a thousand feet wide, Jonah guessed.

There was already a beehive of activity going on across the peninsula. Hundreds of Indians were at work. Some working on lodges, others were working on a great barricade.

"By Gawd, it is true," Henry swore. "I'd never have believed it."

"What?" Jonah asked.

"Look at that wall," Henry said.

Moses picked up on it right away. Warriors were working alongside women and children in the construction of the wall. Jonah took a piece of paper from a leather pouch and with a small bit of charcoal made a crude but good likeness of the barricade. A trench had been dug in a zigzag manner across the widest part of the peninsula. Then a double log wall was raised with rocks and dirt filling the space between the logs. The ends were fitted together like the building of a log house. Loopholes could be seen cut into the wall. At places, it was already eight feet high. Young trees had been cut so that sharp tips were sticking out, making it difficult just getting to the wall. Getting over it would be a nightmare, a deadly nightmare.

Giving Jonah time to make his sketch, Henry finally spoke, "You about done? We have been here longer than I'm comfortable with."

"Just about," Jonah answered and then asked, "How high do you think those rises are? There along the banks."

"Fifty to seventy-five feet there where the river curves," Moses guessed.

"That was what I guessed," Jonah said, making a few more notations. "That's about it," he informed Moses and Henry. Taking the risk, Jonah rose up and took one last look at the stronghold. He saw many things all at once. Large trees grew along the ridge of the tract of land. The winter cold had caused the leaves to fall and the branches of the few hardwood trees looked barren, almost skeletal in appearance. Hunters were riding in with game on pack horses. Smoke from campfires and cook fires rose on a gentle wind. Hundreds, if not thousands, of Indians would be inside those walls when Jackson attacked.

Was it a stronghold or, as Weatherford proclaimed it, a death trap? Jonah shivered. A lot of people would die here. Red men, white men, women and yes, even children. Weatherford was a man with great insight. Could there be a way out?

"Let's go," Henry hissed. "We have been here too long already."

Jonah followed his friends back to the horses. So far, so good. They'd head east toward Georgia, then head north along the Georgia-Alabama border and then turn northwest toward Fort Strother. The time was near. Jackson would march, and soon, Jonah was sure. The great man had other battles to fight. New Orleans and the Redcoats seemed more and more to be in Jackson's thoughts and conversations. *Well, he can have New Orleans*, Jonah thought to himself, *and the Redcoats as well.*

Chapter Thirty

HENRY, JONAH, AND MOSES used the safest, if not the shortest, route back to Fort Williams. While the route was away from the hostile Red Sticks, the group did not let down on their vigilance. Just above Talladega, Henry led the trio westward across the Tallapoosa River and then took a northwest route to Fort Williams. Arriving at the fort just before sundown, it was easy to see something was astir. The fort was a beehive of activity. Spotting one of Russell's scouts, Henry rode over and asked what was transpiring.

"We march out in the morning," the man said as he rushed toward a group forming up.

"You go check in with Andy," Henry said, speaking to Jonah. "We'll take care of the mounts."

Jonah dismounted and headed toward Jackson's headquarters. Captain Stephen Lieupo was exiting the building with a smile on his face. He was limping but smiling. *Good news,* Jonah thought.

After the two greeted each other, Lieupo volunteered, "I've been approved to move out with the group at dawn."

Jonah knew Lieupo had had his fill of being cooped up inside the hospital and fort. He just hoped the trip wouldn't take too much out of his friend. Worried as he was, Jonah didn't want to dampen Lieupo's spirit by asking if he was sure he was up to the trip.

"I'd better check in with the general," Jonah said. "Are you back at our quarters?"

After a confirmation from Lieupo that he was, Jonah said, "Let's sup together tonight."

"It's a deal," Lieupo responded. "Be good to see Moses again."

JACKSON'S OFFICE WAS FULL of officers: General Coffee, Jackson's interpreter, George Mayfield, William Russell, the head of Jackson's scouts. Colonel Thomas Benton, the commanding officer of the U.S. 39th Infantry was also there, with Sam Houston at his side; across from the two stood another officer in the 39th, Major Lemuel Montgomery. Colonel John Williams was the official commanding officer of the 39th, but rumor had it he did not agree with having Jackson as his superior, as he was not regular army. It didn't matter one bit that Jackson was a major general, he was still militia. Therefore, temporary command had been given to Colonel Benton while Colonel Williams went on recruiting service in Tennessee. Jonah couldn't help but think that with the intricacies of military life he was glad he was not on active duty.

Entering the room, Jonah moved over to stand next to Houston. In doing so, the movement caused Jackson to look up. Seeing Jonah, Jackson said, "Well, another piece of the puzzle has shown up."

For the next five minutes, Jonah gave a brief summary of their scouting trip. This was followed by another fifteen minutes of questions and answers, not only by Jackson, but by many of the officers there. Russell's questions were the most specific.

After the questions were finished, General Coffee surprised Jonah, "A very good report, Mr. Lee. Your sketches should prove to be a big help."

Damn, thought Jonah, *had Coffee forgotten about their previous friction or was this his way of being forgiving, his olive branch. Had Jackson said something to his friend privately after their verbal confrontation? Had the man realized in a few days that they'd be in battle and each man's life may depend on the other?* Whatever the reason, Jonah was glad for a civil tone. He would hold no grudges.

Jackson, after making sure there were no more questions, began to speak again, "Your numbers, Mr. Lee, are very much in line with those given by other scouts. The Red Stick towns of Hillabees, New Yorka, Fish Ponds, Oakfuska, and Oakachoy are all deserted. Warriors, women and children are all gone. Menawa has put all of his forces in one fortified camp at Horseshoe Bend. It is impossible to conceive a situation more eligible for defense than the one they have chosen." Jackson continued, speaking to the group, "The skill which they manifested in their breastwork is really astonishing. The breastwork extends across the point in such a direction so that a force approaching would be exposed to a double fire, while they, the Red Sticks, lay entirely safe behind it." Pausing a moment to collect his thoughts, Jackson took a deep breath and ran his hands through his wiry gray hair. With a sigh, the general spoke again, "It will not be an easy task, gentlemen. I fear we may suffer losses, but…if we can defeat the Red Sticks here, gentlemen…" Jackson paused again to let the thought sink in as he pointed to a map laid out across his table. "If we beat them here, the Indian problem will be over in Georgia and Alabama."

"Amen to that," someone said. Jonah did not see who spoke but, Major Montgomery added, "Then it's on to fight the Redcoats."

"Hear, hear," several of the officers joined in. Jonah smiled. It was not hard to get caught up in the moment, but no one was thinking of those who would fall, or were they? Glancing about, Jonah realized Major Montgomery was suddenly very pale. Had he had a premonition? Regardless, he, like all the brave men gathered at this meeting, would answer the call of duty. They always had.

IT WAS COLD WHEN Jackson's army mustered at dawn's early light. The men were fed a hearty breakfast of smoked ham, eggs, hominy grits, hot biscuits, and scalding black coffee that was so thick and strong that Jonah was sure a spoon could stand up straight and not fall to either side.

"Someone must have a flavor for chicory," Lieupo grumbled. "You can't get just plain coffee it seems."

Henry, on the other hand, liked the brew and had a second cup. "It's better with honey," he offered, "but since we ain't got any, sugar will have to do."

Moses had watched the old scout dump at least four spoons into his cup. "Chicory syrup is what he's drinking," Moses chided.

"Don't knock it until you've tried it," Henry quipped.

"Well, remember this day," Lieupo said, "March twenty-fourth in the year of our Lord, 1814."

"What's so big and important about this date?" Henry asked.

Lieupo smiled, "Well, it's the date we march from Fort Williams to our destiny at Horseshoe Bend. But, most importantly is that, with the exception of the coffee, this was the best breakfast we've been served since we've joined up with Andy's army."

This brought a chuckle from the group until Crockett, who had just joined the group, volunteered, "They always feed a condemned man well before they lead him off to his fate."

"Damn, Davy," Henry snarled, "why did you have to bring up such a morbid point?" Dumping the remainder of his cup on the ground, Henry growled, "You done ruined my coffee."

Chapter Thirty-One

THE ENGINEERS WHO HAD departed before Jackson's main army did an outstanding job of widening the narrow Indian trail from Fort Williams to Horseshoe Bend. It was a distance of fifty-three miles if Major Russell was to be believed.

"Damned if this ain't just about a joy ride," Lieupo quipped.

The work the engineers had performed definitely was of benefit to Captain Lieupo but had been absolutely necessary to move Jackson's army. The army now numbered a force of approximately four thousand. This included five hundred Cherokees and one hundred White Stick allies. The U.S. Army 39th Infantry Brigade marched at the head of the army directly behind Russell's scouts. Much to his chagrin, Houston was stuck riding with his unit and not up front with his friends. Bringing up the rear were the two artillery pieces, a six pounder and a three pounder, plus the score or so of supply wagons. The route the army used to reach Horseshoe Bend was known as Weogulfga-Cussetta Trail. Reining in on a small ridge, Jonah, Moses, Henry, Lieupo, and Crockett watched as the mass passed by.

"Lotta good them buggers will be," Henry snarled as the two cannons passed. "They make a lot of noise and smoke and not much more."

Jonah smiled as he winked at Moses. They had already discussed Jackson's lack of big guns as they had studied the Red Sticks barricade during their scouting trip.

"Be nice to have some of General Harrison's field pieces," Moses said, speaking of the heavy cannons used in the northwest campaign.

The army came to a halt and camped that first night in the general area of Sylacauga. That night, Crockett had a crowd gathered around as he told a tale of a Creek woman's divorce. The more the jug was passed, the juicier the tale got. It was a devilish tale of a Creek squaw who had an itch that her husband couldn't keep scratched. Therefore, when the itch became overpowering, the squaw sought relief through some brave who was quite adept at providing the squaw the needed relief. The problem was, the itch got to be more frequent, and so the brave's services were required more and more. These activities, which in the beginning were taken with the utmost care to make sure they were kept a secret soon became common knowledge as the episodes became more frequent. Knowing what was going on didn't bother the squaw's husband in the beginning, he being an older and more realistic man. However, as the meetings became poorly kept secrets, the husband became embarrassed and went to the chief and demanded his wife face a trial for adultery.

"Ever see a trial for adultery?" Crockett threw out to the crowd as he paused long enough to intercept the jug and take a hearty pull. Smacking his lips, Crockett took another lengthy pull, belched and passing the jug continued. "Well, boys, I seed a trial first hand. Young man I was, but I remember it well. The squaw's name was Mary Running Doe." This brought a big chuckle from the group. "The brave's name was Horse." This brought another round of laughter.

"Lying heathen," Henry whispered. "Last time I heard this tale the brave's name was Stag."

"What was the husband's name?" somebody called out.

Crockett laughed in spite of himself as he tried to appear in deep thought. "As I remember," he began, pausing long enough to clear his throat and then continued, "I believe it was Limping Duck." The group roared with laughter.

"Well, he kept that one the same," Henry swore.

As the laughter died down, Crockett continued, "Well, old Chief Running Bear, who was to hold the trial, allowed me to sit in on it, but I was to keep my mouth shut."

"That was a chore, wasn't it?" someone in the crowd threw out, causing another round of laughter.

Crockett took advantage of the pause and grabbed the jug again. Passing the jug on after a big pull, he continued, "Now let me finish."

Henry fished out his pipe and after packing it and lighting up, he whispered, "Here's where it gets good."

"The lodge where the trial was held was packed. Chief Running Bear sat toward the front of the lodge all solemn like. Limping Duck, the husband, stood on one side looking like a burly old bear. The wife, Mary Running Doe, stood to the other side looking all meek and innocent with big brown eyes."

"Where was Horse?" someone asked.

"I don't recall," Crockett answered. "It doesn't matter anyway, as he wasn't on trial. He didn't rape her, she asked for his attention."

"Wish she'd asked for mine," a soldier volunteered.

"Why?" his sergeant asked. "You couldn't scratch her itch any more than her husband did." Laughter erupted again.

"Well, what happened, Davy?" a voice called out.

"If I wasn't interrupted at every turn, you'd know by now," Crockett threw back.

"Hush everybody," the sergeant bellowed. "Let Davy finish his li... tale."

"Well," Crockett said speeding up his tale. "Limping Duck made his complaint to Running Bear. This was done with much shouting and gestures. When the tirade was finished, Running Bear asked the wife if she had strayed. Mary Running Doe nodded yes. Running Bear then asked why she would do such a thing to an old warrior who had provided so well for her. Sheepishly, Mary Running Doe mumbled, "Cause he is old. He can't pee without wetting his moccasins." The crowd howled at this. "The angry old warrior reached over and gave her a slap that made her stumble," Crockett said, trying to rush through his story.

"The chief had no choice but to declare the woman guilty of adultery," Crockett said. Sensing the story was near the end, the crowd became quiet again.

"Outside the lodge, the young warriors packed into a group. The chief drove a stake into the ground and then had an older warrior march off fifty or so yards and drive another stake in the ground. All the while the younger warriors were jumping up and down and joking with each other, bragging about their manliness. The chief then turned to the squaw as the old warrior returned from driving his stake in the ground. Firmly, but with a smile on his face, he ordered Mary Running Doe to strip naked. The squaw defiantly ripped off all her clothes, then went and stood by the second stake. A sight it was too, boys. Now, these stakes were in a meadow and at the other end of the meadow stood a lone, tall pine tree."

"Did they race?" someone called out.

"Hush, idiot," the sergeant said sharply.

"Yeah, it was a race," Crockett said. "Mary Running Doe was given a fifty yard head start as she was at the second stake and the young warriors lined up at the first stake. They would take off at the same time. If she beat the young warriors to the tall pine her husband would have to take her back. If she was caught, he didn't. There then would be a ritual where all the braves would enjoy her favors. After that she would be divorced. Well, Running Bear gave the word and the race was on." Crockett stopped here and during the silence, Henry nudged his companions and winked.

Finally, the silence got to be too much and somebody called out. "Was she caught, Davy?"

Crockett had grabbed the jug again and seemed to be enjoying the silence. Sitting the now empty jug down he replied, "Course she was, you knucklehead. She had an itch that needed to be scratched." The crowd roared again with Crockett's reply. The man who'd asked if she was caught looked sheepish for a bit and then he started laughing.

"What a way to wind up the evening." Hearing the comment, Jonah turned to see Jackson standing there. His permanent scowl seemed relaxed a bit with the hint of a smile. Jackson abruptly turned and walked away speaking to his friend, General Coffee as he went. "Biggest damn liar in Tennessee, that Crockett."

"Tennessee?" Coffee responded. "No, Andy, the world. Crockett is the biggest damn liar in the world."

"I hope Davy don't hear 'em," Moses said.

"Why?" Henry said. "He knows it…takes pride in it, I'd say."

Chapter Thirty-Two

THE ARMY MOVED OUT at dawn the following morning. Many of the men were grumpy, and more than a few had hangovers from the various jugs of corn squeezing that had so liberally been passed around. Jackson, it seemed, had told his officers that a tad of relaxed discipline was in order as long as it didn't get out of hand. After traveling most of the day, they made an early camp near Hollins, and the next night, the twenty-sixth of March, camped near Pinckneyville.

At sunset, Lieutenant Allen asked if he could fire the guns to make sure they were operating as they should be. Jackson nodded his approval but advised the young artilleryman to pass the word first. The camp that night was more subdued than usual. The men knew either from firsthand knowledge or had been told by friends and comrades that tomorrow they would reach their destination...and for some their final destination.

BEHIND THE BARRICADE, SCOUTS had been regularly riding in and reporting the progress of Jackson. *Where is Lumhe-Chati,* Menawa wondered, thinking of Weatherford. His presence as a great war chief would certainly lift the spirits of his warriors. But they would do well without him. The barricade zigzagged across the neck of Horseshoe Bend. Pierced with loopholes, Menawa's warriors wouldn't even have to show themselves as they fired on the white man and his Indian allies. The soldiers would face almost certain death at the hands of his warriors. If only they had more muskets and rifles. The lack of firepower was Menawa's biggest concern. Only about one third of his warriors were armed with firearms, the rest with bows, lances and war axes. Hopefully, it would not get to the point the lances and axes were needed. The bows would prove useful if the enemy got into range.

It was time to speak to his braves, Menawa decided. He climbed up on the wall of the barricade and called his people to him. He spoke of the sign that had been shown to them by Tecumseh. He repeated much of what the great warrior had said when he had visited the southern tribes and preached for harmony and unity. Next, after Menawa had done all he could to inspire the Red Stick warriors, he let Monahee talk. The old prophet told how the Great Spirit had assured him that the long knives could not harm the mighty Red Sticks. Menawa couldn't help but smile. There were too many empty lodges for him to believe that. But let the prophet talk. He wanted to be alone with his own thoughts. As he walked toward the river and his lodge, he heard Monahee's young prophets speak.

The prophets declared the camp to be impregnable. They had vowed the Red Sticks would be invincible to the white man's balls. Well, they had said the same at the Holy Ground and many Red Stick braves had been slain there. Menawa had decided that he put little faith in the ranting of the prophets but it would not be wise to dispute them now. They had the young warriors all believing, so that was all that mattered.

The sound of whoops and joyous cries was suddenly heard toward the front of the barricade. That could only mean one thing. Some of the scouts he'd sent out had located Lumhe-Chati, the Red Eagle, as he was known by the Creek, and Weatherford to all others. Such a deep man, half-white, half Indian. No wonder he was so complicated. He had too many names. It did not occur to Menawa, Emperor of the Red Stick nation, that he too was a half-breed and had been known by many names at various times. All that mattered now was that he was Menawa, and unless mad old Jackson could be defeated, the Indian's way of life, his lands, and his very being would be gone forever. Fate had already dealt the death hand to Tecumseh in the northern lands. Would his fate be the same here? What had Weatherford said about Cholocco-Litabixee? A death trap...a death trap, but for whom? Mad old Jackson's army, Menawa hoped. Where was he now? Was the man having the same sort of thoughts as he? Did their minds follow similar paths? Had Jackson decided to defeat the Red Sticks or die trying? He had the men and weapons. But he had to cross a killing field to reach the barricade, and then he had to breach the barricade. It couldn't be done. The Redcoat agent who had helped with the construction said it couldn't be done. Not under the withering fire his warriors would lay down. But if he did, there was always the river; the river and the canoes that Menawa had built. Even a badger didn't trust himself to only one escape. And Menawa was more than a badger. He was Menawa...a Red Stick warrior.

THE ARMY HAD MADE its camp. Men were going about building fires, taking care of the mules and horses, and some were pitching tents. The tents were mostly for the officers. Away from the center of the camp, Jonah could hear the river as it flowed. The Tallapoosa, so tranquil, was flowing ever so peacefully south. Tomorrow its banks would run red with the blood of opposing forces. Jonah walked down to the edge of the Tallapoosa. He'd been at the routine evening officer's call. Nothing new, other than Jackson had laid down one law: no runners. Any man found deserting or running would be shot down where he stood. No questions asked. Well, that was not unusual. General Harrison had had a man shot for running. Thinking about it brought back other memories...Ana. That was the morning he'd met Ana. Where is she now? Is he as much in her thoughts as she in his? Did she still feel the same for him?

A rustling sound in the cattails brought Jonah out of his reverie. *Not a good place to be mooning away,* Jonah thought to himself. The sound came closer. It was two men. Jonah recognized their voices right off - it was General Jackson and General Coffee. So as not to startle the men and risk getting shot, Jonah deliberately made some noise.

"Who's there?" Jackson called out.

"Jonah Lee, sir," he answered, making his way to the two generals. After a quick greeting the men stood silent.

The wind swirled through the cattails and rattled the canebrake along the river's edge. Jackson finally broke the silence, "Tell me, Mr. Lee, how do we match up to General Harrison's army at the Thames?"

Caught off guard with the question, Jonah took a moment to collect his thoughts. "Until the arrival of the thirty-ninth, I'd say General Harrison's force was made up with more regular army and trained militia."

Jackson nodded, "My army, on the other hand, is made up of farmers, traders, backwoodsmen, river men, gamblers, ne'er-do-wells, and braggarts. All of which are scrappers, fighters, Mr. Lee, men who live to fight. They don't have the discipline or shiny uniforms of the regular army, but there's no backup in them either. We will be victorious tomorrow, Mr. Lee. The Red Stick problem will be over by the time the sun sets tomorrow."

"I'm sure you are right, Andy," said General Coffee. "I don't think Mr. Lee doubts the truth in your words. Do you, Mr. Lee?"

"No, sir. I agree with the general about his men. Remember, sir, I've been in a few scraps with them already and have firsthand experience in regards to their ability."

Both of the generals laughed. "You have indeed, Mr. Lee, you have indeed." The men spent the next few minutes in idle chit chat. Jackson then recommended they return to camp.

As they headed back, General Coffee paused. "I would consider it an honor, Mr. Lee, if you and Moses would be a part of my force."

"Thank you, General. We will be glad to ride with your cavalry."

Chapter Thirty-Three

BACK AT CAMP, JONAH quickly found Moses, Henry, and Lieupo. "Where's Crockett?" Jonah asked. Since they'd left Fort Strother, the four had been together most of the time.

"Russell sent for him, told him to bring his gear when he reported. I 'spect he's sent him off somewhere," Henry said.

"We're to ride with General Coffee's cavalry," Jonah informed Moses.

"That makes three of us," Henry said. "I'm to scout for the general's horse soldiers."

"I'm to be held back," Lieupo groaned. "I'm to be with General Jackson's staff. John Reid caught me as we were leaving officer's call."

Jonah nodded. He knew that while Captain Lieupo wanted to be in the thick of it, he'd be limited by his recent injury. Time would see him back in the thick of it.

"I spoke with Sam," Moses said. "Colonel Benton has requested for, and been given, the honor of having the U.S. 39th Infantry lead the assault on the barricade the next morning."

"Daft, if you ask me," Henry swore. "Charging a stronghold packed with armed Red Sticks." Henry paused to tap his pipe against the heel of his hand, clearing the bowl of burnt tobacco. Knowing the old scout had not finished, Jonah and Moses waited patiently. Putting the stem to his mouth with the bowl pointed toward the ground, Henry gave a quick blow. Satisfied the pipe was clear, Henry spoke again, "Was I in charge of this man's army, I'd spread everyone out so the stronghold would be surrounded and wait 'em out. It wouldn't take long before empty bellies would make the red devils downright docile. I'd shoot or hang Menawa, Weatherford, McQueen, and a few more and then set the rest of 'em loose."

Jonah smiled as he and Moses had discussed a similar action. They had even mentioned it to Sam Houston. Houston was convinced Jackson would never agree with such a plan.

"He'll never agree to a long siege. He's in a hurry to go south and take on the Redcoats. Besides," Houston said in all earnestness, "there's no glory in conquering the enemy through siege. Jackson needs…no demands, a victory."

"Did you put the idea through to our leader?" Moses asked Henry.

"No, Andy ain't got the patience for it. Of course, we could spread everyone out like I mentioned, and then when it got good and dark we could send in a few men with a keg or two of powder placed against the wall. Before we set it off we could douse the barricade with some coal oil, so when the powder went off it'd make a big fire. Even if you just set a keg or two of oil with the powder, when the thing went off it would create a big fire. Of course, we could create a distraction some-where so the boys sneaking in with the powder and oil kegs wouldn't be noticed. Andy could have his cannons set so they were firing off to one side. That would keep the Red Sticks hunkering down."

"Damn," Jonah swore. Henry ought to be a general.

"His plan has merit," Lieupo agreed.

A silence ensued with each man reluctant to break it, all deep in thought. Henry had sat on a log. Now he stirred and was feeling in each of his pockets and finally found what he was looking for, his to-bacco pouch. It was near empty. Noticing this, Moses got up and re-turned with four cigars he'd scrounged away in his saddlebags. Taking the offered cigar, Henry put the tobacco pouch back in a pocket and then removed his pipe from his mouth and tucked it away.

"Store boughts," Henry declared as he looked appreciatively at the cigar. "Don't recall ever having a store bought, certainly not one this fine."

Jonah, Moses and Lieupo watched as the old scout stuck most of the cigar in his mouth and then pulled it out with a twisting motion. He reversed the cigar and repeated the maneuver with the other end. He then leaned forward and took a small burning twig from the fire. After a puff or two he had a good light.

Sighing, Henry leaned back, "A fine cigar, Moses. Much obliged."

"They're from Colonel Lee's stock. They are a mixture of Cuban long leaf filler with a Virginia wrapper."

"I might have known they were from someone who knew his tobacco and not you two. You'd probably smoke rabbit tobacco."

Lieupo, who'd been pulling on his cigar to light it, suddenly choked on tobacco smoke as he laughed at Henry's comment. With tears in his eyes and a smile on his face, Lieupo managed to stop coughing long enough to say, "He's got you two pegged." He then added more wood to the fire, and as it blazed up, the men eased back a bit.

"Moses, you going back to Fort Strother and take up with that pretty Cherokee maiden?"

"Not likely," Moses muttered. "She laid down the law of when I'd have to be back. Set a timetable I'm not likely to keep."

"Humph," Henry snorted. "It's a good thing I didn't have any set time to be back." He paused and seemed to be in thought. Using his fingers he seemed to be making calculations. "God Almighty," he said. "We've been at this six months as near as I can figure. It's hard to see how we've made it this far with all the setbacks old Andy faced. No wonder he craves a big victory. Why, with all the broken promises, bickering officers, lack of food, no supplies, bad powder, and bad guts."

What Henry meant was dysentery, Jonah knew. He remembered the poor state of Jackson's men when he rode in with Moses, Lieupo and the Georgia Volunteers. The army had been out hunting. *What a way to run an army*, he'd thought.

"Short enlistments," Henry was saying. "Men joined up expecting to be home in three months. Off for a lark they thought. It was hardship, not adventure, they found. It came near to having to kill one's own kind to keep desertion at bay. It ain't no wonder we fight tomorrow," Henry said as he laid out his bedroll. "We got to take our frustrations out on somebody. God help them Red Sticks."

Chapter Thirty-Four

JONAH WOKE UP WELL before sunrise. Lieupo was still in his blanket but Moses was rolling up his bedroll. Henry was gone.

"Henry's gone to get water for coffee," Moses said, seeing Jonah's gaze.

Jonah got up and moved into the woods to relieve himself. His body gave a sudden shiver from the early morning chill. Always coldest just before sunup, he'd learned. When he walked back to the fire, Henry had the coffee going and Lieupo was sitting up. Not up, not out of his blankets, just sitting up.

Yawning, Lieupo said, "I guess I better get up and get in uniform. Our general will expect me to be in complete uniform today."

The coffee had come to a boil and cups were being poured. "Don't fill them full," Jonah said, digging down into his bags. He pulled out a shirt. Unrolling the shirt, he produced a small flat bottle of brandy. "A little something for the coffee," he said.

Henry stared up at Jonah as he poured a healthy libation into each of the four cups. "What else ya'll got hidden away in them bags?" he asked.

"That's it, I'm afraid," Jonah admitted.

A THREAD OF SUNLIGHT WAS peeping over the horizon. Jonah could hear the thirty-ninth taking roll call. The sergeant calling roll was a big, beefy Irishman who'd found a home in the army. No more starving in Ireland's barren potato fields. Standing behind the sergeant were the thirty-ninth's officers. Colonel Benton stood at the center of the group with Major Montgomery at his side, and there on the edge of the group was Sam Houston.

"Good morning, Mr. Lee, Moses," Colonel Benton called out. "Make sure you remember us when you next speak to the president."

"I'm sure he will hear of the thirty-ninth's brave exploits long before I see him, sir, but I promise I will pass along how you spear headed today's fight. Indeed, I will consider it an honor, sir." This caused a sudden cheer to go up in the infantry's ranks.

"Well said, sir," Colonel Benton exclaimed as he took a step forward and shook Jonah's and Moses' hands.

"Keep your eye on Houston, sir. I hear there are a lot of lovely maidens beyond the barricade. He might prove hard to restrain."

Another cheer went up with a few hoots and howls. Houston's prowess among the Indian maidens was well known.

"You devil," Houston responded but with a smile on his face.

The artillerymen were hitching up the two small cannons to a brace of horses, and the supply wagons with the powder and balls were being hitched to two teams of mules. John Reid was busy with Jackson's aides. They were striking his headquarters tent. It would be moved and a new command post set up, probably on the rise overlooking the barricade. The cannons would be set up near there as well.

General Coffee was at General Jackson's side and the two appeared to be in private conversation. Jonah and Moses halted at a respectful distance to allow the two friends to complete their conversation in private. Finally, with a handshake and a pat on the shoulder, the men turned.

Spotting Jonah and Moses, Jackson said, "Here are your volunteers, John."

"Good morning, General Jackson, General Coffee."

"And to you, as well," Coffee replied. Using an extended arm and hand with a pointing index finger, Coffee said, "We are forming up over that way a piece. You can go on over. I will be right there."

Coffee's horse was being held by one of the Indian allies. "Cherokee," Moses whispered as the two headed toward Coffee's cavalry. Passing Lieupo, they paused. They had established a solid, hopefully long-lasting friendship with the lanky captain.

"Watch out for Jackson," Moses said. "He'll likely need a good guard before the day is over with." Moses couldn't explain the feeling he had. He had no great love for Jackson's high-handed ways toward the red man, but he didn't want to see harm come to him either. He was suddenly glad Captain Lieupo would be close at hand.

"I wonder where Crockett got off to," Jonah remarked.

"He ain't going to like missing this fight while off doing Russell's errands," Henry said.

Moses replied, "I agree. He ain't going to like missing the big one."

"Maybe he's about," Jonah said.

"Doubt it," Moses replied. "You don't hear him, do you?" It was a chuckling duo that turned the bend in the path and came upon Coffee's cavalry.

The first to greet them was Henry. "You finally got around to moving, I see," the scout growled good-naturedly. Jonah and Moses were introduced to a few of the officers. "This is Eli Hammond. He is in charge of the rangers, and this is Colonel Gideon Morgan, who is in charge of our Indian friends." Turning to another man who had walked up, Henry said, "This is John Ross. He's Colonel Morgan's adjutant. Men, this here's Mr. Jonah Lee and Moses. I don't recollect Moses' last name," Henry said, somewhat embarrassed.

"Lee," Jonah said. "Moses Lee."

Most of the men had heard of Lee and a few had had the opportunity to meet him. They heartily welcomed Jonah and Moses. A man Jonah had heard called McIntosh joined the group. He was in charge of the Creek allies, the White Sticks.

"Would Creeks fight Creeks?" Jonah had asked Moses when he'd heard they would be joining Jackson.

"Think of the Bible," Moses replied. "Think of Cain and Abel." Moses knew his scripture.

THE BEAT OF A drum filled the air and the bellow of a sergeant as he called, "ahh...ten...shun." The thirty-ninth were forming up to march. Hearing the drums, General Coffee pulled out his watch, opened the guard and spoke to no one in particular as he peered at the timepiece. "Six o'clock."

The cavalry mounted up and rode to the clearing. Jackson sat his horse to one side with his aide, John Reid, and Captain Stephen Lieupo just behind him. Jackson saluted Colonel Benton as he rode past. Houston nodded to Lieupo, who nodded back. Sitting on his white horse, Jackson looked more like a tired farmer than a major general. He was becoming a thin, stooped, and worn out looking man. He'd swept his hat off as the group marched by, and his wry, unruly white hair was sticking almost straight up.

Waiting patiently for the infantry to pass, the cavalry held their horses in check. With a windy morning chill, the horses wanted to be on their way. There was much stamping about, with a couple of the horses so agitated they tried to take bites out of their neighbors. One even nipped at Henry's leg, receiving a hearty slap across the nose with the end of Henry's reins for his bad judgment. Finally the infantry had marched on, so with the briefest of salutes, Coffee started his cavalry off at a gallop. Their orders placed them three miles downriver from their present camp. It was a place just below the small peninsula that was situated along the end of the Horseshoe Bend.

Jackson was sure that when the barricade was stormed, the Red Sticks would flee. He had ordered Coffee to spread out his men in a semi circle along the bank of the Tallapoosa River to cut off escape by the Indians. Coffee had a group of seven hundred men with him that was made up of Hammond's rangers, Morgan's Cherokees, McIntosh's Creeks, and Coffee's own men. A formidable force it was. Coffee would have liked to lead the charge over the barricade. However, he'd been friends with Jackson long enough to know once the general had made up his mind, there was no changing it.

The Red Stick squaws and children were down by the river bank collecting water to cook with. Seeing the cavalry on the river's opposite bank sent them into a panic. Dropping their water jugs and skins, they scampered back to the village, spreading the alarm. Hearing the commotion, Menawa emerged from his dwelling, determined yet full of misgivings and doubt.

Chapter Thirty-Five

THE SUN HAD COME up, chasing away the early morning chill. However, it brought with it the buzz of insects. A gentle slap was followed by a soldier's curse, "Damn skeeters. Everything around here either bites you, stings you, or does it damnedest to scalp you." This brought a chuckle from those within hearing. The officers let it go. It was a way for the men to keep their nerves in check. Besides, the Indians knew where they were. To hear laughter from the enemy might increase their anxiety and play on their nerves.

BOOM...BOOM...the cannons fired. The six pounder followed by the smaller cannon. Jonah looked at his watch. It was ten thirty in the morning.

"At the distance they are shooting from," Henry volunteered, "I doubt that little gun could put a scratch on a cat's arse." A bellow of laughter followed the scout's comments.

Speaking to Moses, Jonah said, "That doesn't do the infantry much good, does it?"

The cannon kept up a continuous fire. Even Coffee had snorted, "Damn waste of powder and shot if you ask me." Moses poked Jonah and motioned for him to follow. Moving closer to the Tallapoosa River and easing through the cattails until they were right at the river's edge, Moses said, "Look over there." Not one hundred yards across the Tallapoosa lay canoes, lots of canoes. "If we had those, we could create an assault from both directions."

"You're right," Jonah replied, excitement in his voice. "Let's go talk to the general."

However, the man they ran into, literally collided with, was Colonel Gideon Morgan. Jonah quickly explained about the canoes on the opposite bank. "A few good swimmers could get them and be back in no time. The river is calm and not very wide at this point." Seeing the logic, Morgan nodded. "We were going to tell General Coffee," Jonah said.

Morgan grabbed Jonah's arm and said, "No! He'll never approve of it if it doesn't come from Jackson. Follow me."

Arriving to where a group of Cherokee warriors were waiting, Morgan spoke to them in their language. "Quickly, go get those canoes and bring them to me. Several of you setup a covering fire in case it's needed."

Without hesitation, several of the braves quickly stripped off their powder horns, shot bags, and shirts. They also removed their moccasins and then without hesitation they dove into the river.

"When they get back you can go tell Coffee," Morgan said with a smile. "I'll say the Indians did it on their own if it comes up." If they were successful, Jonah seriously doubted the question would ever arise.

From the bank, Jonah and Moses watched as the swimmers made their way to the opposite bank. Quickly tying several canoes together, they made their way back with a train of canoes pulled behind them.

"Let's get ready," Jonah said. He wanted to be in the first wave to get across the river. Once on the opposite bank, they could set up a perimeter of sorts to cover as more men were landed.

THE RED STICKS WERE grouped by the barricade. The initial fear that had overwhelmed the warriors with the onset of cannon fire was gone. When the balls hit the walls of the barricade, they did little more than chip away at the bark. Flying splinters caused a few minor cuts but nothing more. The younger prophets, all naked and painted red and black, were dancing, shouting, and throwing insults to the white men. Some were even crawling up on top of the barricade making obscene gestures at their enemy.

General Jackson had not sent his army forth yet, but he had deployed a number of sharpshooters, as many as could find good cover. One backwoodsman had had enough of the red devils disrespect. He propped his long rifle on the rock he was hiding behind, checked the wind, and waited. When the next howling, painted devil turned toward him, the sharpshooter took careful aim and slowly squeezed the trigger. There was a delay as the powder ignited, and then the gun bucked with a boom. The sharpshooter quickly slid back behind the rock. His aim had been sure; there was no doubt in his mind. The Red Stick had one dead prophet. Menawa had wondered why Monahee allowed the young men to climb the barricade. The old prophet was dancing and chanting. Seeing the young prophet fall, Menawa grabbed Monahee by the arm and snatched him around, leading him to where the young prophet had landed. Several wild-eyed braves stared down at the body lying at their feet. Disbelief and shock were written all over their faces. The dead prophet lay on the ground, his head turned so the huge hole with his brains oozing out was clearly visible.

"Where's your medicine now, prophet?" Menawa asked, anger in his voice.

The one incident, which could easily have been prevented, did much to damage the Red Sticks morale; it was enough to prove the prophet's words to be false. Menawa flung the old prophet to the wall.

"Quickly, take your follower away from the wall. I don't want our braves to have to see him. It will be bad enough when the attack comes without having to step over that and constantly be reminded the Great Spirit may not be on our side as you promised."

Weatherford stood over to the side. It had started: the demise of his people. He looked around. How quickly the attitudes of the young braves had changed. He could see the fear…the forlorn look. They would fight, fight to the death; they were Red Sticks. They were warriors, but it was over. The battle hadn't even started, but Weatherford knew in his heart it was over. Maybe it was better to die here at Cholocco-Litabixee than to suffer the humiliation that would follow. From the river, the sound of scattered musket fire could be heard. Weatherford closed his eyes. The trap was being shut.

COFFEE WATCHED AS MEN were quickly ferried over to the rear of the Red Stick stronghold. Coffee saw a young officer and ordered, "Take forty men and take that small island." The small island was at the southernmost part of the Horseshoe. Taking and holding it would help cut off the Indians escape.

Lieutenant Jessie Bean saluted and hurriedly ran to where Hammond's rangers were getting into the canoes. Saluting Hammond, Lieutenant Bean quickly explained his orders. Hammond spoke to the Cherokees, again in their own language. Five canoes were provided, and the men crowded aboard, eight men per canoe. Bean turned to thank Colonel Hammond, but he'd already shoved off. The canoe had barely scraped the muddy bank of the island when two men were shot, falling into the muddy water at the river's edge. A brief skirmish ensued, but in twenty minutes, the group had taken the fifteen acre island they'd been ordered to seize. Sending a Cherokee messenger back to inform General Coffee that the small island was now in their hands, the general grunted. He'd sent another force further south, so now he had cut off all means of escape.

HEARING THE INCREASED FIRING from the rear of the village, Jackson gave the order for the thirty-ninth to advance. A rider galloped up to the command tent.

"General Coffee's respect, sir, we've taken the small island. Colonel Gideon is attacking the rear of the village and setting fire to it. He requests another hundred men."

"Very well." Seeing Captain Lieupo at hand, the general said, "Go send the Tennessee militia with this officer and then return." He then turned to Reid, "Tell Colonel Benton to begin the general assault. We have them boxed in."

BEHIND THE BARRICADE, MENAWA was in a quandary. The village was being attacked at both sides. He'd thought the river would protect his back, but he was wrong. What to do? There was Weatherford, he called to him, "Lumhe-Chati, we are being attacked front and rear."

"I told you it was a death trap," Weatherford replied hotly. "The greater force is still from the front. That's where most of our braves must stay. Send a hundred braves to protect our rear. Our women must fight as well."

Menawa barked orders to braves to comply with Weatherford's recommendations. Walking toward the barricade, Weatherford couldn't help but think Jackson's men must have found a way to steal the canoes in order to cross over. Therefore, it was a fight to the death. He would die as he lived, as a warrior. It would be an honorable death.

Lieutenant Sam Houston was kneeling down on one knee. He was ready. He was beyond ready. He, with the others in the infantry, had waited as they were told while the cannons roared and spat forth one ball after another. Yet from his vantage point, there seemed to be very little damage to the barricade.

Major Montgomery kneeled just in front of Houston. Turning, he said, "Ain't no Indian built that wall, Sam."

"Jonah said as much the same," Houston replied.

Looking toward the village, they could see a small plume of smoke. As they watched, the smoke grew in size. They'd been hearing sporadic gunfire. Now it was almost continuous.

"It's time to move," Colonel Benton ordered. Being a stickler for pomp and ceremony, he had the drummers at their drums.

"Twelve-thirty," Major Montgomery volunteered. They'd waited for two hours while the cannons had roared continuously. It was a wonder he could still hear.

"They must have fired a hundred balls," a soldier said.

"Naw...more like seventy or seventy-five," another replied.

"You kept count."

"I tried."

"Up," Colonel Benton gave the order. "Prepare to march. Hold your fire until we are in range. Once we've fired, its cold steel. Alright men, remember the general's eyes are upon us. Now march."

Chapter Thirty-Six

WITH A GREAT ROAR, the United States Thirty-Ninth Infantry Regiment rose and charged. One thousand men charged with the United States flag and the regimental colors at the front. *It had to be a grand sight*, Major Montgomery thought. It would make a beautiful painting, one he'd have an artist paint if he survived.

Hearing the roar, the Red Sticks shouted back, some of them firing too soon. Houston could hear the bangs and saw the puffs of smoke from the barricade's loopholes. As they closed with the enemy, Houston watched as lead balls punched into the earth around them, kicking up dirt. Then it was men the lead balls were hitting, a different sound. A soft thud as the balls impacted with flesh, followed by a cry of pain, sometimes a simple curse.

The thirty-ninth charged on. Men fell, but they continued. One of the flag bearers fell with an 'oomph' to his knees but still holding on to the flag. Another infantry man grabbed the colors and on they went, right into the face of the enemy fire, not withering, not retreating. Houston felt a ball tug at his uniform and a sting in his shoulder. A graze, he thought. One of the officers was waving his saber, shouting encouragement.

They were now very close to the barricade, and the Red Sticks' balls were becoming more accurate, as evidenced by the increase in thuds, cries of pain, and men falling. One officer on a horse was down, the horse shrieking out in pain as it was riddled with balls. The officer was dead before the horse hit the ground. Colonel Benton was still up and mounted. On they charged and then suddenly they were at the breastwork. They...he had made it to the wall.

Muskets protruded through the loopholes, firing and then being pulled back to be reloaded. Sam took a chance and lunged forward, impaling an Indian with his bayonet. The musket was ripped from his hand as his foe fell back. Pulling his saber he lunged forward again, piercing the chest of another Indian.

Major Montgomery was beside him. He was gasping for breath and had smoke stains on his face. "To me," he bellowed. "Come on, men, come on thirty-ninth. Over the top. Come on men."

Looking at the carnage all about him, Houston realized the major was right. They had to breach the wall. Striking down on a musket that poked out of a loophole, Sam then slashed at the arm trying to retrieve the weapon. With a cry of pain, the bleeding arm was jerked back. Sharpshooters had moved in close and were now keeping up a steady fire aimed at the loopholes. The smoke was now dense and not only burning the eyes but causing men to cough and choke.

Major Montgomery climbed, clawed, and pulled his way to the top of the breastwork. Elated, he waved his sword back and forth, urging his men onward. "Up and over," he called. The men gathered and started to climb when a musket fired, followed by the sickening sound of a thud. Major Montgomery's hand went to his head and he fell backwards, dead, his body thudding into the ground.

"You murdering heathens," a sergeant bawled. "You done killed my major."

With that, men flooded the wall. Men at the base pushing others up and over. Sam Houston was one of the first over, followed closely by a score of others. Revenge and murder burned in the hearts of the men from the thirty-ninth. Musket balls and arrows struck the men as soon as they were over the wall. Houston felt a sharp, stinging sensation and knew he was hit but not bad. Menawa and Weatherford were both at the front of the mass.

Two soldiers fired at Menawa at the same time. Both balls hit the emperor in the chest, and he went down. He was helped to his feet by other braves. Weatherford swung his war ax, crushing the skull of one of the soldiers who had shot Menawa. A sergeant lunged at Weatherford with a bloody bayonet. Weatherford retreated. Some brave threw a tomahawk at the sergeant, but it was a weak swing, as Houston cut down with his sword, nearly severing the brave's arm. More and more of Jackson's men scaled the wall. Bodies, some dead, some wounded, bodies of both the Red Sticks and the soldiers began to mass up, causing enemy and friend alike to fall over each other.

War whoops, shouts, cries of pain and curses filled the air. Shoulder to shoulder, men fought with muskets, tomahawks, war axes, fists and blades. The Creeks held for a time, but as more white men came over the wall, they retreated. A group of soldiers on top of the wall all fired at once. A dense smoke now gathered at the bottom of the wall. Weatherford tried to counterattack, but it was no use. A warrior, who was braver than most, rose and shot at Houston. Sam felt the ball hit him, but he was in a fighting rage. He swung his sword with all his might at the Indian. Blood spouted from a severed neck artery, and the hot blood hit Houston's face.

"Down, down," came the order again. White men dropped at the order and another thunderous volley was fired into the Red Sticks who had tried to withstand the attack. Most of these were now down, writhing in pain or kicking as spasms racked their body just before they breathed their last. Beneath this mass lay Menawa, wounded nine times but still alive. Alive even after the rush of soldiers coming over the wall trampled his riddled body. Where is Lumhe-Chati, he wondered. He had seen the war chief make the counterattack. Was he down, was he dead? Hopefully, he would escape from this...this death trap.

Looking about, Menawa could see the blood-soaked ground was strewn with bodies, some in heaps, mangled bodies heaped upon others. The battle still raged on. It was behind him now, more toward the village and the river. If he could move, this would be a good time. "Oh, Great Spirit," he prayed, "help me escape."

JONAH, MOSES, AND A large group of Hammond's rangers had attacked the rear of the village. At first, there were just a few answering shots from Red Stick braves, who had spied them. The fighting then picked up but had not reached its height.

"We need more men," Colonel Morgan swore and sent a runner with the request to Colonel Coffee. The runner chose to take a canoe rather than swim the river.

Most of the Cherokees were now there, and the fight increased but with only pockets of resistance. So far, it had not gotten hand-to-hand. Muskets banged and arrows flew. At some point, one of the lodges caught on fire, and then more and more lodges started to burn. Most of the smoke drifted toward the barricade. With the increase in burning lodges and smoke, more braves raced to the rear and the fighting increased. At one point, a group of squaws and children ran from a lodge toward the river. Several Cherokees turned to fire at them. Moses shoved one of the Cherokee braves down, shouting, "No!" They got the message right away. This big black warrior would not tolerate harm being done to women and children. The only reaction from the Cherokees was to turn their attention back to the Red Stick braves. After an hour, the fighting had become constant. At times, it was hand-to-hand as the muskets and long rifles became too hot to fire.

"How long do you reckon this will go on?" Henry wheezed. The smoke from burnt gunpowder and that from the burning lodges made one's eyes burn and water; stopped up a man's nose and made it hard to breathe.

Jonah splashed water from a canteen on his face and wiped it dry with a dirty sleeve. He rinsed out his mouth with a swallow, spit and then took a drink. He was behind a deadfall with ten or twelve other men including Colonel Morgan.

"Where are the damn reinforcements?" Colonel Morgan snorted.

"If they don't get here soon, we don't have much of a choice," Henry coughed. Seeing Jonah's questioning look, he added, "Go for a swim or get scalped. More braves are coming over the ridge."

"Get ready men," Morgan ordered.

Jonah was not sure Jackson would send more to the rear. A high-pitched, hotly contested battle was going on at the front of the wall. God help those men. God help Sam Houston. There was no backup in the man; he was a fighter to be sure. He wouldn't stop until he was severely wounded or dead. A shot was fired, kicking up bark and stinging Jonah's face. *Keep your mind on the business at hand,* he thought to himself.

"Here we go again," Moses cried.

Round after round was fired until the Red Sticks were too close to reload, then it was hand-to-hand. Moses swung his rifle like a club, splitting a brave's scalp and downing him as the warrior flung a war ax, just missing Henry. The old scout yelped but wasn't injured. Jonah was tied up with another brave, who had him by the hair with one hand and a tomahawk in the other. The Indian was naked, painted red and slick. Jonah could feel himself losing his grip on the wrist that held the Indian's tomahawk. He fell backwards to the ground and kicked upward, causing the warrior to fly up and over Jonah. Jonah quickly grabbed his knife from his belt sheath and gave it a throw. The blade penetrated the Indian's eye, causing him to scream and run. He tripped over a limb, fell face first and didn't move again. Jonah picked up his long rifle to reload. The fight was temporarily over.

A cheer went up. Turning toward the noise, Jonah's group could see the reinforcements had arrived. Seeing the new men, the Red Sticks gathered and almost in military fashion fired two quick volleys followed by flying arrows. Hearing an 'oomph', Jonah turned and saw Colonel Morgan fall. Quickly, he ordered the men to drag the colonel behind a tree. Blood poured from Morgan's scalp and Jonah thought him dead until the colonel moaned, turned his head and tried to sit up. Henry poured water over the wound and somebody offered a rag that was not too dirty. Within no time, he got to his feet, dizzy at first and then he seemed fit.

"Let's move out," Morgan said. "It's time to take to those blame red devils."

With that, the Cherokees were turned loose and the Red Sticks now had to defend themselves from two fronts. Determined, the men reloaded and moved out. The fight was straight ahead.

Chapter Thirty-Seven

WOUNDED TWICE, SAM HOUSTON was carried from the field of battle, protesting all the way, shouting, "I can still fight." His protest did little good. Weatherford watched Houston being carried away. He liked the man the Cherokees called Colonneh, or Raven. Too bad they had not joined with the Red Sticks. With Colonneh and his Cherokee friends, they could have carried the day. They could have defeated old mad Jackson and ended the white man's greed and stealing of the Creek's lands. Their lands would be next, Weatherford was sure. Jackson would not be satisfied until all the Indian land belonged to the white man. More firing and the cries of battle were coming from the river. He had seen Jonah and the black warrior. He'd also seen the black warrior stop the Cherokees from making war on Red Stick women and children. It was a good thing, because he had drawn a bead on the black warrior. Seeing his actions, Weatherford picked another target.

Other squaws had not been so lucky, having been killed, some even raped before being killed. What would Jackson think of that, his men molesting Indian women? He'd seen Jackson riding about on his horse. Many had shot at the man but his spirit had protected him, as not one shot had found its mark. Weatherford had two-dozen braves with him. They had hacked loopholes in this lodge that they were holed up in, pouring forth a path of death and destruction to any of the enemy who drew near.

"Lumhe-Chati," a brave called to his leader. "We are out of powder and ball. All we have left are empty muskets, tomahawks, our knives and a war ax. Do we rush the white men and fight to the death?"

"No," Weatherford replied. He was tired...wounded and tired. He'd fought all day. "It's getting toward dusk," he said to his followers. "All brave warriors. We will leave this place. Bring what you can. We have done all we can do. If we like, we can fight another day."

"The prophet said we would be protected here. The white man's bullets would not harm us. Is it wise to leave, Lumhe-Chati?" the brave asked.

"Where is the prophet now?" Weatherford asked.

"He is dead."

Weatherford nodded. "He was wrong about this place. Now he's dead wrong. We will not throw away our lives because of a dead prophet."

The sun was going down quickly. Weatherford instructed his men to pick up any powder, shot or food they passed but to not waste time in doing so. Easing out of the lodge, the Red Sticks stuck close to the ground with an occasional brave dipping down and picking up something that would be useful.

MOSES WAS TIRED. HE'D just escaped being brained by a young brave throwing a rock at him. Not wanting to kill the youth, he reversed his long rifle and jabbed the brave in the chest with the butt plate. The boy fell down gasping, the wind knocked out of him. Jonah was swinging his rifle as a club. His target was a brave who had Henry pinned down and was sitting on the old scout, trying to free his knife hand. The barrel hit the brave at the base of the skull, breaking his neck instantly. Henry scrambled to his feet.

"I'm out of powder," he swore.

"I'm low as well," Moses said.

Jonah walked over to where a dead Indian lay and took his powder horn and tossed it to Henry. "Not much," he said as he made the toss.

"It's getting too dark to see much," Henry swore.

Jonah nodded and then hissed, "Down, there's a swarm of Red Sticks."

Ducking low, the three loaded as quickly as they could. It was easy to see they were outnumbered three to one.

"Where are our men?" Henry cussed.

"Hush," Jonah snapped.

A brave who was in the lead stopped as his followers kept going. He peered toward Jonah and his friends for a moment and then rose up. It was Weatherford. His braves had all continued on. Seeing this, Jonah stood. Both men stared at each other. Weatherford raised his hand ever so slightly and Jonah returned the gesture. Hearing noise, Jonah looked over his shoulder. Soldiers were coming up the rise. He turned back and Weatherford still stood there. Jonah motioned for him to go and pointed over his shoulder at the reinforcements coming. Weatherford nodded, waved again and was gone.

"Who was that?" one of Morgan's officers asked as he approached the three men.

"Not sure," Jonah replied. "I was trying to clear the smoke so I could see."

"What smoke?" the young lieutenant asked.

"What smoke?" Henry repeated. "Where you been, boy? It's been such a haze we could barely see."

"It's cleared now," the lieutenant replied.

"Wind carried it away," Moses said. "A minute ago you couldn't see the hand before your face. Look a yonder, Lieutenant; it's like a fog drifting toward the river."

"I see it now," the lieutenant admitted. "I'm to tell you to hold your fire. General Jackson is sending up a white flag to see if the Red Sticks will surrender."

"They ain't let up yet," Henry volunteered.

"Well, you just hold your fire for now," the lieutenant said, acting important.

"Got to," Jonah said. "Unlike some, we have been fighting all day. Our powder horns are dry and we're nigh out of shot." This brought a chuckle from the men escorting the young lieutenant.

"Yo' paw know where you're at?" Henry asked. The escort soldiers lost it, busting out with laughter at the old scout's comments.

"I'll have you whipped," the boy said to Henry.

Taking a step forward Jonah said, "You better watch your lip, sonny. That ole he coon has been fighting all day. I imagine he's tuckered out so he won't take much sass. Were I you, I'd go on about your rat killing while there's enough of you for your daddy to recognize."

"I ain't afraid of some old no account…" the boy never finished his sentence.

WHAP!!! Jonah had slapped the young lieutenant before he knew what he'd done. Collecting his temper, Jonah hissed, "My name is Jonah Lee, should you feel the need for satisfaction."

"No, sir," the young lieutenant said. He'd been assigned to the general's staff and had heard Captain Lieupo speak of Jonah Lee, the president's man. "Let's move out, men," he managed and then quickly went to do as ordered.

IT WAS NEARLY PITCH dark when Colonel Morgan's men made it to the camp. Men were still walking about the Horseshoe with torches. Jackson had ordered that an exact count of the Red Sticks' dead be made. To keep an accurate count, the tips of the dead braves' noses were cut off as they were counted. Two hundred women and children had been taken prisoner. When the counting was done, five hundred and fifty warriors had been killed within the barricade with three hundred or more killed down by the river. Some had died trying to escape down the Tallapoosa. Neither Menawa's nor Weatherford's body could be found among the dead or the prisoners. Of Jackson's army, forty-seven men were killed, and one hundred-fifty nine were wounded. Some, like Sam Houston, had been wounded more than once. Among the Indian allies, twenty-three were killed and forty-seven were wounded.

Later that evening, the mouthy young lieutenant showed up where Jonah, Moses, and Henry had set up camp. Seeing the young lieutenant first, Moses nudged Jonah and whispered, "Trouble."

Henry was lying in his bedroll and with a groan sat up. The lieutenant walked up and paused for a moment and then in half a whisper managed, "I apologize for this afternoon, sir. I was out of line."

"Think nothing of it," Henry answered before Jonah could speak. "Sit down," Henry invited.

Sitting down, the now smiling lieutenant asked, "Ya'll are friends with Captain Lieupo, ain't you?" When they all admitted they were, the lieutenant said, "He's a hero now."

"Do tell," Jonah said.

"Yes, sir. He saved the general's life."

This sounded good so Jonah asked, "How so?"

"During the fighting, every now and then someone would bring in a prisoner to be questioned. Not much good it did since we already knew as much as the prisoners did. Still anyway, they kept bringing the red devils in for questioning. Finally, they brought in this Creek brave who recognized the general. Before anyone knew what was happening, he grabbed a knife he had hidden and lunged for General Jackson. Seeing this from the corner of his eye, Captain Lieupo kicked a table over in front of the Creek brave tripping him. Then Chief Junaluska got hold of the fool. The general would have been a goner for sure had not Captain Lieupo tripped up the rascal."

"Well, good for Lieupo, I guess he's strutting."

"No, sir, he fell and busted his arse when he kicked the table over. He's up and about, but he ain't strutting. He's sore as hell if you ask me." Now it was Jonah, Moses, and Henry who busted out laughing.

"I'd give you a snort if I had one," Henry finally managed. He had laughed until he cried. "Trouble is, we are dry. Not a snort to be had."

"That's alright," the lieutenant said. "I got a bottle." This set the laughter off again.

Boy's got promise, Jonah decided, as he took a swig of the offered bottle.

Chapter Thirty-Eight

HEARING THEIR FRIEND SAM Houston had been wounded not once, but twice, Jonah, Moses, Henry, and a limping Stephen Lieupo made their way to the hospital tent to see their friend. Jonah had a slash on his upper arm that continued to ooze in spite of a makeshift bandage. Jonah had attended an officer's call an hour earlier; Jackson was elated, a victory...a resounding victory. His only remorse, other than the loss of life of the men in his army, was that neither Menawa nor Weatherford had been killed or captured.

I HAVE HAD CONFLICTING REPORTS," Jackson had said at the officer's call, slamming a stack of papers down on his makeshift desk. "Some say Weatherford was not even at Horseshoe Bend. Others say he was and that he'd been wounded more than once." After pausing and taking a drink of water, Jackson spoke again, "I tend to think he was not present." Jackson's words were the ones that would be considered gospel.

Jonah knew better, but for some reason held his silence. Across the table, Jonah saw Colonel Morgan. The man made an almost imperceptible nod. He, too, knew the truth but kept silent.

"What we do know is that Menawa was there and several witnesses say he was wounded multiple times. In spite of this, we have no body." Jackson's voice was raised and his irritation at not having either Menawa's or Weatherford's person or body was evident.

"You know how these Indians are, Andy. They likely drug his body off somewhere or even throwed it in the river," John Coffee said.

"Well, it would have been a damn sight better if we'd had the devils," Jackson said.

"Regardless, it was a solid victory," Coffee said. "The Red Sticks are broken."

This seemed to cheer up Jackson. Looking up, he saw Jonah. "Colonel Morgan tells me it was you who spotted the canoes and recommended the attack from the rear, Mr. Lee."

"I may have been the one who spoke to the colonel, sir, but others had come upon the same idea."

"Ever so modest, Mr. Lee. It's no small wonder the president keeps you. You are content to do your duty and let others bask in the light." The general paused while he took another sip of water. Setting the glass down, he said, "I hear it was much the same at the battle of the Thames where another took credit for killing Tecumseh."

"I don't recall anyone actually taking the credit, sir."

"And I don't recall them actually denying it either," Jackson responded.

I wonder where he got his information, Jonah thought. *Had Captain Hampton told Captain Lieupo?* Jonah didn't think so. It came to him then: Captain Clark. More than likely, it came from him. He had mentioned his relationship with Hampton.

"Colonel Morgan nevertheless gives you the credit for the idea," Jackson was saying. "He also said you and Moses likely saved his life when he was wounded." The colonel still wore a bandage on his head, albeit a clean one now.

"The colonel was only dazed, sir, he was able to fight on."

"Thanks to you, Moses, and Henry," Morgan said.

"Yes, well as I understand it," Jackson said, "I'm convinced your efforts played no small part in our victory. I have already said as much in messages to Governor Blount, John Armstrong, and our esteemed President." Apparently noticing Jonah's wound for the first time, Jackson said, "Make sure you visit the surgeon, Mr. Lee. It appears your wound needs tending. Besides, Houston is over there making a fuss to be set free. Maybe your presence will calm him down a tad."

ENTERING THE HOSPITAL TENT, the group could see Houston propped up on his cot. He was speaking to several of the hospital staff. Houston had paused in his narration and seemed to shudder. "Senseless, so many killed, absolutely senseless."

The surgeon handed Houston a glass filled with an amber liquid. "Take a swallow of this, Sam." Houston took a sip, paused and then downed the liquid. Setting the glass down, he looked at the surgeon, who said, "Medicinal...purely medicinal."

One of the surgeon's attendants said, "Go on, Lieutenant Houston, and finish your story."

Lieutenant...did he say Lieutenant? Sam must have gotten promoted, Jonah thought. *He had been an ensign.*

Sam took a deep breath and let it out slowly, "The sun was going down and it set on the ruin of the Creek nation. Where, but a few hours before, a thousand brave warriors had scowled on death and their assailants, there was nothing to be seen but volumes of dense smoke rising heavily over the corpses of painted warriors and the burning ruins of their fortifications." Houston had leaned forward as he spoke. Now he laid back, his thoughts heavy on his mind and on his heart.

Sensing the need to break the mood, Jonah swallowed and called loudly, "Houston! Sam Houston, I know you're lazing about in here somewhere." Over here came the reply. "I might have known if a man needed care he'd have to pry the surgeon away from you. Tell me, sir, is Lieutenant Houston grievously wounded or is he shirking?"

Alarmed at first and then realizing the men were friends, the surgeon responded, "Wounded? Yes, but not so bad that he will miss his duty for more than a week."

"Less," Sam interjected.

Seeing Jonah's wound, the surgeon said, "Oh my, you are in need of attention." Splitting Jonah's shirt sleeve, he cleaned the wound while the friends talked. "This is more than a superficial wound," the surgeon advised. "It will need ligatures to close it. Bring a lantern over more closely," he said as he dabbed at the blood and proceeded to sew up Jonah's wound.

Grimacing as the needle punctured the skin, Jonah cursed, "Damn, is that the only needle you got? It feels as big as a goose quill, and dull to boot."

"Now, Mr. Lee, surely after what you've been through today, this is minor."

"Humph," Jonah snorted. "That was done in battle. It happened so fast I didn't have time to feel it. But you, sir, appear to take delight in torturing a wounded soul."

Tying a suture, the surgeon spoke to his attendant, "Lewis, see if there is any of the brandy left, and if so, pour our wounded warrior a snifter. Maybe that will restore some of his fortitude." The last was said as the surgeon punctured the skin again, placing another stitch in the cut.

Seeing the glass of brandy, Henry reached out and took it. He quickly downed the fiery liquid and handed the empty glass back.

Jonah glared at the scout, "Damn you, you worthless sod."

"I...I have been wounded too," Henry declared. "It's me innards."

In spite of himself, Jonah smiled. Then, as the rest of the group burst out in laughter, the surgeon took the opportunity to puncture the skin, placing another stitch in the wound.

"Damn you all," Jonah growled.

Chapter Thirty-Nine

THE NEXT TWO WEEKS were filled with preparation to return to Fort Strother. The return trip was slow and arduous. The rough road caused wagons loaded with wounded men to lurch and bounce about. The cries of pain filled the air at such times. More than one wound busted open, causing the surgeon to rush about trying to take care of the wounded men.

"General Jackson," one of the surgeons begged. "Can't you just let us lay over for a few days? Even one day would be a help."

"The Coosa River is not far. We will camp there, even though it's early in the day," Jackson relented.

Jonah thought to himself, *the man does have a heart*. For some reason, Jonah was suddenly glad that he had taken part in something that would go down in history. Would his name be mentioned? Probably not, but it was enough to know that he was there; that he had been given the honor of serving with a great general...no, a great man. Sitting there astride his horse, Jonah thought of Jackson's accomplishment.

Before this campaign, he'd never before commanded an army. Never had a militia officer, general or otherwise, commanded a regular army regiment. Being a military historian of sorts, Jonah could not recall where a militia general had directed an assault upon a fortified enemy stronghold. Jackson was a natural leader; a man of cunning, an aggressive man with the will to achieve against all odds. A man who would not put himself or his welfare above that of his men. He was a leader who faced hardships head on with his men, yet a man who could be callous and ruthless when the need arose. Andy Jackson, mad old Jackson, the Indians called him. And now some were calling him old Hickory.

The president had asked Jonah to be a calming force in regards to Jackson. How do you calm a tornado? Jonah thought. You don't, you get the hell out of the way and wait until it blows itself out. *I have failed at this assignment*, Jonah thought. Then he recalled interceding when Jackson had considered having the captured Red Stick warriors executed.

S IR," HE HAD PROTESTED. "I beg you to reconsider. Not only is it inhumane, but it would be sending the wrong message. Word would surely get back to Menawa and Weatherford. If they should have any white captives, you can bet they'll die a horrible death." Jonah could see his words were not having the effect he wanted. So in desperation, he said, "Right now, sir, you have won a tremendous victory. Wouldn't you want to go down in history as Jackson the victor rather than Jackson the butcher?"

Rage flew over Jackson's face as he stood to his feet, knocking his chair backwards and over. Jackson's aide, Captain Reid, and General Coffee were present. Their faces were white, aghast that anyone would speak to Jackson in such a manner. Not that they didn't agree with Jonah.

Jackson glared at the man who dared to speak to him so. Jonah stood his ground. After an awkward moment, Jackson's red face began to turn back to normal. "You are a man of conviction," Jackson said. "You're not afraid to stand up for what you feel is right. Once again, I see why Madison has such a trust in you. You are a determined man, much as I am. I respect your fortitude, Mr. Lee. I can see where you are right and I thank you for being so honest and forthright. I am proud to have you as a part of my command." He then turned his attention to other matters, thereby dismissing Jonah.

"That took guts," Captain Reid said. He had followed Jonah outside the command tent. "You have done what others have failed to do, and that's change the general's mind about something. You are now ahead of the game, but I caution you not to push it. President's man or not, Jackson will tolerate only so much."

Not yet sure why he said what he did, Jonah stopped suddenly and faced Reid. "Nor will I, Captain, nor will I."

In the end, Jackson ordered the captives be taken under guard to Huntsville. Jackson was emphatic in his orders that the Indians be treated humanely or the guards would answer to him personally. Jonah had tried to hide his smile, knowing that the last had been for him.

THEY MADE CAMP BY the Coosa River, and immediately the wounded were taken from the confines of the wagons and laid out in the sun. There were still a few hours of daylight left. Moses rode up to where Jonah was sitting. Some of the wounded had died during the march and more were likely to follow.

"War is never pleasant," Moses said speaking softly. How many times had he and Jonah been involved in battle and so far had never been seriously wounded? Yet there were men like Lieutenant Moulton and Major Montgomery of the thirty-ninth who fell in their very first engagement. You never knew when it was your turn. Did you go home and sit in a rocker on the porch and be content to say, "I did my part." *I think not*, Moses decided. That day might come, but not while his country needed all her men to fight for her freedom. *Freedom, how powerful a word*, Moses thought, *how powerful the meaning…freedom.* He lived a life of contentment and freedom. Fate had played him an ace card…the Lees. But what about so many of his kind, the Negro and the red man? Neither part of his ancestry was free.

The Creeks had slaves, captured and bought, as did many other tribes. Men, women, and children held in bondage. Was that not what the biblical Moses was supposed to have done, lead his people out of bondage? Here it was over eighteen hundred years later and people were still slaves. Would it change? Colonel Lee and Mama Lee said it would. It would have to. It's not a perfect world, Mama Lee had said more than once. Life is not always fair. Was it fair to push the red man from his lands? Both he and Jonah had decided it was not. But it was a part of life, a fact. The Red Sticks would now push west or south into Florida. Hopefully, they would go away far enough they would find peace, at least for a while.

The talk now was of pushing south toward New Orleans, to fight the British. At least, that was against an enemy trying to take their country, their homes. Not some red man who was just trying to protect what had been his for a thousand years. Damn the British, the French, and even to a degree, the Spaniards. All of whom at some time or another had instigated the Indian to do their dirty work. Each time it was the red man who died and who suffered. Was it like the Israelites in the Bible? They were meant to suffer for all of time. Moses wasn't sure. Some things were beyond him, but he was glad he'd not have to shed any more Indian blood, God's will.

Chapter Forty

S AM HOUSTON WAS NOT a patient man. He had tried to follow the doctor's orders. Indeed, he had as much as he could without going absolutely crazy. But he'd had enough, enough of lying on the cot, enough of lying in a bumpy wagon. Enough of eating watered down soups and of being constantly scolded by the surgeon or one of his attendants every time he turned around. Dammit, he was not made to lie about. He needed fresh air, needed to be around other men, and he needed a horse to get as far away from these nagging medical people as he could. Limping from his tent, he found a saddled horse tied to a rope where the mules had been hitched at the noon halt. Throwing his walking stick down, he pulled himself into the saddle. Riding away, he could hear shouts from the surgeon ordering him back. Ignoring the surgeon, he rode on up the line.

Spying familiar faces, he rode up to them. Houston still had a dressing over his shoulder where he'd been shot twice, and one over his thigh where he'd been struck by an arrow. There was a paleness to his face, and he looked gaunt but he felt much better now than in recent weeks. Captain Stephen Lieupo saw his friend riding toward them and spoke to Jonah and Moses, alerting them of Sam's approach.

Pulling his horse up, Houston said, "Place was getting to me. Smelt like death and decay. I had to get shut of it."

Of the three, Captain Lieupo understood best where Sam was coming from. He'd been there. An aura of death seemed to hang over the hospital tents and then the wagons like a cloud, a black cloud. He couldn't get away fast enough, either.

"Whose horse did you steal?" Jonah asked.

"I don't know. Hopefully, I can find mine and send this one back before they hang me." This got a chuckle from the group, none of whom missed the 'send the horse back' and not 'take the horse back'.

"We got word by some of Russell's scouts that the Red Sticks are gathering for another fight," Jonah told Houston. "The general says if they are foolish enough to wait till we get there we'll give them the fight. Henry didn't think it was likely they'd hang around, however."

Jackson had taken a longer but much easier route for the return trip. When they reached the fork where the Coosa and Tallapoosa Rivers came together, he ordered a halt. With the scouts reporting that the Red Sticks were again gathering, Jackson made camp and ordered a new fort be built on the site where Fort Toulouse had been built. The French had built the fort in 1717. The stockade was turned into a trading post serving the Creeks until 1763, which was when the French and Indian War was decided in favor of the colonials and the British. The fort was left to ruin after the cannons were spiked.

Within no time at all, the sound of axes rang out, along with the sound of trace chains and the braying of mules as logs were snaked to where the fort was being constructed. Word came in that the number of Red Sticks being seen was diminishing. Finally, Henry rode in and said the Red Sticks had taken flight, as the area around the Holy Ground was deserted.

It was here, during the final stages of construction of the new fort, that a solitary figure rode through the gate. It was just at dusk. Dismounting, the Indian handed the reins of his horse to an Indian known as Big Warrior. "Ah, Bill Weatherford, we have got you at last."

Jonah and Captain Lieupo had just left Jackson's tent. Hearing Weatherford's name, Jonah did an about face and headed in the direction of the voices, with Lieupo close behind.

"You damned traitor, if you give me any insolence, I will blow a ball through your cowardly heart," Weatherford snarled.

Hearing the interchange, Jackson came running out of his tent. Jonah closed with Jackson, wondering how the hell the war chief of the Red Sticks could just ride in. It would have been easy for him to murder Jackson.

"How dare you, sir, ride up to my tent after having murdered the women and children at Fort Mims."

Colonel Hawkins, who had been in Jackson's tent, eased up beside Jonah, his hand on the handle of the pistol tucked in his sash. Jonah whispered, "Easy now, Weatherford does not appear to be up to mischief."

Weatherford looked at Jackson and the gathering crowd. Seeing Jonah, Weatherford's gaze paused and a slight smile of recognition came to his face. Turning his attention back to Jackson, the Red Stick warrior, known as Lumhe-Chati and Red Eagle, stood tall, showing no signs of fear as he spoke: "General Jackson, I am not afraid of you. I fear no man, for I am a Creek warrior. I have nothing to request on behalf of myself, you can kill me, if you desire. But I come to beg you to send for the women and children of the war party, who are now starving in the woods. Their fields and cribs have been destroyed by your people, who have driven them to the woods without an ear of corn. I hope that you will send out parties who will safely conduct them here, in order that they may be fed. I exerted myself in vain to prevent the massacre of women and children at Fort Mims. I am now done fighting. The Red Sticks are nearly all killed. If I could fight you any longer, I would most heartedly do so. Send for the women and children. They have never done you any harm. But kill me if the white people want it done."

"Kill him! Kill him! Kill him!" Jonah was amazed at the vehemence in the crowd. He took a step forward and turned toward the crowd. They would not kill Weatherford if he could help it. Pushing through the crowd, there came Moses, Lieupo, and much to Jonah's surprise,

Henry. They all sidled up next to Jonah. Though a weapon had not been drawn, the meaning of the four's stance was obvious.

Jackson's voice roared out, "Silence," he commanded. When the crowd hushed, he spoke again, very emphatic in his words and his tone, "Any man who would kill as brave a man as this would rob the dead."

There was much muttering and grumbling but the men turned and shuffled off. Jackson then invited Weatherford in for a glass of brandy. Seeing Weatherford gaze back toward Jonah as he made his way to the tent, Jackson called out, "Mr. Lee, would you care to join us?"

Before the night was over, the three had established a friendship that would last each man until his dying day.

Chapter Forty-One

THE DAYS AND WEEKS after the battle at Horseshoe Bend and the surrender of Weatherford seemed to crawl by. The construction on the new fort was finally completed. Even though it was basically on the same site as Fort Toulouse, which the French had built in 1717, the men wanted to rename it. To honor their victorious general, the new fort was named Fort Jackson. Crockett returned from wherever he'd been and cussed a blue streak at having missed the battle. Some stated he'd shied away from the battle. Those that said this did not do so within Crockett's hearing. Jonah did not believe this. Knowing the man as he did, he was sure Crockett would have been in the thick of it. Even with Crockett's presence, the days were getting very monotonous, as life tends to get after such an event.

There had been a few skirmishes where patrols were either attacked or they encountered and attacked a band of Red Sticks. These small bands usually consisted of no more than two or three, up to a dozen or more. The attacks usually ended quickly. The patrols had suffered a few wounded but no deaths. A few Indians were taken prisoner. It was from a captive that Jackson learned how Menawa escaped.

During the dark of night, before the soldiers got to the pile of bodies under which Menawa lay, he was able to crawl out. Blood had clotted and dried so that his body was stiff. He had been shot by soldiers at least seven times and had received cuts and bruises on top of that. However, with seven musket balls still in his body, he managed to crawl and stagger his way to the river. He latched onto a floating log and drifted down the river past Jackson's sleeping sentries. Filled with fever, his body in torment from his wounds, Menawa was pulled from the river and cared for by some friends. When he was able to travel, he made his way south to join the Seminoles in Florida.

Jackson was livid to hear the Creek emperor had escaped. The news that the Creeks were joining the Seminoles, who were attacking isolated American settlements, made Jackson more resolved in his determination to go into Florida. "First things first though," Jackson said, meaning the British. He busied himself preparing a document of capitulation for the Creeks and a treaty of peace for all the tribes.

Hearing and then reading the documents, Jonah was appalled. The words Weatherford had spoken when the cold weather had them held up at the trading post were coming true, all too true. After reading the document, Jonah was unable to hold his tongue. In front of Captain Reid, General Coffee and others, Jonah slammed the document down on the table, causing a glare from Jackson and stern looks from the others.

"General, I cannot believe what I'm reading. This is an absolute travesty. It sends the wrong message, sir. Not only to the Red Sticks, but to the Indians who were our allies. General, it's...it's a slap in the face. You, sir, if you proceed with this, have betrayed all of our allies. You are sending the wrong message, General, one I do not believe the president will endorse."

Jackson's face was red, his fist were balled up but rested on the table as he leaned forward. "I've heard no dissent from my other officers," Jackson snarled.

"Your officers," Jonah threw back. "If I was assigned under your command, I might not speak either," he replied. "Not that I'd think any different. Besides, sir, I'm not sure you have the authority for such a treaty."

"That's right," Jackson said. "You work for someone on a more lofty level. I forgot. But you must remember, Mr. Lee, I've been given command over the entire south by Mr. John Armstrong, our Secretary of

War. He and I are usually of the same mind. With my new assignment, I believe I, until instructed otherwise, can make such a treaty. I also have the authority to deal with any treasonous acts I might encounter."

Taking a breath, Jonah knew it would be better to hold his words but his conscience wouldn't let him. "I understand that, General. But from where I stand these documents are exactly that, treason. I would find it hard to sleep, and worse yet, I'd find it hard to meet my maker if I didn't speak out against what I consider a tragedy."

"Well, Mr. Lee, I salute you for that, sir," Jackson's voice had lost its hostility. "I do not feel the same as you do, sir, and surely history will decide. As you say, if I'm wrong, I will have to stand before my maker and answer. However, with the influx of settlers, even with the war going on, I feel what I'm doing is in the best interest of our Indian friends. However, to show you I hold no grudge against a man who disagrees with me and is willing to speak his convictions, I will allow you to write your comments to our president and put them along with my dispatches."

"Thank you, sir."

"You are a mind after my own heart, Mr. Lee. We might not always agree, but I believe your presence has been for the better." With that, Jackson dismissed everyone.

J ONAH HAD WRITTEN HIS dispatches but had not heard from the president or secretary of war. Jonah had decided that if he'd not received a reply by the second week of July, he'd pack up and head home. He and Moses had talked about this on a few occasions. Other than spending time with Stephen Lieupo, Sam Houston, Crockett and, of course the scout, old Henry Parrish, they had little to do. Time was growing heavy on their hands.

The Alabama sun was bright. The sky was blue and free of clouds. Most of the men around Fort Jackson had hunted for a little shade.

As the day dragged on, a few energetic souls put fishing line on cane poles, dug some worms, and found spots to go fishing. What they were looking for were areas that provided shade from nearby trees and cast a shadow over the river. The fish tended to migrate to these shaded areas. Bream and catfish seem to be plentiful. Henry pulled in a cat that weighed at least ten pounds.

"He'll do for filleting," he told Moses, who also had a pole and was sitting close by. "What I like," Henry continued, "is about two, maybe three pounders. No bigger than three pounds anyway. They are the tastiest when cooked right. Now, it ain't everybody can cook 'em right. Not like my Linda. She'll collect bacon grease and then put it into a big old deep iron skillet. She'll take them old cats and dip them in a bowl of corn meal and sprinkle a dab of salt on 'em and then drop the fish into the hot sizzling grease. She'll let it set there a bit and then flip it over. When it's golden brown, she'll take them out. You can just pull the meat right off the bones. She leaves the tails on, and when they're fried up right they're right crunchy. Of course, them big old cats are too big for the pan. So after I gut and skin the big ones, we fillet them. No bones in the fillets when I do the cutting. Course, like I said, I like the smaller cats, even if you do have to be particular about the bones." Henry took a deep breath and let go a sigh. It was almost like he smelled his wife's cooking. "Sometimes, she'll fix cornbread and other times, she will make corn dodgers. Of course, she always fixes grits. Hot buttery grits with salt and pepper. As good a eating as a body could ask for."

"Mama Lee puts cheese in her grits," Moses said. "That seems to make 'em better."

"Don't know how they could be any better, but I'll mention that to Linda."

"What do you like to sop your bread with, wild honey or molasses?" Moses asked.

"Oh, honey any day. Makes no difference what kind of bread, I'll take honey."

"Well, Mama Lee fixes some good blackberry jelly and she'll make fig preserves. They always go good with morning biscuits."

Bang! Bang! The sound of gunshots interrupted the conversation on foods.

"Best we skedaddle to the fort," Henry said, laying down his pole and picking up his long rifle.

"I'm with you," Moses declared.

PART V

Chapter Forty-Two

THREE RIDERS ENTERED THE fort. Two had been wounded by gunshots. One of the wounded was Captain Gregory Clark. He'd been shot in the thigh and shoulder. The stain on his britches and the dressing tied around the wound indicated a large loss of blood.

"I thought we'd shook them," he whispered, his chest heaving as he spoke.

"Who?" Jackson asked. He'd recognized Captain Clark from previous encounters.

"British agents and their Indian friends," Captain Clark said.

"Let's get this man to the surgeon," Jackson ordered.

"Wait," Clark gasped. "We have to get word to Washington…" He had passed out without finishing his sentence.

"Take these gentlemen here to the surgeon at once. Now be a good man," Jackson said, as Clark was rousing up. "Let the doctor fix you up and we'll see about Washington."

The third man, the one who hadn't been wounded, was dressed in homespun attire. He was Clark's scout and had been with him when they had visited Fort Strother. Walking up to the man, Henry greeted the scout. "Lucky as usual, ain't you, Ledbetter?"

A grin appeared on the man's face. "Henry, I figured your scalp would be hanging from a Red Stick's lance by now." The two men shook and hugged each other.

"This is my sister's oldest boy," Henry volunteered. "He doesn't like his given name, so we just call him Ledbetter. Of course, they's a lot of men with the same first name. Some of 'em even famous like. Named after Francis Marion," Henry whispered to Jonah. "He thinks Francis is a woman's name, so he tells folks to call him Ledbetter. Big as he is, most folks don't argue, 'cepting his maw and pa."

Ledbetter took care of the horses and made his way over to where his uncle camped. He greeted everyone, took an offered cup and didn't draw it back when a jug was handed forward to add a little something extra to the coffee. Somebody pushed an empty crate forward and Ledbetter took it and sat down. He lit his pipe and, with little coaxing, told of their ordeal.

"We have been after that blame British agent that got away at Fort Deposit. Captain Clark was close to hemming him up a few times but he always got away. Finally, at Mobile, we caught the rascal. Only his friends came right after us. A few times we thought we'd lost them and then there they'd be. We took fresh horses a couple of times, once at gunpoint. It ain't right to pull on one's own kind, but we had to have those horses. With the fresh horses, we put distance between us. We held up in an old hunter's shack one night. It was raining and we figured it was safe. Thought the rain would wash out our tracks. It was here that Captain Clark got to go through the prisoner's things. Some of it was in a code, but other parts of it were written plain. There was even a drawing of the barricade at Horseshoe Bend. Captain Clark knew in his heart the barricade had been designed by an engineer. It weren't built by an ignorant savage, he'd said. Anyway, the captain found a leather pouch. It had an official looking seal on it like the Redcoats use. Captain Clark unrolled the pouch and after a few minutes sat back and swore. They plan to attack Washington, he said. The British Navy is getting together a force, and they aim to attack and burn Washington. He then rolled up the pouch and put it in his shirt. He was putting the rest of the stuff back in the saddlebag when a shot come through the window. It hit the captain in the shoulder. The British agent, seeing the opportunity, tried to run out the door. He snatched open the door and was blasted back in by his own men. They must have thought he was one of us. We hunkered down and realized the floorboards had huge cracks in them. Captain Clark kept up a return fire while me and Langford, that's the other scout, ripped up the boards. After a while, the firing stopped. Somebody said that they'd give us ten minutes to think about it, and then they were coming in and no mercy would be given. We propped the dead agent up next to the window so it looked like somebody was there. We even propped a stick on the window hoping they'd take it as a rifle barrel, and then out we went. We found their horses and waited. When the shooting started we hit the saddle and lit out. Thought we'd got shed of them until we spotted them about a mile back. The captain was shot in the leg and Langford in the back. We lit a shuck then at a bend pulled up behind a rock. The captain's leg was bleeding pretty badly. We waited until they galloped by and then I rolled up a spare shirt and tied up the captain's leg. Langford put a handkerchief inside his shirt. We eased out and made our way through the woods until we got to the fort's clearing. We didn't know a new fort was here but it sure was a welcomed sight. We figured them agents were hiding somewhere, but our only chance was to run for it. Had we called for help, they'd have found us before help arrived anyway. So we just kicked our horses and here we are."

"That's quite a story," Jonah said.

"Yeah, it is. But the captain says we gotta get these plans to Washington," Ledbetter said.

"Well, he ain't in no shape to ride," Henry volunteered.

"That's true," Jonah replied. "But we are." Moses shook his head. He knew things had gone smoothly for too long. Turning to Captain Lieupo, Jonah asked, "You up to a long ride, Steve?"

Chapter Forty-Three

THE TRIP FROM FORT Jackson to the Lee home in Thunderbolt was a much more relaxed trip even though it was a hurried one. The Indian danger was gone, the weather was much nicer, and they didn't have a bunch of young militia replacements to slow them down. Jonah had spent a couple of hours talking with Captain Clark before they started their trip. Clark, propped up in bed, had dictated a report to be given to the Secretary of War, John Armstrong. Jonah had written the report and Greg had signed it. After the report had been completed, a fair copy had been made of the correspondence the British agent had been carrying. Captain Reid had undertaken that chore. The copy was given to Clark, who swore it was a true and certified copy. He signed the copy, Gregory Clark, Captain, USA.

Jackson had said, "Well, I guess that's better than Gregory Clark, Spymaster." This brought forth the chuckle he knew his comment would receive.

The discussion then turned to the best route to Washington. Much discussion was given to an overland trip, but then Clark had felt there were too many unknowns to guarantee a safe, expedient passage overland the whole way. Therefore, it was decided to travel back to Thunderbolt and obtain transportation to Washington aboard one of the many ships that could usually be found in Savannah or nearby ports. The trip would be faster and they could keep an eye out for British ships.

The arrival at the Lee home was met with joy and excitement. The family had just sat down for the noon meal when one of the colonel's hounds started barking, which caused every other dog on the place to take up the howl. The colonel stepped out of the kitchen door just in time to see three weary riders on worn out horses ride into the backyard.

"Mattie," Colonel Lee called, "tell mama her boys are home and you go ahead and fix three more plates."

Exhausted, Jonah, Moses, and Stephen Lieupo put smiles on their faces as hands were shook, backs were slapped, and hugs given. Collard greens with ham hocks, green beans, hominy and fresh cornbread and ice tea were served.

"That was worth coming home for," Moses declared.

"That's the truth," Stephen Lieupo added.

"Is that chocolate cake?" Jonah asked.

"It sure is," the colonel answered. "Your mama's own thirteen layer cake."

That was Jonah's absolute favorite cake. Mama Lee didn't do much of the cooking at this point in her life, but she still enjoyed making desserts.

"Tomorrow I'll fix Moses an apple pie," Mama Lee said. This brought a sudden silence from Jonah, Moses, and Lieupo. Sensing the silence, Mama Lee looked up. Tears came to her eyes, "You ain't even going to be here a whole day," she managed.

At that moment, Jonah didn't care if the British set the world on fire. He and Moses looked at each other, reading the other's thoughts.

"We ain't going nowhere, Mama, not if you are going to fix apple pie," Moses said smiling, trying to relax the mood.

"That's right," Lieupo chimed in. "I had some of your pie at Christmas and you poured a sweet cream over it. I can tell you one thing, this old soldier ain't going anywhere when there's the promise of apple pie."

THE SLOOP, *SPARROW*, TUGGED at her cable. The tide was on the turn and the captain waited impatiently as bags were tossed unceremoniously from his gig up and onto the sloop's deck. Next came three men: one wearing the uniform of a captain in the army, the second a fearsome looking mixed breed, and the third was a white man who could only be Colonel Lee's son. The army officer appeared to have been wounded, as he moved with a limp. He was agile enough to climb the battens and into the entry port, however. The black, mixed breed was dressed very well, as well as Colonel Lee's son. He didn't carry himself as a servant, so he must be of some importance. Jonah, that was the colonel's son's name; he looked very much like his father. He was the spitting image of a much younger Colonel Lee.

"Welcome aboard, gentlemen. I'm Harvey Jordan, captain of the good sloop, *Sparrow*. My first mate is Mr. Bryant Hays. This is our steward, Sam. He will help you get your things stowed and show you your cabin. As you can see, the tide waits for no one, so I must be about my duties."

No sooner had the anchor been lifted than the *Sparrow* drifted with the tide. The hands knew their jobs. The triangular mainsail was hoisted and the jib was hauled taut. Mr. Hays took the wooden tiller in his rough, weathered, bear-like hands. The light wind filled the sails and the ship was underway. Hays moved the tiller and the ship answered. God willing, they would be in Washington in a few days.

THE *SPARROW* WAS A small ship, a sloop his father had said, "She's only sixty feet long, and it takes only a handful of men to sail her. I think her captain will be willing to provide passage to Washington."

"How can you be so sure?" Jonah asked his father.

"Because I'm the major stockholder," the colonel replied.

This was a new revelation. Jonah knew his father had other interests than the plantation, but he'd never have guessed he'd been interested in maritime trade. This had all come to light the evening they'd gotten home. Under the pretense of seeing about the horses, the men had walked out to the stables. Jonah had already summarized his time with Jackson, ending with the Battle of Horseshoe Bend and the eventual surrender of Weatherford.

Once at the stables, Jonah filled his father in on Captain Clark's capture of the British agent and finding the documents he carried. Jonah let his father read the copy of the document. After handing the document back to his son, the colonel cleared his throat and spat. One of the cur hounds dodged at just the right time to keep from getting splattered.

"Time is certainly a concern," the colonel said, talking to himself. He was silent a moment as though in deep thought and then spoke to his son. "I may have a solution for you. You boys go get cleaned up and spend time with your mother."

"Yes, sir," Jonah responded, almost in military fashion. As he left the stable, he heard his father call, "Otis, come here. I got an errand for you to run."

S AIL HO."

"Where away?" Captain Jordan asked.

"Two points off the starboard bow," the lookout called.

Having spent time aboard Commodore Perry's ship, Jonah knew another ship had been sighted.

"Keep a fine lookout," Jordan bellowed. For the next few minutes, the captain paced the deck. He then walked over to where the first mate stood talking to a man holding the tiller. Jonah couldn't hear what was being said but could tell the captain was nervous.

"Deck there! She's a British ship, Captain, a frigate and she's changed her course, and she's bearing down on us."

"Damnation," Jordan cursed.

Hays hawked and spat over the side. He was a short man whose full head of black hair blew with the wind. "They ain't got us yet, Cap'n. Be dark in another thirty minutes."

A sound not unlike thunder seemed to roll across the waves. "She's fired a gun," the lookout called down.

"Damn waste of powder and shot," Hays offered.

Sparrow slipped into Chesapeake Bay just as the sun sank over the horizon. The frigate had fired once more but she was nowhere close to being within range.

"Do we anchor tonight?" Jonah braved the question. He'd heard Captain Jordan talking about ships running aground. This close to his goal, Jonah didn't want to wind up on a sandbar or worse...a prisoner on some British warship.

When the British warship had been sighted, the captain had recommended putting a shot in a bag, and if it looked like they were to be taken, put the incriminating documents in the bag and toss it over the side. The cover story would be Captain Lieupo, having been wounded, was going to be invalid out of the service. Jonah, with Moses as his servant, was looking for his lost love that was said to have family in Washington. Jonah felt his chest heave at the mention of his lost love.

The *Sparrow* made good time and luck was with the ship. Off the mouth of the Potomac River, Captain Jordan decided to drop anchor for the night.

"You never know what we'll run into," he said. "I'd not want to risk the ship or our lives. I think we're safe from the British but we'll keep a night watch. Tomorrow we'll go up river."

After a cold meal, the men sat back and smoked cigars or pipes. "I wonder how Henry is doing," Moses said. "I wonder if he's home yet or if Russell talked him into hanging around."

"Not much to hang around for," Lieupo responded.

"Nothing but the British and New Orleans," Jonah said, joining in the conversation.

"I wouldn't be surprised if he decided to go home," Moses said.

"What surprised me," Lieupo said, "was Crockett coming back."

"Me too," Jonah and Moses replied in unison.

"I hope Captain Clark mends," Jonah said as he threw the nub of his cigar over the side. Though they'd only spent a limited time together, he truly liked the man. "I'm turning in. Hopefully, we'll get to Washington before the Redcoats do."

"Be a damn big rush for nothing, if we don't," Lieupo replied. Yawning, he looked at his cigar and sent it over the side. "Tastes terrible," he groaned, "keeps the skeeters away, but it tastes awful."

Chapter Forty-Four

THE ROAD INTO WASHINGTON was a mess. Jonah had used his letter from the President to obtain three horses. It was better than walking but not much faster. The road was virtually choked by people in a panic: refugees with carts, bedding, and livestock; infantry soldiers and artillery pieces heading toward the city. A mass of frightened humanity.

"I guess the word got out the British is coming," Lieupo stated.

"It would appear so," Jonah replied.

"Humph," Moses snorted. "I'd be headed to the woods, not trying to use some bogged down road."

Jonah nodded in agreement and eased his horse off the side of the road, and in single file, the three made better time. Once in the city of Washington, it got worse. There were far more people in uniform, but uniformed or not, the people moved around aimlessly, with looks of disbelief and fright on their faces.

Pushing their way through the crowd, braving angry looks and curses, the three made it to the government buildings, one of which housed the secretary of war. Out of concern for their horses, Moses waited outside with his long rifle in his arms.

Looking back as they made their way up the steps, Captain Lieupo said, "It'd take a brave...or a foolish soul to think he could steal our horses with Moses standing guard."

Jonah smiled but continued up the steps. He'd never known anyone to take something from Moses that he'd not been willing to give.

Inside the building it was a beehive of activity, uniformed soldiers issuing orders and instructions to junior officers. Jonah and Lieupo shoved their way up to a desk where a regular army major seemed to be controlling the entry for the main offices.

"We need to see Mr. Armstrong," Jonah said, getting straight to the point.

"And so do half the people in Washington," the major said, not looking up.

"I suggest, Major, when you're speaking to a presidential agent, you at least show a degree of courtesy," Lieupo stated in a firm military manner.

Hearing this, the major stood up, not at attention but showing a degree of deference. He eyed Lieupo for a second and then looked to Jonah. "You have some identification, I suppose," the major questioned.

Jonah had been prepared for this, having seen all the urgent activity inside the building. "I do," he replied, handing forth the envelope with the presidential seal emblazoned on it.

The major, seeing the envelope, didn't even open it. "Well, sir, you won't find the secretary here. He left, headed toward the president's house, not thirty minutes ago."

"Thank you," Jonah said as he turned and hurried out of the building. "Do you know where the president's house is?" He asked Lieupo as they descended the steps.

"It's not far," Lieupo said. He paused, putting his arm on Jonah's shoulder. When Jonah stopped, Lieupo pointed off, down Pennsylvania Avenue. The nation's capital was under construction. The unfinished building rose up above all the other structures in the area. "It is to be a grand building," Lieupo said. "The capital of freedom and democracy, built on the backs of free and brave men who were not afraid to risk their lives for liberty and independence. Now, not even forty years later, we're fighting the battle all over again."

Jonah felt a lump in his throat as he looked at the sad face of his friend. Captain Stephen Lieupo had fought hard and bravely for his country. He had been wounded and would bear the results of those wounds for his entire life. But there was no backup in the man. He'd do to stand in the line of battle with. As Moses would say, 'And that's the gospel.'

Continuing down the steps, Lieupo asked, "Do you reckon it'll be there tomorrow?" Jonah didn't answer, he didn't need to. They both knew the answer to that.

❧

THE THREE MEN PUSHED and bullied their way to the president's house. Just before they got there, they had to stop while a cavalry detachment rode by, followed by a regiment of infantry. Bringing up the rear was more artillery. The sound of horses' hooves and jingle of trace chains was immediately replaced by the rumbling sound of wheels of the gun carriages.

Watching the group go by, Lieupo turned to his friends and with a concerned voice said, "Damn, Jonah, they are headed in the wrong direction. They are headed toward Fort McHenry and Baltimore."

"Hell's fire," Jonah swore and kicked his horse into motion, knocking bystanders asunder.

"Sorry," Moses yelled, looking back at the people rising from a muddy street.

Once at the president's house, Jonah swung down and bounded up the steps. Two army guards blocked his way. He pulled his letter out and shouted, "Out of the way, this is an emergency." The guards didn't move and the metallic click of musket hammers being pulled back added meaning to their determination.

Slower, but just as determined, Captain Lieupo mounted the steps as fast as he could. "At ease," he bellowed. Military experience by the guards had its desired effect. Huffing and puffing, Lieupo ordered, "Go get your officer now, we'll wait here." Turning to Jonah, Lieupo said,

"Getting shot on the steps of the president's house won't solve a blast-ed thing." Seeing the truth in his friend's words, Jonah gave a sigh and managed a smile.

It didn't take long for the guard to return with an officer, who after introductions and a quick glance at Jonah's papers, admitted the men in the house. They were made to wait in the foyer while the officer hurried off. In less than a minute, John Armstrong himself came to collect the two. "This way," he said after a quick handshake.

Armstrong led them into a room where President Madison stood by a window. His wife, Dolly, sat in a chair and Captain, no, now Major, Hampton, stood.

Without waiting for the usual greetings, Jonah said, "The British aim to attack and burn Washington."

Immediate silence. Not a word was spoken as the room's occupants stared at Jonah in disbelief, if not outright horror.

Finally, Hampton spoke, "Are you sure, Jonah, you have evidence of this?"

Jonah took the document out. Untying the strings and unrolling the leather, he handed the document to Hampton.

"You are certain of this," Hampton said, after reading the docu-ment and handing it to the president and secretary of war.

"Captain Clark is, sir. British agents shot and wounded the captain trying to get it back."

"Damnation," Armstrong swore. "I'm sorry, Mr. President, I was certain Baltimore was the target."

Two things then happened. The president's butler announced that dinner was ready and another officer rushed into the room. The offi-cer, a colonel, was in charge of the president's security detail.

"Mr. President, a dispatch rider has just arrived. The British are almost at the mouth of the Potomac. It's a whole damn fleet, Mr. President, including troop ships. We have to get you and Mrs. Madison out of the city, sir. It's very possible the Redcoats could be in the city before nightfall."

Turning to his wife, President Madison told her to get together a few things and go with the colonel. He then called for his aide and ordered him to collect anything vital to the country and go with the colonel as well.

"What about you, sir?"

"What about me?" the president repeated the question. "I'm going to fight the British."

Chapter Forty-Five

A S THE GROUP MADE ready to leave, a messenger arrived to inform them that Brigadier General William Winder, who had been put in charge of the defense of Washington, called for an emergency meeting. Soldiers were dispatched to round up key members of Madison's cabinet. A quick meeting ensued in which Winder met with the president, secretary of war, and members of the president's cabinet that could be found on short notice. At the meeting, it was decided the first line of defense had to be Bladensburg.

Pausing, the president looked at the men around him. "If the battle is lost, if Washington is taken, we will meet at Frederick."

Seeing the questioning look on Jonah's face, Lieupo leaned over and whispered, "Maryland." Jonah nodded but didn't speak.

As the group mounted, another dispatch rider rode up. Seeing the president, he was not sure whom to address. He'd been sent to give his message to the adjutant for the secretary of war.

Impatiently, President Madison ordered, "Speak up man, we haven't got all day."

"Yes, sir." He handed the president a folded paper and blurted out, "The British have moved up the Patuxent to upper Marlborough and towards Bladensburg. General Stansbury plans to take up a defensive position on the western bank of East Branch River and try to keep the British from crossing the bridge."

"How many men does he have?" Madison asked.

"Fourteen or fifteen hundred I'd say, sir, and it's said Commodore Barney is coming with four hundred of his sailors."

"I hope Tobias can hold them off," the president said, using General Stansbury's first name.

"To hold the bridge would be good," Armstrong volunteered. "But if not, it must be burned."

"That's a ninety-foot bridge," Hampton said. "It would need to be blown apart, not burned."

T HE VILLAGE OF BLADENSBURG was a ghost town, abandoned. Not a person stirred. Not a farmer, merchant, man, woman, or child. Worse yet, Jonah thought, not a single soldier. They finally spied a cavalry detachment, and with orders from Madison, they fell in behind his group. They encountered a few militia stragglers who fell in as well, but being on foot they were soon left far behind.

A few hundred yards from the bridge, Stansbury's cannons came into view. Fresh dirt embankments marked the position of each gun. Seeing the president, a group of Maryland militia stood up and began to cheer. Madison waved and soon General Stansbury made his way over to the president's group. He handed his telescope to President Madison, who scanned the surrounding countryside. An unending line of Redcoats was marching toward the bridge. If the bridge fell, so would Washington.

"Your orders, Mr. President?"

Looking down at Stansbury, Madison said, "Fight the British, General, don't mind me, just fight the damn Redcoats." Stansbury saluted, did an about face and hurried away.

"Mr. President, there's an old barn over there, sir, that will offer a good view and afford a degree of protection."

"I'm not here as a spectator, Major Hampton. I'm here to fight."

"I understand, sir, but the general can't fight his fight if he's worried about you."

"You also have to think of the country, sir," Jonah said, not sure if he should speak. "Take a moment to think, Mr. President, if you are captured by the British, it will be an end to the war. All will have been for naught."

A whistling sound passed overhead and followed by a large bang. "What the devil?" Armstrong questioned.

"It's those new rockets the British have. They're called Congreve rockets."

"Thank you, sir, Commodore." Barney had approached the group without being detected, as all were intent upon the enemy.

"My pleasure, Mr. President."

"Commodore," Major Hampton said, "this is Mr. Jonah Lee, a good man and a dear friend. Next to him, looking as fearsome as ole spit himself, is another friend, Moses. And last but not least is Captain Stephen Lieupo. Captain Lieupo is on assignment from the war department." In other words, Jonah thought, Captain Lieupo is a spy.

The sound of cannons roaring and the crackle of muskets and pistols began to fill the air, followed by more of the whistling of the Congreve rockets.

"If you'll excuse me, Mr. President, I fear I hear the call of duty."

"Of course, Commodore...Joshua, take care."

"Thank you, Mr. President, I will. And you take care as well."

The firing picked up, but even over the sound of gunfire, the beat of British drums could be heard. And with the sound of drums, a sinking feeling engulfed Jonah. There was no way they would defeat three or four thousand trained British troops. Maybe with someone like Jackson in command, or even Joshua Barney, but the battle was lost... Washington was doomed. They'd fight, but the end results would be the same.

"Better to fight like the Indians," Moses whispered. "Hit hard but run before the British can recover, and then hit them again on another day." Lieupo raised his eyebrows but didn't speak.

Round after round roared from the big guns on the American side, only to be answered by the British. Soon, a haze of spent gunpowder drifted on the slight breeze. Men sweated as they fired, and their faces were blackened by the smoke. Thirst dried out their mouths but there was no time to quench it. No canteens were available, only powder and shot. Then, with a bugle blaring and the tempo of the drums increasing, the Redcoats charged...with a bone-chilling roar they charged.

Sitting on a skittish horse, Jonah watched the battle unveil. The American cannons roared, spewing a fiery hell at the Redcoats. Jonah noted some of the guns were naval guns from Barney's emplacements. Still the Redcoats came, their flags flying, bayonets shining in the late summer sun. On they came, when another deafening roar came from the American guns. This time the entire British front line fell. Brave men down and dead from the hell belched forth from the American guns. The line began to stagger and fall back, but British officers made their way to the front, braving a hail of certain death from musket's fire. Men continued to fall, and the advance slowed but didn't stop, didn't retreat. As soldiers fell, others would fill the gaps. The line was widening as more of the British were sent to the front. They couldn't hold for long. The Americans would be outflanked and surrounded.

BOOM...BOOM...BOOM...The air was rent with the thunder of big guns firing. It was Jonah who recognized the different sound, having served a short while with Perry on the Great Lakes. "Canister or grape," he volunteered. "Someone, maybe the commodore, has ordered the firing of canister. It's more deadly to the infantry than balls."

"God, I hope he has a wagon full of it," Hampton said.

This time the British line broke and the Americans advanced. A short, grim, hand-to-hand battle ensued. Men were hacked down by swords. Bayonets impaled their foes, a Redcoat officer's face exploded as a musket ball hit him. Without thinking, Jonah kicked his horse forward, only to have a hand reach out and take the reins.

"No, Jonah. Today, you...we are spectators. I don't want you down there in a battle we can't win." Jonah looked at Hampton. At first he felt anger, and then common sense took hold and he relaxed. He was not the only one who knew the battle was lost.

No sooner had the Redcoats been driven back, than a new column was formed and the advance was on again. American guns continued to fire, until one by one they grew silent.

"What in damnation is going on?" a frustrated Armstrong spoke out. "Why have they stopped firing?"

Jonah knew, as did Moses and Lieupo; Hampton also knew. "They can't fire, Mr. Secretary, they are out of ammunition."

"Send for more then," Armstrong exploded.

"It's no use, John," the president spoke in a disheartened, but resolved voice. "There is no more ammunition. It's been sent to Baltimore."

CRACK...THUD...Moses yelped and ducked down. Without realizing it, the president's party was now within musket range of the British. Lead balls thudded into the plank walls of the barn.

"It's time to retreat," Hampton said, his voice was stern and final.

The group waited while Jonah dismounted and looked at Moses' arm. His muscle in the upper arm had been creased and slight ooze came from it. Madison handed Jonah a handkerchief to tie around the wound.

"Humph," Hampton grunted. "If it'd been me the ball would have missed. My muscles and arms ain't near as big as my friend here."

Moses smiled, "At least I got a keepsake," pointing to the handkerchief.

Epilogue

THE ROAD BACK TO Washington was filled with those fleeing the battle for the first mile or two, and then it thinned out. President Madison sent a galloper to make sure his wife had heeded his instructions.

A smile crossed his face; a gathering had been planned for the evening. "Forty guests, as I recall. I suppose it will have to be postponed," he said, getting the chuckle he knew his comments would bring.

When the group approached the president's home, Mrs. Madison was handing a huge picture of George Washington to the butler to be put in the carriage. Jonah was surprised at how little the First Lady had packed.

Seeing his gaze, Mrs. Madison said, "Important things, Mr. Lee. In the end, you realize there is very little that can't be replaced." She then pointed at the painting of George Washington. "But that's one of them. I'll not let some Redcoat brag about taking it."

A man came out with a basket of food. "I can't think of anything else, Madame."

A colonel helped Mrs. Madison into the carriage and then climbed into the driver's seat. "It was a pleasure meeting you, Mr. Lee. Perhaps we can meet again in a more relaxed time," she said.

"Thank you, Madame. I will look forward to it."

"It's Dolly, Mr. Lee, my friends call me Dolly."

"Then it's Jonah, not Mr. Lee."

"I will look forward to our next meeting, as well," President Madison said. "John said he was sending you to New Orleans to keep Jackson in line."

"I will go if that's your wish, Mr. President, but other than yourself, I don't know anyone who could keep General Jackson in check."

"Do you think it was wrong to give mad old Jackson command of the south?" Madison asked.

This question took Jonah by surprise. First, where had the president heard of the Red Stick's name for Jackson and second, what did he truly think of Jackson being in overall command? After a long pause to collect his thoughts, Jonah responded, "If I wanted a battle won, I could certainly send mad old Jackson." Jonah couldn't resist the use of Jackson's Indian nickname. "However, I must say he treated the Indians most unfairly."

Armstrong, who Jonah was sure agreed with Jackson, started to interrupt, but the president held up his hand, quieting him. "Mr. Lee has the floor," he said.

"I feel, sir, you must be prepared for possible fallout from Jackson's actions if he treats our other allies as he did our Indian friends." Taking a breath, Jonah exhaled and continued, "I realize, sir, we are living in desperate times. The enemy is virtually at our door. So I must say I think choosing Jackson was not only the right choice, it was the only choice."

"I am heartened by your words, Mr. Lee. I will be in touch, God's will. But for now, I must bid you a hasty good-bye."

"Good-bye, Jonah."

"Good-bye, Dolly."

THE MEN WATCHED AS the president and his cavalry escort rode out of sight. Armstrong held his hand out to Jonah.

"The president has already told you where we'd like for you to go. Just so you know, General Jackson had much to say about your character, all of it good. He said you were a born leader, a fighting man's man, one who he could count on to give him true counsel. He also said you were not intimidated by him one bit. Coming from Andy, that speaks volumes."

Jonah thought for a moment and then said, "If it's your wish, John, I will accompany Jackson."

Moses, who had kept silent for most of the time since they had been in Washington, spoke, "How can we deny a request from the secretary of war."

Armstrong smiled but bowed his head. After a moment he looked up. "In all probability, it will soon be former secretary."

Lieupo started to say something but, seeing Major Hampton's faint shake of the head, closed his mouth.

"Things have been difficult," Armstrong continued, "but I thought I could help the president and help win the war. I never imagined all the obstacles I'd face. In truth, Jonah, I did not think the British would attack the city. Baltimore is a much more strategic target."

"It's not which was the most significant target," Jonah said. "They were going after the one with the most semblance, the target that would strike a blow to the general morale of our country."

"Well, all they've done is piss me off," Lieupo declared.

"That's two of us," Moses joined in.

"I think most Americans will feel that way," Jonah said. "But take heart, John, the only man I know that was perfect was sent to the cross."

"And rose again," Moses added.

"I don't know," Armstrong said. "Take care Jonah, Moses, Captain Lieupo. I appreciate your service and your loyalty." With that, he turned his horse to ride away.

"I'll be along in a minute," Hampton called.

"There goes a dejected man," Moses said. "He's in a bad way."

Major Hampton nodded and then spoke to Jonah. "I have not forgotten about Anastasia. In fact, our search has gained momentum now that a friend of yours has added resources at his disposal to the search."

"A friend?" Jonah questioned.

Nodding, Hampton smiled. "A powerful friend. Colonel Mentor Johnson is a man who is loyal to his friends. I told you that back at the Thames."

"How is the colonel?" Jonah asked.

"He's recovering. He's not well yet, but he is recovering. I had the opportunity to sit down with the colonel a few months ago, and he was most shocked and concerned about Anastasia's welfare. He started where you left off. He sent men to follow each branch of the river. When he got positive news, he sent a whole squadron of men down the river on the trail. It is now believed that Anastasia is in or around New Orleans. It is feared she is not entirely free to come and go as she pleases. This came from a man in Natchez who spoke rather than lose his tongue. Unfortunately, he did gain another chin." This was said while making the motion of a knife slitting a throat.

Lieupo gave an involuntary shudder and said, "Damn."

"These men are to locate Anastasia but not try to take her unless her life appears to be in danger. The men have been told you will be arriving in New Orleans with Jackson's forces," Hampton said.

"Hence, my assignment," Jonah said.

"We had to find a reason for you to be there, Jonah," Hampton said. "No one expects you or anyone else to control Jackson. You may have the opportunity to make counsel, advise the general at times. But that's not your prime objective. You are to go rescue your woman. You are not to put yourself in harm's way. You get Anastasia and you go back to Georgia. Have a slew of grandchildren for the colonel and Mrs. Lee."

Hampton turned to Lieupo, "You are to be my eyes and ears, Captain. I will send you a means by which you can contact me. You may even look over your shoulder and find me standing there. In the meantime, if something is urgent, send it to Colonel Johnson's home in Kentucky. He will see that I get it forthwith."

Jonah couldn't help but think how Mentor Johnson still had his hand in things, much as he did in the northwest, if not more so.

"Captain Clark will join you in New Orleans if he recovers from his wounds soon enough. He has thoughts of forming an alliance with the pirate, Laffite. If you take a roundabout trip, you will find the *Sparrow* pulled up in a creek waiting on your return. I have a man waiting on you at the edge of town to guide you." Smiling, Hampton continued, "I told him he'd not mistake the three of you. Mostly as Moses would stand out, no offense meant."

"None taken," Moses assured Hampton.

Extending his hand, Hampton shook each of the three men's hands and said, "God's speed. Good luck and give Anastasia a big kiss for me. I expect an invitation to the wedding."

"I'll name my first born after you," Jonah called as his friend rode away.

Jonah looked at his friends sitting astride their mounts next to him. "Shall we be on our way?" he asked, feeling for once that there was hope in locating Ana. In the distance, the sound of gunfire could be heard. Washington would be in British hands by nightfall. There was little that could be done about that, he knew. But hopefully Ana would soon be in his arms. There was a lot he intended to do in that regard.

Appendix

TREATY OF FORT JACKSON

Articles of agreement and capitulation, made and concluded this ninth day of August, one thousand eight hundred and fourteen, between major general Andrew Jackson, on behalf of the President of the United States of America, and the chiefs, deputies, and warriors of the Creek Nation.

WHEREAS an unprovoked, inhuman, and sanguinary war, waged by the hostile Creeks against the United States, hath been repelled, prosecuted and determined, successfully, on the part of the said States, in conformity with principles of national justice and honorable warfare—And whereas consideration is due to the rectitude of proceeding dictated by instructions relating to the re-establishment of peace: Be it remembered, that prior to the conquest of that part of the Creek nation hostile to the United States, numberless aggressions had been committed against the peace, the property, and the lives of citizens of the United States, and those of the Creek nation in amity with her, at the mouth of Duck river, Fort Mims, and elsewhere, contrary to national faith, and the regard due to an article of the treaty concluded at New-York, in the year seventeen hundred ninety, between the two nations: That the United States, previously to the perpetration of such outrages, did, in order to ensure future amity and concord between the Creek nation and the said states, in conformity with the stipulations of former treaties, fulfill, with punctuality and good faith, her engagements to the said nation: that more than two-thirds of the whole number of chiefs and warriors of the Creek nation, disregarding the genuine spirit of existing treaties, suffered themselves to be instigated to violations of their national honor, and the respect due to a part of their own nation faithful to the United States and the principles of humanity, by impostures [impostors,] denominating themselves Prophets, and by the duplicity and misrepresentation of foreign emissaries, whose governments are at war, open or under-stood, with the United States. Wherefore,

1st—The United States demand an equivalent for all expenses incurred in prosecuting the war to its termination, by a cession of all the territory belonging to the Creek nation within the territories of the United States, lying west, south, and south-eastwardly, of a line to be run and described by persons duly authorized and appointed by the President of the United States:

Beginn at a point on the eastern bank of the Coosa river, where the south boundary line of the Cherokee nation crosses the same; running from thence down the said Coosa river with its eastern bank according to its various meanders to a point one mile above the mouth of Cedar creek, at Fort Williams, thence east two miles, thence south two miles, thence west to the eastern bank of the said Coosa river, thence down the eastern bank thereof according to its various meanders to a point opposite the upper end of the great falls, (called by the natives Woetumka,) thence east from a true meridian line to a point due north of the mouth of Ofucshee, thence south by a like meridian line to the mouth of Ofucshee on the south side of the Tallapoosa river, thence up the same, according to its various meanders, to a point where a direct course will cross the same at the distance of ten miles from the mouth thereof, thence a direct line to the mouth of Summochico creek, which empties into the Chatahouchie river on the east side thereof below the Eufaulau town, thence east from a true meridian line to a point which shall intersect the line now dividing the lands claimed by the said Creek nation from those claimed and owned by the state of Georgia: Provided, nevertheless, that where any possession of any chief or warrior of the Creek nation, who shall have been friendly to the United States during the war and taken an active part therein, shall be within the territory ceded by these articles to the United States, every such person shall be entitled to a reservation of land within the said territory of one mile square, to include his improvements as near the centre thereof as may be, which shall inure to the said chief or warrior, and his descendants, so long as he or they shall continue to occupy the same, who shall be protected by and subject to the laws of the United States; but upon the voluntary abandonment thereof, by such possessor or his descendants, the right of occupancy or possession of said lands shall devolve to the United States, and be identified with the right of property ceded hereby.

2nd—The United States will guarantee to the Creek nation, the integrity of all their territory eastwardly and northwardly of the said line to be run and described as mentioned in the first article.

3d—The United States demand, that the Creek nation abandon all communication, and cease to hold any intercourse with any British or Spanish post, garrison, or town; and that they shall not admit among them, any agent or trader, who shall not derive authority to hold commercial, or other intercourse with them, by license from the President or authorized agent of the United States.

4th –The United States demand an acknowledgment of the right to establish military posts and trading houses, and to open roads within the territory, guaranteed to the Creek nation by the second article, and a right to the free navigation of all its waters.

5th—The United States demand, that a surrender be immediately made, of all the persons and property, taken from the citizens of the United States, the friendly part of the Creek nation, the Cherokee, Chickasaw, and Choctaw nations, to the respective owners; and the United States will cause to be immediately restored to the formerly hostile Creeks, all the property taken from them since their submission, either by the United States, or by any Indian nation in amity with the United States, together with all the prisoners taken from them during the war.

6th—The United States demand the caption and surrender of all the prophets and instigators of the war, whether foreigners or natives, who have not submitted to the arms of the United States, and become parties to these articles of capitulation, if ever they shall be found within the territory guaranteed to the Creek nation by the second article.

7th—The Creek nation being reduced to extreme want, and not at present having the means of subsistence, the United States, from motives of humanity, will continue to furnish gratuitously the necessaries of life, until the crops of corn can be considered competent to yield the nation a supply, and will establish trading houses in the nation, at the discretion of the President of the United States, and at such places as he shall direct, to enable the nation, by industry and economy, to procure clothing.

8th—A permanent peace shall ensue from the date of these presents forever, between the Creek nation and the United States, and between the Creek nation and the Cherokee, Chickasaw, and Choctaw nations.

9th—If in running east from the mouth of Summochico creek, it shall so happen that the settlement of the Kennards, fall within the lines of the territory hereby ceded, then, and in that case, the line shall be run east on a true meridian to Kitchofoonee creek, thence down the middle of said creek to its junction with Flint River, immediately below the Oakmulgee town, thence up the middle of Flint river to a point due east of that at which the above line struck the Kitchofoonee creek, thence east to the old line herein before mentioned, to wit: the line dividing the lands claimed by the Creek nation, from those claimed and owned by the state of Georgia. The parties to these presents, after due consideration, for themselves and their constituents, agree to ratify and confirm the preceding articles, and constitute them the basis of a permanent peace between the two nations; and they do hereby solemnly bind themselves, and all the parties concerned and interested, to a faithful performance of every stipulation contained therein.

In testimony whereof, they have hereunto, interchangeably, set their hands and affixed their seals, the day and date above written.

Treaty with the Creeks, Fort Jackson, 1814.

Signatories

Andrew Jackson, major general commanding Seventh Military District, [L. S.]

TustunnuggeeThlucco, Speaker for the Upper Creek, his x mark, [L. S.]

MiccoAupoegau, of Toukaubatchee, his x mark, [L. S.]

TustunnuggeeHopoiee, Speaker of the Lower Creeks, his x mark, [L. S.]

MiccoAchulee, of Cowetau, his x mark, [L. S.]

William McIntosh, Jr., major of Cowetau, his x mark, [L. S.]

TuskeeEneah, of Cussetau, his x mark, [L. S.]

FaueEmautla, of Cussetau, his x mark, [L. S.]

ToukaubatcheeTustunnuggee of Hitchetee, his x mark, [L. S.]

Noble Kinnard, of Hitchetee, his x mark, [L. S.]

HopoieeHutkee, of Souwagoolo, his x mark, [L. S.]

HopoieeHutkee, for HopoieYoholo, of Souwogoolo, his x mark, [L. S.]

FolappoHaujo, of Eufaulau, on Chattohochee, his x mark, [L. S.]

PacheeHaujo, of Apalachoocla, his x mark, [L. S.]

Timpoeechee Bernard, Captain of Uchees, his x mark, [L. S.]

UcheeMicco, his x mark, [L. S.]

YoholoMicco, of Kialijee, his x mark, [L. S.]

SocoskeeEmautla, of Kialijee, his x mark, [L. S.]

ChoocchauHaujo, of Woccocoi, his x mark, [L. S.]

Esholoctee, of Nauchee, his x mark, [L. S.]

YoholoMicco, of Tallapoosa Eufaulau, his x mark, [L. S.]

StinthellisHaujo, of Abecoochee, his x mark, [L. S.]

OcfuskeeYoholo, of Toutacaugee, his x mark, [L. S.]

John O'Kelly, of Coosa, [L. S.]

EneahThlucco, of Immookfau, his x mark, [L. S.]

EspokokokeHaujo, of Wewoko, his x mark, [L. S.]

EneahThluccoHopoiee, of Talesee, his x mark, [L. S.]

EfauHaujo, of Puccan Tallahassee, his x mark, [L. S.]

Talessee Fixico, of Ocheobofau, his x mark, [L. S.]

NomatleeEmautla, or Captain Issacs, of Cousoudee, his x mark, [L. S.]

Tuskegee Emautla, or John Carr, of Tuskegee, his x mark, [L. S.]

Alexander Grayson, of Hillabee, his x mark, [L. S.]

Lowee, of Ocmulgee, his x mark, [L. S.]

NocooseeEmautla, of ChuskeeTallafau, his x mark, [L. S.]

William McIntosh, for HopoieeHaujo, of Ooseoochee, his x mark, [L. S.]

William McIntosh, for ChehahawTustunnuggee, of Chehahaw, his x mark, [L. S.]

William McIntosh, for SpokokeeTustunnuggee, of Otellewhoyonnee, his x mark, [L. S.]

Done at fort Jackson, in presence of--

Charles Cassedy, acting secretary,

Benjamin Hawkins, agent for Indian affairs,

Return J. Meigs, Agent of Creek nation,

Robert Butler, Adjutant General U. S. Army,

J. C. Warren, assistant agent for Indian Affairs,

George Mayfield, Alexander Curnels, George Lovett, Public interpreters.

Historical Notes

THIS IS THE SECOND in a trilogy based on the War of 1812. It was Tom Gruden's brainchild that I was happy to be a part of. Tom passed away before the first book was published, but I felt compelled to write the trilogy as we discussed.

The War of 1812 is often referred to as the forgotten war. The first War of Independence and the Civil War seemed to overshadow the importance of sacrifices made during its brief duration. As the War of 1812 has been overshadowed, so have the struggles and sacrifices of the men fighting the "Creek War;" both red and white men.

As Americans pushed westward, the Indians were pushed from their native lands. This was especially true for the Creek Nation in Alabama. As the Battle of Horseshoe Bend took place during the War of 1812, and since numerous characters who took part in the battle would be forever remembered in the history of our nation, I decided to center book two of my trilogy around this battle.

I have tried to remain very accurate to the details and timeline for the events that took place in this book. But, remember this is a work of fiction based on historic fact. I make no claim that it is purely factual.

While I do not always paint Jackson in the best light, especially in his dealings with Indian allies, I must say I find him to be a brave and magnificent leader. I know of no other American leader who was faced with such great odds and still obtained the success that Jackson achieved. A man who was plagued with wounds from dueling, near starvation for lack of supplies, faced with expiring enlistment contracts and mutiny, jealousy from regular army officers, he beat all that opposed him and won at all levels. He beat the Red Sticks and the British. He also beat the Spanish and the Seminoles in Florida. Finally, he beat his political opponents and became President of the United States.

John Coffee was Jackson's lifelong friend and commanding officer of the cavalry. He started out with the rank of colonel but was promoted to general. Captain John Reid was Jackson's aide and friend.

In regards to other main characters in this book, I encourage the readers to read about these brave men. Sam Houston became a legend in Texas and was the Republic of Texas' first president, after winning their independence from Mexico.

Davy Crockett will be forever remembered for dying at the Alamo. However, while some put him at the Battle of Horseshoe Bend, I could find no record of it. He was a part of Jackson's forces and served as a scout with Russell's scouts before and after the battle however. Crockett was a known storyteller and served as a representative of Tennessee in the Congress. Jackson's army was made up for the most part of militia. Volunteers from Tennessee, Georgia, and a few from the Carolinas who were brave, but poorly trained men. Most of whom were also poorly disciplined. Davy Crockett was one of the Tennessee volunteers.

It was not until the arrival of the 39th United States Infantry, in February 1814, that Jackson had an army that he could truly go to battle with. After a riff with Jackson, the 39th's commanding officer assigned himself other duties.

Major Montgomery of the 39th was killed, shot in the head as he climbed over the barricade at Horseshoe Bend. The city of Montgomery, Alabama was named in his honor.

William Weatherford, aka. Red Eagle, aka. Lumhe-Chati, lived for years after the Battle of Horseshoe Bend. As he promised Jackson, he gave up his war ax. He did not flee Alabama and join the Seminoles in Florida as many other Red Sticks did. This group included Menawa, who survived his wounds at Horseshoe Bend but died fighting with the Seminoles against Jackson some years later.

The Creek Nation was considered one of the civilized tribes. They lived much as whites, married white women, and a good many characters mentioned in this book were of mixed heritage. A number of them were Scots. These included William Weatherford, whose family, especially his grandfather, was very well-to-do. Menawa was part Scottish, and Peter McQueen was also of mixed blood. The Creeks planted fields, raised livestock, and owned slaves. Until pushed by the white man's greed and westward expansion, as well as being supplied by Spanish and British agents with weapons and talk of war, they would have lived in peace indefinitely.

While the burning of Washington only takes up a small part of this book, it was an important part of the War of 1812. No other enemy has since caused so much destruction to our capital. We have, however, been attacked; I'm sure no one has forgotten 9/11. Our Pentagon was attacked and received heavy damage. An attack planned for the Capital did not take place. Therefore, the British burning of Washington, D.C. was the only time in our history in which the nation's capital was laid to ruin.

John Armstrong did resign the office of Secretary of War on the fourth of September, 1814, shortly after the city was burned. He was replaced by James Monroe, who became the fifth president in 1816. He was the last of our founding fathers to hold the office.

Finally, I'd like to say I probably spent more hours in researching this book than any I have ever written. I went through thousands of sheets of printer paper and several ink cartridges, and I read numerous books written on the war. These were listed in *Remember the Raisin*. Therefore, to give you but a few resources in which to read further is not reasonable. I will say that the great-grandson of William Weatherford has a good website. He was kind enough to respond to my emails. Don C. East also has a few articles on the web that gives a good overview and I recommend it. Tennessee history also provides a good outline of the events that lead up to the Battle of Horseshoe Bend and a good synopsis of the battle itself. Remember that Crockett, Houston, and Jackson were all from Tennessee.

About the Author

Michael Aye is a retired Naval Medical Officer. He has long been a student of early American and British Naval history. Since reading his first Kent novel, Mike has spent many hours reading the great authors of sea fiction, often while being "haze gray and underway" himself. This is his second novel on the War of 1812.

Acknowledgements

Thanks to Chris and Jay, the good folks at Bitingduck, for continuing to work with me and bring my stories to print. You are a really great team, and I feel lucky to have you in my corner.

Greg Clark, your smile and energy is contagious. Thanks for lunch.

George, Jim, Alaric, and Bill, where would I be if it wasn't for old salts such as yourself willing to advise and answer my questions.

www.ingramcontent.com/pod-product-compliance
Lightning Source LLC
Chambersburg PA
CBHW070504030726
47503CB00004B/1157